BENEATH THE LEMON TREES

EMMA BURSTALL

Boldwood

First published in Great Britain in 2024 by Boldwood Books Ltd.

Cover Design by Head Design Ltd.

Cover Illustration: Shutterstock and iStock

A CIP catalogue record for this book is available from the British Library.

Paperback ISBN 978-1-83561-537-9

Large Print ISBN 978-1-83561-538-6

Hardback ISBN 978-1-83561-536-2

Ebook ISBN 978-1-83561-539-3

Kindle ISBN 978-1-83561-540-9

Audio CD ISBN 978-1-83561-531-7

MP3 CD ISBN 978-1-83561-532-4

Digital audio download ISBN 978-1-83561-533-1

Boldwood Books Ltd
23 Bowerdean Street
London SW6 3TN
www.boldwoodbooks.com

To eleven very special women (aka The HSs – you know who you are). Thank you for all the wonderful walks and talks and for introducing me to stunning Crete.

PROLOGUE

Katerina opened her laptop and squinted at her inbox. There was one new message, which she clicked on, but her eyesight was poor and she couldn't read it.

Frowning, she cast around for her glasses. They weren't on the rough wooden table, where she'd set her laptop, nor on the floor by her feet.

Muttering to herself, she rose and hurried a few paces across the flagstones. She'd kicked off her woollen slippers and the ground felt hard and chilly.

'Ah!' she cried triumphantly, picking up the glasses, which were lying on the stone worktop next to the sink. They were covered in smears, which she wiped on the bottom of her black skirt.

Glancing out of the little window, she noticed a mangy brown dog peeing down her pots of beloved crocuses.

'Buzz off, you pesky mutt!'

She banged on the glass with her knuckles and the dog slunk away, but not before scratching at the ground with its back legs, kicking up dirt.

Katerina growled, a bit like a dog herself, before pushing the glasses up her long straight nose and settling down again.

A few strands of wiry grey hair escaped from her bun and she blew them off her face with one big puff, but they only settled back in the same place.

Dear Miss Papadakis…

She sniffed. Well, whoever it was had made their first error. Katerina might be a widow, but she was definitely not a 'Miss'.

Careless of the writer not to check. People were so sloppy nowadays. But she supposed it wasn't exactly a hanging offence. She read on…

Forgive the short notice, but I'm looking to book a villa for two weeks in May, for myself and my two children plus my friend and her two children.

We need four bedrooms minimum – one for me, one for my friend, Louise, one for our boys, age nineteen and sixteen, and one for our fourteen-year-old girls.

We just wondered, Villa Ariadne looks absolutely lovely and perfect for our needs. Is it by any chance free?

The writer went on to give her preferred dates over the half-term holiday and mentioned she'd never been to Crete before and had always wanted to visit.

Blah, blah. They were all the same, trying to wheedle themselves into Katerina's good books, just so they could get the weeks they wanted.

The final paragraph, however, made the elderly woman pause…

My family and I have been through a difficult time and we're badly in need of a break!

The exclamation mark struck Katerina as a somewhat clumsy attempt to lighten the sentence. She wasn't fooled. When a woman told a complete stranger she'd been through a tough time, she was rarely exaggerating.

The writer signed off as Stella Johnston. Katerina pushed back her chair and closed her eyes. Her hand went instinctively to the right-hand pocket of her skirt, where she felt for the woollen pouch containing a miniature vial of olive oil, some dried laurel leaves and a silver pendant with a double-headed Minoan axe: her lucky talisman.

It was comforting to squeeze the pouch and feel with her fingertips for the objects inside. She took several deep breaths and tried to focus on the word 'Stella'.

S T E L L A. She mouthed the letters, then whispered them out loud, one by one, almost reverentially, waiting for an image to form in her mind – of what, she had no clue.

At first, she could see nothing, only the letter shapes, but then gradually they started to jumble up, whirring round her brain like dirty washing in a machine: the pale-blue sleeve of a man's shirt here, a brown corduroy trouser leg there.

The motion made Katerina feel sick and she longed for the whirring to stop. When it finally did, the letters seemed to come to a standstill right before her eyes, only they weren't in the correct order.

Now they spelled ALTELS. Her English was good, and she was pretty sure there was no such word; it meant nothing to her.

Squeezing her eyelids tighter still, she forced herself to concentrate even harder. It made her head throb; it was quite painful.

All of a sudden, a sense of calm came over her, like a gentle breeze fanning her face and neck. She exhaled, long and slow.

'Of course,' she said at last, with a relieved smile. She nodded, as if in response to some comment or other, though she was quite alone. 'Let's wait and see.'

On opening her eyes again, she hit the 'reply' symbol at the top of the email and wrote back immediately.

Dear Mrs Johnston

(Not 'Miss', whatever the woman's marital status. There were children, after all.)

I'm delighted to say you're in luck! Villa Ariadne is indeed free between those dates... If you need a taxi transfer, just let me know your flight details at least a week before your arrival and I can arrange it for you... I look forward to welcoming you to our beautiful island...

Closing the laptop once more, Katerina stayed at the table for several minutes deep in thought, her elbows resting on the hard surface, chin in her hands.

May the eighteenth? That was only two months away. She'd better let the others know the villa wasn't available after all; she'd kept them hanging on long enough.

There were always plenty of enquiries, mostly from Brits, plus a few French and Germans. She didn't advertise; she waited for them to find her, then Villa Ariadne made the final call, so to speak.

It was rarely wrong, though it took its time and of course, you could never predict how things would pan out.

The sound of tinkling goats' bells drifted through the gaps in the window frames: the goatherd taking the animals downhill to be milked.

Time for a cup of mountain tea, Katerina decided. And perhaps a little *Kalitsounia*: a pastry filled with sweet cheese, cinnamon and lemon zest. She made these herself and never grew tired of them, though she tried to limit herself to one a day; she didn't want to burst out of her clothes and have to buy new ones.

After stuffing her feet in her slippers, she walked over to the tap, filled a small saucepan with cold water and lit the gas ring with a match.

You could never call her life dull, she thought with some satisfaction as she blew out the match. She might be in her eighties, but there were always new people to meet, fresh stories waiting to be told.

As she popped the saucepan on the heat, she found herself thinking about the crisp white sheets and pillowcases folded neatly in her linen cupboard. They were deliciously light and would smell heavenly, having been hung out to dry in the lemon grove, warmed by the Cretan sun.

She'd make up the beds in plenty of time and put a few sprigs of lavender under the pillows, some wildflowers on the dressing tables. And she'd make more *Kalitsounia* as a welcome present.

She could do that for them, at least, along with some of the other nice little touches the guests so appreciated. The rest, of course, was out of her hands.

1

The housekeeper was older than Stella had imagined with thick grey hair poking out from under a dark-blue headscarf, knotted beneath her chin, and tanned wrinkly skin.

She looked fit, though: short, slim and wiry. She was wearing a white blouse and smart navy trousers, and brandishing a piece of paper with Stella's name on. She gave a small polite smile when she spotted the group coming off the ferry.

'Thank goodness,' Stella said, stopping for a moment to wave at Katerina, before dragging her brown wheelie suitcase across the tarmac. It was ridiculously heavy; she'd packed in a rush and chucked everything in. 'I was worried she might have forgotten about us.'

'She's ancient,' said Hector nastily. He was Stella's nineteen-year-old son.

'Shh. Don't be rude.'

'What happens now?' He knew perfectly well; Stella had told him a hundred times.

'We walk to the villa. It's about a mile.'

'A mile? You've got to be fucking joking.'

He'd been extremely unpleasant since they left home at the crack of dawn this morning – in fact, ever since Stella had tried to lay down the law some weeks ago and insist he join them on holiday.

Of course, she'd hoped he'd come about eventually and start to enjoy himself, but he was stubborn as hell and the signs weren't good.

Her eyes started to fill up and she realised she could easily cry. She mustn't. Once she started, she might never stop.

'Why can't we drive? Haven't they heard of cars? This place is a shithole.'

Stella's features seemed to slide down her face and the corners of her mouth drooped. She was sick and tired of having to be strong. If he only knew how close she was to cracking...

Louise, who was just behind, came to her rescue.

'It'll be good to stretch our legs, Hector,' she said briskly. 'We've been sitting for so long. Look! What a stunning place!'

She gestured to the turquoise bay and painted wooden boats, the sparkling white buildings with bright-blue windows and the dry rocky mountains rising up behind them.

'I like the fact there are no roads. You can only get here by boat, you know. It feels like a world away from London.'

Hector was about to answer back but was interrupted by laughter and they all turned to look. A group of youths were standing by the quayside, wolf whistling at the two girls trailing behind Louise's sixteen-year-old, Will.

He had his head down, pretending not to notice, while his sister, Amelia, and Stella's daughter, Lily, egged on the youths, flicking their long silky hair and giggling, lapping up the attention.

Louise raised her eyebrows. 'We'll have to keep an eye on those two minxes!'

Stella giggled, despite herself.

They were just a few short paces from Katerina now and she hurried forward to greet them. Holding out both hands, she took Stella's in hers and squeezed tight. Her grip was remarkably sure and strong.

'You had a good journey, I hope? You must be tired. Welcome to Porto Liakáda!'

Will and the two girls, both fourteen, wanted to stop for a drink in the town before heading for the villa. Tables and chairs were spilling out of bars with brightly coloured awnings. It all looked very tempting, but Louise was having none of it.

'C'mon. Let's drop our bags first, then you can explore as much as you like.'

Katerina led the way towards a flight of steep, narrow stone steps between two buildings, bounding up the first few as if she hadn't even noticed they were there. Then she stopped suddenly, realising Stella was struggling with her heavy suitcase.

Louise, having perfected the art of capsule wardrobe packing, had a neat carry-on, while the younger ones wore trendy backpacks.

'Here, give that to me.' Katerina reached out to grab Stella's luggage, but she shook her head.

'I can manage, honestly. I shouldn't have brought so much stuff.'

Will, who was of average height and athletic looking, like his mother, offered to help instead, but Hector hung back.

'Why don't you take one end, Hector, and Will can take the other,' Louise said firmly. 'Just till we reach smooth ground again.'

Lily and Amelia chatted excitedly all the way up, but the others were mostly silent. The steps were extremely steep and even without her bag, Stella soon felt out of breath and her legs ached.

At one point, she stumbled, banging her knee on the step above. Pain whipped through her body and she closed her eyes, wincing.

Louise spun round.

'Are you okay?'

Stella nodded. Her knee was throbbing but there was nothing to be done. She'd no doubt have a big ugly bruise there tomorrow, to add to all the others.

Her mind flashed to Al. He used to tease her because she was constantly covered in bumps and bruises. He said she looked like the kid at school who was always getting into scraps.

In the early days of their relationship, he used to say, only half joking, people would think he'd beaten her up. She could still picture him lying in bed with her one lazy Sunday morning. They were on their first proper holiday together, in Barcelona. They'd just made love and it was hot, so they'd thrown off the covers and were sprawled, side by side, only their thighs touching, listening to the steady slowing of their heartbeats.

After a few moments, he'd rolled over, propped up on one elbow, and begun to count her scratches and bruises, kissing each one ever so softly 'to make it better'.

He could be so tender like that, with the children too. When they hurt themselves, they always wanted him to treat the wound, not Stella. They said he was calm and gentle and they barely felt it, whereas she could freak out at the sight of blood and make them more anxious, too.

A wave of sickness came over her. *Al. Don't think about him.*

Rubbing her knee, she rose and gave a brave smile before ploughing on. Soon, even super fit Louise was panting and had to slow down. Katerina, meanwhile, sprang on, oblivious, until she reached the top.

'That's the hardest part done!' she cried, turning round. She wasn't smiling but Stella noticed her black eyes sparkling with amusement.

She must think them a soft lot; she probably skipped up and down those steps every day without even thinking about it. No wonder Cretans were renowned for their longevity.

When at last everyone had joined the housekeeper at the summit, there began a long, slow ascent up a gravelly donkey track.

Assorted trees dotted the dry landscape – pine and olive, lemon, orange and fig – along with myriad wildflowers: pink, blue, white, yellow and purple. The scent of wild thyme and sage filled their nostrils, and at one point, Katerina paused to point out some rough wooden beehive boxes, stacked one on top of another on a stony plateau.

Painted in vivid primary colours with metal catches on the front, they looked very jolly, like Jack in the Boxes.

'We make the best honey in the world,' Katerina announced proudly. 'Because of our wide variety of trees and flowers, and our temperate climate.'

'I hate honey,' muttered Hector, but she didn't seem to hear.

A herd of goats, with jangling gold bells round their necks, were perched on rocks a little way off. On spotting the group, they bleated loudly. It was a pitiful, wavering sort of sound, a series of cries of varying pitches, high and low.

A few of the animals turned tail and scrambled higher up, but once they realised the strangers weren't a threat, they went back to munching on the blades of grass growing between the rocks.

Dragging her heavy suitcase, Stella berated herself yet again for packing so badly. May was one of the best times to visit Crete but it was still hot, much warmer than she was used to, and she was uncomfortably sweaty in her jeans and long-sleeved white cotton top.

Up to now, they hadn't seen a soul. Soon, though, they came to a tumbledown stone cottage with a rusty, vine-covered pergola outside, providing some shade.

The brown painted shutters were open downstairs and glossy red tomatoes were drying on a large tray on the front step.

At the side of the house, an elderly bent woman in a black head-scarf was tending to a flock of chickens beside a rickety wooden henhouse. Some items of white washing were hanging on an olive tree nearby.

The woman nodded and grinned as they passed, revealing black stumpy teeth.

'That's Eleni Manousaki,' Katerina whisper-shouted, once they were out of hearing. 'She lives alone, like me. Her husband died years ago and they didn't have children. She's got bad arthritis. She knows I'm just up the road if she needs anything, but she hates interference. She seems to manage remarkably well, the poor old thing.'

Stella smiled to herself. Katerina must have been about the same age as her neighbour, but clearly considered herself in a different league entirely, and far more youthful.

It was humbling to think how hard both women's lives must be, up here on the rocky mountain, and how doughty and cheerful they seemed.

'When will we be there?' Lily whined. Stella dropped back to walk beside her daughter and Amelia. Both girls' heads were bowed. Their moods had taken a nosedive.

'Not long now, I'm sure,' she reassured, but really, she had no idea. Maybe a mile meant something different in Crete. Maybe they'd be walking for hours. Perhaps this whole trip was a terrible mistake and they shouldn't have come.

The donkey track curved right then left and on they trudged without speaking. The silence was broken at last by a cry from Katerina.

'This is it! We've arrived!'

She'd come to a sudden halt and was pointing ahead. Everybody stopped and stared too. The gravelly track petered out a few feet hence and became a rough sandy path, lined with gnarled old olive trees.

At the very end was a set of tall, shiny black metal gates and behind them loomed an imposing building made of the same grey-beige stone as Eleni's cottage.

Now the goal was in sight, the group's pace quickened. Even Hector started to hurry, picking up one end of Stella's case without being asked when she struggled to drag it across the sand.

Soon, Katerina was pulling a big bunch of keys from her trouser pocket and placing it in a large black lock. The metal gates were very heavy. Undaunted, she turned round, bent almost double, and used all the strength in her back and legs to force them open.

'This way,' she said firmly when Amelia and Lily started to wander across the gravel courtyard in the wrong direction. 'Stay with me or you'll get lost.'

The villa did indeed look like the sort of place where you could easily lose your way. The main part was a tall rectangular tower, with an archway in the middle leading to the front door. On either side were two lower, two-storey sections, with windows upstairs and down.

It was an old building that seemed to have been lovingly renovated. There were no cracks or gaps in the stonework and the sky-blue shutters and front door looked freshly painted. Giant terracotta pots in the court-yard had been carefully filled with interesting-shaped palms and colourful blooms.

Stella was about to ask about the history of the place, but Katerina got in first.

'Sections dates back to 1462,' she said. 'It was built by the Venetians, but has been much modified since. The current owners have taken care to bring it up to date while retaining most of its original charm.'

Louise cocked her head to one side, her interest piqued.

'Who are the current owners?'

Stella had been wondering the same thing; she hadn't seen any mention of them on the villa's website. Katerina was already striding up the stone steps to the front door, however, and didn't reply.

'Be careful. They're quite steep.'

As soon as the door swung open, Amelia and Lily pushed ahead, followed by Stella, Louise and the boys.

Gazing round, they could see they'd entered a wide, open entrance hall, with a high ceiling, smooth, whitewashed walls and cool, cream-coloured marble floor tiles.

In the centre was a polished dark wood table on which sat a chunky, greenish-grey ceramic vase with a round bottom and narrow neck.

A number of curved archways led off the hall into smaller rooms, one with a TV and some comfortable-looking dark-red armchairs, just waiting to be sat on, another with a desk, more chairs and an antique wooden table with a fancy chessboard on top.

Another bigger arch behind led into the dining room with a rectangular, pale-grey marble table in the centre. It could probably have seated at least twelve people and must have been incredibly heavy to lift. To Stella, it seemed to represent strength and permanence. She liked it.

The open-plan layout of the property created a sense of space and light, while the little nook-like rooms round the atrium seemed to beckon you in.

Stella took a deep breath. She'd picked well; the villa was serene, comfortable and beautiful. Thank God one thing, at least, was going right.

They left their bags on the floor and followed Katerina to the yellow and white kitchen at the back of the house. It was spotlessly clean and appeared to have everything they needed. There was even a tree outside the open window, giving off a heavenly scent of lemon blossom.

Next, they went upstairs to see the bedrooms, which were simply but tastefully decorated with linen blinds in deep shades of red, orange and blue, original paintings and wooden floors scattered with rustic, woven rugs.

The best ones had balconies and views of the mountains, town and sea.

Louise turned to Stella and smiled.

'Happy?'

'Very. It's gorgeous. Surely I'll be able to relax here?'

Katerina fixed on Stella with beady black eyes, before glancing away. She was shrewd, for sure, the type who didn't miss much.

Louise insisted Stella take the biggest room with the best view. Once the others had picked where they'd sleep, they all strolled downstairs again into the wraparound garden.

On one side of the house was a swimming pool, which looked out over the ocean, and on the other, tucked away in a private stone court-yard, a square-shaped plunge pool, decorated in beautiful blue and white mosaics and surrounded by lush green plants and trees.

There was a paved area for alfresco eating, and a grassy patch near the main pool with wooden sun loungers half shaded by greenery. The thick yellow cushions on the seats looked soft and inviting. Stella decided this would be where she'd take her novels and try to read.

Her focus had been so poor of late, she'd found herself getting through entire chapters without having absorbed anything. She longed to lose herself once more in a really good story.

Her mind flitted again to Al. He'd always loved the type of lazy holiday where you couldn't do much because of the heat; you just sat around the pool with your nose in a book.

She could see him now, sprawled on a lounger in his bright-red swimming shorts, which Lily dubbed 'disgusting', because he'd picked them up cheaply in a supermarket, along with the groceries.

Actually, Stella had quite liked them, or him in them, anyway. He was still a good-looking man: tall, broad-shouldered and handsome. She hadn't minded the extra roll round his tummy or the love handles; they were part of him, as much as his hazel eyes and infectious laugh.

Remember the bad stuff, she told herself: the rows, the attention seeking, the clinginess, the constant desire for reassurance – and sex, when that was the very last thing on her mind. She couldn't cope with his needs on top of everything else.

'C'mon! Hurry!'

Lily's voice brought her back to the present. Lily was pulling Amelia's arm, trying to drag her indoors to get changed for a swim.

Stella glanced at Louise. 'D'you fancy a dip?'

'To be honest, no. I want to unpack and get myself sorted.'

Katerina cleared her throat, which made Stella jump; she'd forgotten she was there.

'If there's anything else you need, please give me a call.'

The housekeeper's English was heavily accented, but faultless. 'I don't live far, just twenty minutes away, up the mountain.'

'Your house is even higher up than this?' Stella was amazed. 'How do you manage? How do you get your shopping up?'

She was already slightly worried about lugging groceries from town herself, even with the others to help.

Katerina shrugged. 'It's not hard. I don't need much. I have a goat and I make my own yoghurt and cheese. I buy olive oil and honey from the farmer and there's plenty of fruit on the trees. The rest I can carry.' She smiled. 'I'm used to walking everywhere, as you've seen.'

She was about to leave when she remembered something.

'You don't need to water the garden, unless you want to, of course. There's a very good sprinkler system which comes on automatically first thing in the morning and late at night. Oh, and I've left some supper in the fridge – lamb cutlets with beans, and a feta salad. I also brought eggs for breakfast, some bread, orange juice and *Kalitsounia*. These are traditional pastries. I made them myself. I hope you like them. You'll find coffee and mountain tea in the cupboard above the sink.'

'Thank you. You're very kind.'

Stella had eaten a little on the plane, but that was hours ago. She didn't feel hungry, but guessed the others might be. It couldn't be far off suppertime. The sun was just beginning to sink and the air felt cooler.

'Shit.'

They turned to see Hector, sitting cross-legged on the rustic wooden table they'd probably be eating at later. He had a cigarette in his mouth and was lighting match after match, but the wind kept blowing them out.

Stella's face fell again; he was determined to cause her maximum embarrassment. All he did was throw poisoned darts at her, dripping with anger and resentment.

Katerina would have been well within her rights to tell him off for putting his feet on the table. If she disapproved, though, she didn't show it.

'Be careful,' was all she said. 'The land is so dry; we get a lot of wildfires.'

He grunted an acknowledgment of sorts; at least he'd heard.

When Katerina turned back to Stella, her features looked softer suddenly, her eyes less beady, her nose less sharp.

'I hope you have a good night's rest. I think you'll like it here, all of you. Villa Ariadne is a very special place. It's like nowhere you've ever been before.'

2

'Will you be okay?' Louise placed a hand on her friend's arm and left it there for a moment.

They were just outside Stella's bedroom door.

'Fine thanks, honestly.'

'Good. Let's leave the kids asleep tomorrow and go for an early walk. We can talk properly then.'

It was a relief when she'd gone. Stella sat on the end of her bed and stared out of the window. The shutters were wide open and the sky was a rich, velvety black, sprinkled with sparkling stars.

All she could hear was the faint chorus of buzzing cicadas. She wasn't sure she'd ever stayed anywhere as quiet, but she didn't find it troubling. It seemed to wrap her in a comforting cocoon, providing a welcome layer of protection against the harsh daytime world.

Her mind, usually so noisy and intrusive, was a little quieter too, as if darkness had lowered the volume to a level she could just about cope with; for once, she didn't feel the urge to try to run from her thoughts, anyway.

Drawing up her legs, she hugged her arms in tight and rested her chin on her knees until a sharp pain made her pull back. She'd forgotten she'd tripped on that step earlier in the day. A big bruise was already blossoming.

Replacing her chin gingerly on the other knee, she relaxed again. She'd showered earlier and put on her pale-pink cotton pyjamas, which felt cool and soothing against her skin.

They'd been a present from her oldest and dearest friend, Harriet, many moons ago, and Stella wore them every night, except when they were in the wash. They seemed to bring the two women just that little bit closer.

Stella still missed Harriet so much. It was more than eighteen months since she'd died, but the grief never seemed to ease.

Everything had happened so fast. Prior to the summer before last, Harriet had just seemed a bit down, complaining about feeling super tired. Her irritable bowel syndrome had flared up again and she had stomach pains and was losing weight without meaning to.

Stella urged Harriet to see her GP, but she insisted she was too busy at work; and anyway, her doctor would only say the same stuff as usual – find ways to relax, do some exercise, avoid foods that trigger the IBS, and so on.

If Stella had known what she knew now, she would have tried to force the issue, but Harriet had a stubborn streak, which was partly what made her such a successful lawyer, and Stella knew she'd be difficult to budge.

After a few weeks had gone by and the symptoms still hadn't improved, in desperation, Stella had secretly phoned Harriet's husband, Jon. She was hoping he'd succeed where she'd failed, but Harriet dismissed his concerns, too. Even her seventeen-year-old daughter Jemima's pleas fell on deaf ears, until she noticed her mother's skin had turned a strange yellowish colour, along with the whites of her eyes, and insisted she must see her GP.

By then, Harriet had put up with her symptoms for three or four months. She hadn't told anyone she'd also been throwing up several times a day and had diarrhoea, on and off, too.

When she finally saw her doctor, she was given an urgent referral to a specialist. Stella could still picture Harriet's face when she told her the news.

'It's such a bore,' she'd said, frowning with irritation. 'They want to see me next week. I've had to cancel a very important meeting with a client, plus lunch with a former colleague I haven't seen for ages. I really wanted to catch up with her and she's quite difficult to pin down. I'm sure it's just my wretched IBS playing up again.'

She and Stella were having coffee in a venue halfway between their southwest London homes. It took them both about fifteen minutes to get there and it had become something of a Saturday morning ritual, followed by a stroll in the nearby park.

'I'm sure you're right, but it's best to get checked out,' Stella had said with a reassuring smile. In truth, though, fear fluttered in her stomach and all of a sudden, she felt horribly cold.

She'd offered to go with Harriet to the hospital, but Jon wanted to take her. The results came back within days and the news was devastating: Harriet had Stage Four pancreatic cancer. It had already spread to her liver and lungs and the only thing they could offer was palliative care.

At first, Stella couldn't take it in.

'There must be something they can do – chemotherapy, radiotherapy?' she'd asked Harriet dumbly. Jon was holding his wife's hand on the sofa in their sitting room, having just returned from the appointment with the consultant. He couldn't look Stella in the eye.

Harriet was as pale as a ghost but seemed eerily composed.

'I've got six months to a year,' she said with a paper-thin smile. 'Rubbish, eh? I'd better make the most of it.'

In the event, she died in just over three months. During that time, Stella visited most days and came up with a list of enjoyable activities to entertain her friend and help take her mind off the grim reality of what was happening. She splashed out on tickets to the opera, and they spent self-indulgent afternoons in the theatre and cinema, catching up on old movies they'd never seen and watching some they practically knew off by heart.

They drove to the beach in Stella's open-top Mini, singing along to the radio, with the heating up full blast and Harriet wrapped in blankets with a hot water bottle on her lap.

In the last few weeks, when her condition had deteriorated to such a point the pain was too difficult to manage at home, she was transferred to a hospice. Heartbreaking as this was, Stella was determined to stay upbeat for her friend's sake. She gathered together the phone numbers of all Harriet's friends and family and set up a WhatsApp group to make sure they worked together and she was hardly ever alone.

Next, she compiled a list of Harriet's favourite music and sat, holding her hand, while they listened to each track. Sometimes they were joined by Jemima or Jon; at other times, it was just the two of them.

She bought fresh flowers for Harriet's bedside and lit soothing candles in the evening, scented with some of her favourite fragrances: grapefruit, lemon, orange and pomegranate. When Harriet couldn't face eating, Stella made cooling smoothies, which she could drink from a special non-spill cup with a straw.

Stella probably felt closer to Harriet in her final days than she'd ever been before. They chatted about all manner of subjects, from things they'd done together to books, poetry, politics and world events. But most of all, they talked about Jon and Jemima, and Stella promised faithfully she'd look after them.

'Jon's going to be lost,' Harriet had said. 'He can hardly boil an egg and he's hopeless round the house. I'm not even sure he knows how to use the washing machine. Jemima will be incredibly sad, of course, but she's young and strong and she's got lots of friends, thank goodness. She'll be okay. It's Jon I worry about more.'

'You mustn't fret,' Stella had replied, moistening Harriet's dry lips with lip balm and popping an ice cube in her mouth for her to suck on. 'I'll show him how to use the washing machine and cook simple meals. He and Jemima will always be welcome at my place, and I'll plan some nice things for them both. I won't leave Jon to grieve by himself.'

When the end finally came, Stella was holding Harriet's hand on one side of the bed, while Jon and Jemima held the other. Jemima looked achingly like her mother, with pale-grey eyes, straight blondish-brown hair, high cheekbones and a small, slightly arched nose.

Her face was flushed and she was shaking with the effort of trying not to cry. Stella's heart went out to her even as she thought any minute her own might break into a thousand little pieces.

As Harriet's breathing became more laboured, Jemima told her mum she loved her and Stella gently stroked her friend's hair.

Finally, she whispered to Harriet that she could go now and promised again she'd look after her little family. Harriet gave a deep, rattling sigh, a single tear trickled down her hollowed cheek – and she was gone. No one spoke a word until the nurse came into the room and confirmed what they already knew.

'She's at peace now.'

Stella and Harriet had known each other since they were babies and had lived close to each other all their lives. Both only children; they were like sisters, really.

Their mothers had met at a local antenatal class and become firm friends. The girls were always in and out of each other's houses, and the families went on many holidays together. Losing Harriet was like falling from a plane and Stella was still going down, wondering when she'd hit the ground.

A bat fluttered so close to the open window, she could see its tiny black eyes and translucent wings. She feared it might enter the room, but it swooped up into the sky and disappeared from view.

After marvelling at its speed and gracefulness, she resumed her train of thought. The aftermath of Harriet's death had been horrific. Jon had been so maddened with grief that for a time, Stella thought he might take his own life. She'd been the one who'd looked after Jemima, talking with her for hours, trying to make sense of what had happened, organising lunches and dinners, trips to the theatre and cinema, anything to take her mind off her sorrows.

Stella had arranged counselling for her, attended meetings at her school, discussed university options and bought new clothes to cheer her up.

It was utterly exhausting and she felt guilty for neglecting Hector and Lily, but what choice was there? Harriet would have done the same for Stella's kids.

When Jemima started university in September, nine months after her mother's death, things had become a little easier. She seemed to settle in well, but Stella still worried about her and Jon and felt duty-bound to keep a close eye on them both.

No wonder she was hard up. She'd stopped pushing her catering business –Deliciously Yours – and orders were right down. It was only thanks to a few faithful friends that she had any work at all.

The phone pinged beside her on the bed and she hesitated for a moment before picking it up. She'd learned to dread texts since Harriet died. They were almost always from someone needing something.

To be fair, her friend, Alisha, had kindly messaged to wish her a happy holiday.

> Hope you have a great time – you deserve it XX

Another text was from her GP, reminding her about her next smear test. Ugh. Then there was a message from Al.

Stella inhaled sharply. What did he want? She thought they'd agreed to no contact for a while, or at least only in an emergency. Just below was something from Jon, so she opened that instead.

> Hi Stella, I hope you've arrived safely. I'm really struggling today. Can we have a chat? Sorry to bother you on holiday. Thanks. Jon.

A weight seemed to settle on her, like a monkey on her shoulder. She snapped on the lamp next to her bed and blinked in the sudden brightness.

No longer wrapped in her protective cocoon, she felt exposed and vulnerable again. More wants, more needs, but how could she refuse?

Opening her Recent Calls list, she quickly found the number.

'Stella?' She could sense his relief. 'I so wanted to talk to you... Thanks for calling... I've been feeling so lost... Missing Harriet... I still don't understand...'

For a while she just listened with eyes closed, making sympathetic noises every now and again: 'Mm', 'I understand', 'Of course'...

He'd said the exact same things to her many times, but that didn't lessen the weight of his suffering now.

He was like a toy – a car or train, perhaps, with a coiled spring inside that needed to unwind fully before it would grind to a halt.

Stella found herself picking at a scab on her lower arm. She couldn't recall how or when she'd got the cut. Anyway, it didn't hurt.

At last, his talking began to slow.

'Enough about me.' He sighed. 'How are you? What's the place like?'

She looked down at the scab and frowned. Blood was oozing from one corner of the wound, threatening to make a mess of the beautiful white sheets. She should have left well alone.

Glancing round in vain for a tissue, she realised the only thing for it was to lick her arm clean. The metallic taste of blood made her nose wrinkle.

'Stella? Are you still there?'

'What? Yes, sorry. It's beautiful here.' Already, fresh droplets of blood were appearing, like little crimson bubbles on the surface of her pale skin. 'The house is gorgeous. It feels weird being away, though. Also, Hector's being really difficult. I hope I've done the right thing, making him come.'

Jon coughed. She could imagine him knitting his brows and smoothing down the unruly tufts of brownish-grey hair that grew on either side of his bald patch.

'You needed a holiday, Stella.' He'd adopted his stern headmaster's voice. He was the principal of an academy in south London.

'You must look after yourself. You've had so much to deal with recently. Try to relax.'

'It's not that easy—' she began, but he'd already moved on.

'I should probably get away myself for a while,' he mused. 'It might help. I can't imagine what it would be like without Harriet, though. I'm not sure...'

His voice tailed off and Stella felt a whoosh of compassion; she wanted to give him a great big hug to take away the pain.

He was alone and lonely. Once, it had been Jon and Harriet; now it was just Jon. The couple had talked about travelling round Australia in a camper van when Jemima left home. So many dreams, never to be fulfilled.

'How about going to see Jemima in Exeter?' Stella suggested. 'You could have a long weekend there, maybe find a nice hotel for you both, or a bed and breakfast by the sea?'

Jon hesitated for a moment while he thought about it.

'It's a tempting idea,' he said eventually, 'but I don't want to cramp her style. She'd feel she had to look after me the whole time rather than go out with friends. I don't want to be a burden to her. She's got enough on her plate with her studies and all her clubs and social activities and things.'

Stella sighed. 'I guess.'

She was tired and had run out of inspiration. She felt deflated and a bit of a failure, but Jon seemed content just to have her ear.

'Thanks for being so kind and lovely, Stella,' he said warmly, before giving a great big yawn, which made Stella yawn, too. 'We'd better both grab some sleep now. I'll call you again tomorrow, if that's okay. Honestly, I wouldn't be able to get through any of this without you. I'd be a total wreck.'

* * *

After hanging up, Stella fell asleep quite quickly, but woke again at around 2 a.m. and was unable to drift off for quite some time.

It had been the same story back home, ever since Harriet's diagnosis, and Stella had become accustomed to listening to music or playing silly games on her phone in the wee small hours. If she lay wide awake for too long, her worries would grow so huge, she'd feel suffocated.

Tonight, though, instead of turning on the light, she tossed off the covers, because she was too hot, and was content to let her mind wander. It took her back to a happy weekend she'd spent with Al, Harriet and Jon some four years ago, before life had turned upside down.

It was February time. There was no special occasion, but it was so rare for the two couples to be together without the children, they'd decided to push the boat out. Harriet knew a lovely old hotel in a small market town in north Norfolk, not far from the beach. They'd driven from London together in Harriet's smart black four by four, with Jon at the wheel, and had hardly stopped talking and laughing from the moment they left to the moment they arrived back home.

Al, an architect, had been particularly busy on a big extension project for a wealthy, demanding Surrey couple. Meanwhile, Stella's decision to advertise her business in a local glossy magazine had resulted in a raft of new orders. They'd hardly seen each other, they were both exhausted and a break was just what they needed.

It was Stella who'd suggested the trip over lunch at Harriet and Jon's one Sunday, and the pair had leaped at the suggestion.

'How about staying somewhere near Holkham beach?' Harriet had said. 'It's one of my favourite places. It shouldn't be busy at this time of year.'

Stella and Al, who'd never been to that part of the UK before, had felt quite giddy with excitement when they'd said goodbye to Hector and Lily and driven off, waving from the car windows until they were out of sight.

Al's parents, who lived near Oxford, had agreed to come to London to stay with the children, then fifteen and ten, and Stella knew she could relax, because Hector and Lily would be well looked after and they'd all have fun.

Hector, who was playing a lot of rugby back then, had a wide circle of friends, was doing quite well at school and bar the odd strop, was good company and loving at home most of the time. There was no indication of the angry, troubled young man he'd become. And Lily was just, well, Lily: sweet, a bit silly, boisterous, thoughtful and keen to please.

The two couples arrived at the hotel at lunchtime and immediately ordered food, wine and beer in the cosy main bar, which had comfy leather sofas, exposed beams and a roaring open fire.

Some other guests sitting nearby, a chatty, sixty-something couple, had an elderly Border terrier called Bobby, which had lost its back legs in a car accident but still managed to whiz round on a special sort of trolley-cum-wheelchair.

It scooted off to the reception area a few times, where staff kept a big jar of posh doggy treats on the counter. Harriet got into hysterics when Bobby's doting owners, Dave and Pat, confessed their pet was very fussy and would only eat organic treats and drink filtered water.

Tears started to roll down her cheeks when Pat also revealed the dog had a girlfriend, a cocker spaniel aged thirteen, named Mavis. She even produced a photo of her with Bobby to prove it.

Bobby, with a neatly trimmed grey muzzle, puffing out his chest, and with his gleaming back wheels proudly on display, appeared to be grinning like a Cheshire cat at the camera. He was fit, trim, and looked very pleased with himself. All he needed was a bow tie to complete his dapper look.

Poor Mavis, on the other hand, resting on her haunches, with her head lowered and a soulful look in her eyes, was showing her age.

'She's got next to no teeth, bless her, but Bobby doesn't mind. We often meet her in the park near our house. She and Bobby rush round and play together like pups. I think he wears her out, actually. You should see them!'

Stella, who was beside Harriet on the sofa, nudged her in the ribs to try to calm her down, but it only seemed to make matters worse. The hysteria was infectious and soon, Al was shaking with laughter, too. Pat and Dave didn't seem bothered. Perhaps they were used to such daft reactions.

'Bobby used to love the sea,' Dave went on seriously. 'We bought him a wetsuit, so his fur stayed dry. The poor chap can't go in the water now, though. His wheels might rust.'

Fuelled with food and booze, Stella, Al, Harriet and Jon had left the hotel, still giggling, and gone for a walk round the town and across the fields, where they'd seen Muntjac deer and flocks of wild geese feasting on beet tops left on the soil after harvest.

Stella bought an overpriced sweater in a boutique shop, before they'd all rolled home to wash and change for dinner. Stella and Al had a luxurious walk-in two-person shower. Of course, one thing led to another and they were soon having noisy, enthusiastic sex. You'd think they'd been stranded on separate desert islands for weeks on end.

They were late down for supper and it was obvious what they'd been up to from their flushed cheeks and secret little smiles. Jon, meanwhile, looked like a cat who'd got the cream, while Harriet, acting prim in a vintage white lace shirt, her hair in an elegant up-do, fooled absolutely no one.

'Go on, admit it, you've been at it like rabbits,' Stella whispered teasingly in Harriet's ear.

Harriet patted her hair and pretended to be shocked.

'I don't know what you're talking about.'

She picked up the drinks menu before clearing her throat and declaring in a rather loud voice, which made Jon wince: 'I need a HUGE cocktail. What about the rest of you? A Harvey Wallbanger, Stella? Or have you already had one?'

She loved being outrageous, especially after a few drinks.

In fairness, it was Harriet and Stella who got on best. Jon and Al had to work a bit harder in each other's company, being very different characters. Al loved a good laugh, and people generally warmed to his easygoing manner and engaging stories, peppered with the occasional risqué joke. Jon, by contrast, tended to be quiet, serious and analytical.

Al called him a 'nitpicker', but never to his face. He knew how important the friendship was to Stella, and fortunately the two men found just enough common ground to keep them engaged.

Harriet always said Al brought out Jon's lighter side and it was true, he certainly laughed a lot more after a few hours in Al's company. They all did.

'I still don't really understand why Harriet's with him,' Al had commented when he and Stella had finally got to bed that night. 'He's definitely punching above his weight. She's so lively and interesting, but he really is a bit of a bore.'

'He's very knowledgeable,' Stella replied, carefully taking out the silver earrings which Al had bought her for her birthday and putting them on the bedside table.

'Yes, and he loves to show it. He completely lost me when he started talking about biofuel technologies and kilowatts per tonne of corn. Honestly, I nearly nodded off.'

'You'd want him on your team in a quiz, though. And he's a good father. I reckon he keeps Harriet steady. She could be a bit flighty and impulsive before she met him. She got herself into quite a few scrapes, especially with men. He makes sure her feet stay firmly on the ground.'

Al looked doubtful. 'He ticks her off like one of his pupils. Did you notice his reaction when she was talking about Harvey Wallbangers? I'm sure he'd have said something if we hadn't been there. I don't know how she can stand it.'

'P'raps she likes it,' Stella replied mischievously.

'What? You mean it's part of their bedroom repertoire? Jon smacking her with a ruler and making her write lines in the nude? I don't think so. He wouldn't have the imagination.'

Stella snorted with amusement, before cocking her head on one side and giving her husband a playful grin. 'Ooh, I'm not convinced. Maybe he's a dark horse. You never know what might go on behind that stern headmaster's exterior. Still waters can run deep.'

3

It seemed she'd only just dropped off again after her sleepless spell when she was startled from her drug-like doze by a loud knocking. It took her a few moments to remember where she was.

'Stella? Are you awake? Can I come in?'

Louise. Stella sat up quickly, smoothing down her hair with the palm of a hand and rubbing a forefinger under each eye to remove any traces of yesterday's mascara.

Louise must have been up a while and looked fresh and bright. Her fair, shoulder-length hair was damp from the shower and she was wearing denim shorts and a clean white vest top, which showed off her toned arms.

She was only five foot three, slim and athletic but definitely a woman, with a small waist and bigger boobs, hips and thighs. Everything was firm and in proportion and she cycled, swam and lifted weights to keep it that way.

Some of Stella's friends, including Harriet, thought she was too perfect and a bit of a smarty-pants to boot, but Stella disagreed.

She'd met Louise on the very first day of secondary school. She'd been feeling lonely and lost without Harriet, whose parents had decided to send her somewhere else.

Louise had come straight up to Stella, bold as brass, after a PE class and asked if they could be friends. She'd always been brave like that. Stella had been thrilled, said yes, and they'd pretty much stuck together for the next eight years.

Funnily enough, Louise and Harriet had tolerated one another but never really gelled; Stella suspected there might have been some jealousy involved. But there was no need, as their paths didn't often cross. Louise was Stella's school friend and Stella saw Harriet at weekends and during holidays.

Everyone seemed to think Louise was super self-confident, but Stella was as familiar with her vulnerabilities as her strengths. She'd wiped away Louise's tears when she was dumped by her first boyfriend and, later, cheered her up when she failed to get into the university she really wanted.

Louise had done the same for her, and occasionally being bossed around seemed a small price to pay for such a long friendship.

Perching on the end of the bed, Louise peered at Stella and pulled a concerned face.

'Bad night?'

Stella gave a wry smile. 'Do I look that awful?'

'Not at all—'

'It's okay.' Stella smiled. 'I woke up and couldn't get back to sleep for ages. I had my eyes closed, though, and I was remembering a lovely weekend we had with Harriet and Jon in Norfolk before she became ill. At least I got some rest.'

'Poor you.' Louise's complexion was so clear and her face so smooth, you'd never think she'd recently turned fifty. She had a light tan left over from a Caribbean holiday with the children in January, and her small, intelligent blue eyes, set quite close together, sparkled with life.

Her hair was naturally fair, she wore little makeup and might have been described as an English rose, were it not for the rows of little gold hoops and studs that glinted all the way up and down the outer edges of her ears. There must have been six earrings on each side. Some had teeny-tiny gold pendants; others were studded with semi-precious stones.

They were intricate and subtle, and Stella often noticed people looking at them. She found her own gaze wandered that way, too. The earrings gave Louise an air of appealing quirkiness, which Stella envied. She couldn't seem to find time to put on any earrings. Sometimes, she even forgot to brush her hair.

'Do you want to skip the walk and try and get some more sleep?' Louise asked now, but Stella shook her head.

'Let's go before it gets too hot. It won't take me long to dress.'

* * *

Her heart leaped when they closed the black iron gates behind them and set off along the sandy path into the Cretan countryside.

It was only 8 a.m. and the sun was already shining. The air felt crisp and the cloudless blue sky looked fresh and cool. Spiral spiders' webs, covered in shimmering dewdrops, dangled like scraps of lace from the olive trees lining the way. Tiny wild orchids and blue pimpernel peeped through the vegetation on either side, which was so dense, at times they felt as if they were walking through a giant salad bowl. The scent of wild herbs filled their nostrils, and birdsong filled their ears. The din was so lusty and joyful, it was almost as if the birds were performing a roistering oratorio just for them.

They kept to a slow, steady pace. They weren't in a rush and wanted to soak up their surroundings. Stella circled her head and shoulders a few times to loosen her muscles and ligaments, all the while keeping an eye out for roots and stones.

She was wearing loose khaki shorts, a white short-sleeved shirt and thick socks tucked into sturdy brown walking boots. Her hair, which was mid-brown and jaw-length, was really too short to tie back, but she'd pulled what she could into a funny, stubby ponytail.

Several inches taller than her friend, she felt pale and unattractive by comparison. Stress had made her weight fall and now her hip bones protruded and her once voluptuous breasts had all but disappeared.

It didn't feel like her body any more, but then almost everything else had changed, too, so she wasn't much surprised.

'I think I did the wrong thing, making Hector come,' she said, aware of the sound of their boots scrunching on sand, rocks and pebbles. 'I hope he doesn't spoil things for everyone.'

'He won't.'

Stella smiled gratefully. Louise was doing her best to be positive, but it couldn't be easy. She'd have had a much better time if she and her kids had gone away on their own.

'How often does Hector see Al?' Louise asked, nudging the conversation on.

Stella took a sip of water from the plastic bottle she was carrying.

'A lot. Two or three nights a week at least and pretty much all weekend. I'm sure he'd live there full-time if there was an extra bedroom. Al just couldn't afford a bigger place, on top of our mortgage. The rent's huge as it is.'

'Does Hector still blame you for the split?'

'Oh yes.' Stella swallowed. 'He idolises Al. I don't think he'll ever forgive me.'

'It seems so unfair.'

Stella frowned. It was true she was the one who'd wanted the separation, but only after the atmosphere at home had become so toxic, it was impacting on everyone. It took two to create a mood like that. Why couldn't Hector understand?

She knew he was insecure, in part, at least, because Al wasn't his real father. He was a drunk named Robin who'd left when Hector was just eighteen months old. Stella had cut off all contact to protect her son and Robin had died of alcoholism a few years later.

Of course Hector had been affected by the split, and Stella had struggled, too. Then when Al had come on the scene some two years later, he'd literally scooped them both up and the world had brightened.

Ever since, Al could do no wrong in Hector's eyes. He was the knight in shining armour, the conquering hero who'd always treated Hector as his own.

He *had* been an amazing stepdad, but Hector wasn't a child any more. He was old enough to realise no one was perfect and he should be able to see things from Stella's viewpoint, too.

Instead, he'd dropped out of university and was mucking about. His former school friends had largely turned their backs and he no doubt blamed her for that as well.

'I could have a word with him if you like?' Louise suggested. 'He might listen to me. Don't worry, I'll choose my words carefully. It might be worth a try?'

Stella frowned. 'Thanks, but I don't think it's a good idea. Not at the moment, anyway. He'd assume I put you up to it, which would make him even angrier, if that's humanly possible.'

Going down the mountain was quicker than walking up and they soon came to the spot with the brightly coloured beehives.

Stella was keen to lighten the chat, but Louise had other ideas.

'How's work going?' she asked, flicking off a fly, which had landed on her shoulder.

The question was undoubtedly loaded; Stella knew her friend too well.

'Really bad.' She pulled a face. 'To be honest, I might wind up the business and look for something else.'

Louise went quiet with disapproval. She'd always been ambitious and had carved out a successful career in public relations. She didn't believe in quitting; the word wasn't in her vocabulary.

'You need to market yourself again,' she insisted, sounding slightly exasperated, because once Harriet's funeral was over and the dust had settled, she'd been repeating the same mantra over and over. Stella might have felt hurt by her tone, but she told herself Louise was only trying to help.

'I can give you a hand if you want. You've got a great little business but you need to kick start it again and shout about it more.'

'I know.' Stella sighed. 'The problem is, my heart's not in it any more. Since Harriet died, I haven't been able to summon up much enthusiasm for anything. Maybe I should find a mundane nine to five job that won't require much brainpower. I like the idea of being able to leave everything behind at the end of the day.'

'You'd get bored very quickly doing a mundane job. Throwing yourself into your business again might take your mind off what's happened.

You worked so hard to get to where you were. It'd be tragic to walk away now.'

She was probably right, but it wasn't what Stella wanted to hear. It was all very well telling her to buck up, but Louise hadn't lost her oldest friend and separated from her husband, all in the space of eighteen months.

In fact, sometimes, Stella suspected Louise didn't fully grasp why she was still grieving for her friend or her marriage at all; it was almost as if she expected her to be over everything by now.

It was just the little things she'd say, like, 'Harriet had a good life, even though it was cut short. I guess it was her time to go,' and, 'You'll come through this; be strong.'

Stella ignored the comments because they weren't meant to be hurtful; they were just clumsily worded. It did make her wonder, though, whether Louise had ever really loved anyone as much as Stella had loved Harriet. Perhaps all her relationships, male and female, were less intense and that bit more superficial.

'Hey! Look!' she cried, relieved to spot a distraction. 'I think that's the start of the steps.'

'So it is. Let's grab a coffee in the village before we explore.'

Once they reached the bottom, it wasn't difficult to find their way round Porto Liakáda as it was so small. The low-lying buildings, all white with blue windows, were set like an amphitheatre round the crescent-shaped bay, with tall date palm trees rising majestically between them.

The one main street was right on the waterfront, and it was here that the two women sat in a café at a table overlooking the pristine turquoise waters of the Libyan sea.

Fishing boats of different shapes and sizes bobbed in the harbour while some way off, royal blue and white umbrellas and matching sun loungers dotted the small pebbly beach.

For now, it was deserted, but rows of yellow kayaks and white paddleboards for hire suggested this state of affairs wouldn't last long.

They ordered coffee and a *Bougatsa* to share, as recommended by their waiter. They weren't sure what to expect and it turned out to be a delicious pie made of crunchy filo pastry, filled with local *mizithra* cheese and sprinkled with sugar.

It disappeared so fast, they soon ordered another, and when Louise had finished her final bite, she stared mournfully at the empty plate. 'I'd happily have that for breakfast every day.'

It was still early and the shops were only just beginning to throw open their doors. A handful of folk in summery clothes were ambling up and down the main street, as if waiting for the action to begin.

The sun was getting hotter by the minute and Stella remembered she wasn't wearing sunscreen. With her pale skin, she'd burn in no time.

Rising, she tried to move her chair under the parasol, but was interrupted by a loud yell, which made her jump.

Glancing down, she could see what appeared to be a child on the ground beneath her seat. He was on his knees, his top half hidden under the table, his rear end squirming. She was so astounded, she wondered for a few seconds if she were imagining it.

'OHMYGOD!' The words tumbled out in a rush.

She tried to whip the chair out of the way before realising the child was trapped between its metal legs.

'Aargh! Are you all right?'

Her heart was thumping so fast, she'd forgotten where she was. There was no need to worry, though, because the boy understood her English perfectly.

'You might've broken my arm,' he said angrily after finally managing to reverse out of his prison and sit back, rubbing the sore bit. 'You should watch what you're doing.'

Stella was too anxious to be offended. Frowning, she squatted down to his level, apologising profusely. 'I'm so sorry. I really am. Can I take a look?'

The boy, somewhat mollified, sat up straight and extended one skinny arm, which she examined carefully.

To her great relief, the chair seemed to have left nothing more than a red mark, and the arm and hand were working perfectly.

She inhaled deeply, realising she'd been holding her breath.

'It seems okay, thank God. No serious damage.'

'It still hurts. You should be more careful.'

Now she could see him better, Stella realised he could only be seven or eight, but he didn't seem at all shy.

He was a scrawny little thing in a grubby white T-shirt and blue shorts. His bare feet were grimy too. His hair was very dark, almost black, and the fringe was so long and shaggy, she wondered how he could see out of it.

Jutting his chin, he started to lecture her on her bad behaviour. Now it was her turn to be annoyed.

'What were you doing under my seat anyway? You shouldn't have been there.'

Before he could answer back, they were interrupted by a shout.

'Oi! Meaty! Come here!'

Stella swung round to see a big blonde woman in a flowery dress running towards them. She was red-faced and her features were scrunched so tightly together in a frown, you could hardly make them out.

As soon as she was near enough, she grabbed the boy's wrist and yanked him up sharply.

'I told you not to go out without shoes,' she snapped, slapping him on the side of the head before he could duck. 'You might've stepped on broken glass, then you'd be sorry.'

'Ma! There isn't any broken glass!'

The boy tried to wriggle out of her grasp but she hung on tight.

'Get back home before I *really* lose my temper.'

As she started to drag him away, he hollered something about his ball being under the table. It seemed he'd been trying to reach it when he got trapped.

His mother shook her head. 'You should look after your possessions. Scrabbling round like that under the poor lady's feet. She probably thought you were trying to steal her bag!'

She was wearing quite a lot of shiny blue eye shadow and Stella decided she must have been in a rush this morning, as one eyebrow was darker than the other.

'Say sorry,' the woman barked, glaring at her son, who goggled in dismay.

After repeating herself to no avail, she tried to cuff him again, but this time he managed to twist from her grip and bob out of the way in the nick of time.

His mum lumbered towards him like a great grizzly bear. The boy glanced round, searching for an escape route, but the tables were quite close together, and besides, he had Stella and Louise to contend with.

Realising the game was up, he muttered an apology but it was so quiet, you could scarcely hear.

His mum took another menacing step forwards.

'I'M SORRY!' he said, louder this time because he was panicking.

'You don't sound it.'

'I AM!'

Stella was beginning to feel a little sorry for the boy. His mum even scared *her*. Bending down to look under the table, she spotted a yellow tennis ball. 'Is this what you were after?'

The boy's face lit up in a grin, revealing a funny gap in front where only one of his permanent teeth had come through.

As soon as he'd grabbed the ball, he scurried off into the distance while his mum turned to Stella, mismatched eyebrows raised.

'He's a right little devil. Sorry for all the trouble. His name's Dimitrios, but we call him Meaty 'cause he can't get enough of the stuff. Lamb, chicken, pork, you name it, he'll eat it. You wouldn't think so by the size of him, would you? He's all skin and bone!'

She had a Yorkshire-sounding accent and spoke so fast, Stella had some difficulty keeping up.

'I'm April, by the way, April Vasilakis,' she went on, barely pausing for breath. 'I run the supermarket over there with my husband, Georgios.'

She pointed to a small store set back from the waterfront where a stout middle-aged man was wheeling out displays of fruit and vegetables on a black shelving unit.

'That's him, my hubby.' She grinned and waved and he waved back.

Now she'd stopped frowning, Stella realised the woman was really rather pretty. She had a round face, a small, squashy nose and sparkly grey eyes. Her bleached blonde hair was in a loose twist, secured on top with a tortoiseshell clip.

Louise, who'd been quite quiet till now, sipping her coffee and taking everything in, piped up, 'I'm guessing you're British. Where are you from?'

She looked amused; she was clearly enjoying herself. It wasn't every day you came across characters like Meaty and his mum.

April said she was born and bred in Leeds.

'I met Georgios when I was nineteen. I was on holiday here with my mates and, well, we just clicked. It was only supposed to be a summer romance and I'm still here twenty-five years later, with four kids, two dogs, two fat cats and a hamster. How did that happen!'

She had a throaty, infectious laugh, which made her shoulders jiggle up and down. Stella and Louise laughed, too.

She said she lived above the shop and Stella's gaze drifted to the two small windows above the supermarket. She found herself wondering how everyone fitted in.

April must have read her mind.

'It's a bit of a squeeze, but it's home to us. We've got two Bernese Mountain Dogs. They're quite big and hairy. They sleep on the balcony in summer but in winter, they insist on kipping on our bed, along with the cats!'

Georgios had finished putting out the display stands and customers were already going in and out of the supermarket, but April seemed in no rush to leave. Perhaps she was a little homesick, as she talked a lot about the UK.

'I love it here but I do miss cheese and onion crisps!' she said mournfully.

She was so chatty, Stella feared they'd never get away, but when Louise told April where they were staying in Porto Liakáda, she fell silent.

'It's a big old place,' she said at last. 'Do you like it?'

Stella was surprised. How could anyone *not* like such a stunning house with two pools and breathtaking views?

'It's really lovely,' she replied, meaning it.

April nodded, but her grey eyes were clouded with doubt. 'It's so big, I should think it's a bit like a maze in there. I'd get lost.'

Stella hoped she'd be able to tell them who owned the place, but April said she couldn't help.

'They might be an older couple, I don't know. I think they're Greek, but no one from round here's ever met them, as far as I can tell. A few years back, they brought in a team of builders from Athens to do the place up. Some of the workers used to come to the village, but even they didn't know a lot. They were happy because they got free housing and were well paid. That's all they cared about. Some people round here say it's weird to buy a place like that and never visit.'

Her hand shot up and she fiddled with the clip in her hair, catching a few loose strands.

'Even old Mrs Papadakis, the housekeeper, never talks about them,' she added, before clearing her throat. 'To tell you the truth, I sometimes wonder if they exist at all.'

4

'She's a real character! So's her son. I bet that flat's noisy when all the family's at home.'

Louise hooked an arm in Stella's as they left the café after paying the bill.

April was newly positioned in her shop doorway when they walked past, with a toddler playing at her feet.

On catching sight of Stella and Louise, she bent down to pick up the child, balancing him on her hip and waggling his wrist to make his chubby hand wave.

He was in nothing but a nappy and T-shirt and was tanned and a bit grimy, with lots of messy black hair, like his older brother. He looked cute and rather grave, which made Louise and Stella smile.

'God knows how she copes with four kids,' Louise whispered. 'Two seems like a lot to me.'

'I suspect they don't wash much,' Stella replied dryly, remembering Meaty's grubby feet. 'But I'll say one thing, she's certainly doing a great job with their English. Meaty's totally fluent – he's even picked up her accent!'

It was a relief to escape the heat and stroll up the main street, which was shady and cool by comparison. They had to watch where they were going, though. The place was quite crowded now and stands were spilling out on either side of the walkway, displaying rows of brightly coloured clothes, hats, jewellery, beach bags and postcards.

Louise stopped a few times to look at cheesecloth shirts and gold earrings, while Stella was more interested in the food stalls, selling local honey and olive oil, bunches of fresh herbs and bags of spices, shelled almonds, walnuts and bottles of Cretan raki, a type of very strong, clear brandy.

Seeing the nuts reminded her of a delicious Greek basil, walnut and feta pesto, which she used to make. Al and the children loved it. They'd have it with pasta or jacket potatoes, for a simple weekday supper.

They were also keen on her classic moussaka, with cinnamon spiced lamb, aubergine and a creamy, nutmeg-spiked sauce. Al used to ask her to make extra so he could take it to the office and have it for lunch the next day. She'd always pop a few homemade sweet treats in his bag, too, as a surprise.

She'd honed her skills at a top London cookery school after A levels, having decided to forgo university in favour of following her passion – food. After that, she'd worked at several leading restaurants and established quite a reputation for herself as a sociable, hard-working, creative chef who specialised in seafood and game.

She went back to it after Hector was born, but found the hours hard to manage. Her then husband was drinking heavily, so she couldn't trust him with the baby, and when the marriage started to implode, it became clear she'd need to be at home much more.

Luckily, she had a little money saved to start her own venture, and Deliciously Yours was conceived on the back of an envelope in her kitchen. It wasn't easy running a business as a single parent, but her mother and father helped with childcare, and friends, including Harriet and Louise, rallied round and kept her sane.

'This is *Diktamo*, or Dittany in English. It only grows on the mountains and gorges of Crete.'

The male stallholder held up a small white bag for Stella to sniff. It had a strong, distinctive, aromatic smell, something like oregano mixed with lemon.

'It is very good for the stomach, the digestive system, good healing qualities. You want some?'

Stella hesitated. She could find a recipe when she got back to the villa and surprise everyone tonight or tomorrow with a new tasty dish. She used to enjoy doing that. Reaching in her bag for her purse, she was about to pay when something Al once said rang in her ears and pulled her up short.

'You never cook any more, you just buy ready meals. It's not good for the children.'

It was one of the last things he'd uttered before he left. That and, 'You're spending all your time with Jon and Jemima. What about Hector and Lily? What about *me*?'

She'd felt guilty, but instead of talking things through and trying to find a compromise, she'd been defensive and mean. She wasn't proud of herself, but in her mind at that time, Al should have seen how stressed she was and backed off.

'You're so selfish,' she'd snapped. 'Everything's about you.'

He'd looked hurt. 'That's not true.'

'Yes, it is. I'm trying to support my best friend's poor family and all you can think about is your stomach. You're a grown man; you can make your own fucking meals from now on.'

It was almost the last straw. Ever since they'd met, cooking his favourite meals had been one of the ways she'd shown him how much she loved him.

That night in bed, when he'd tried to get close to her and she'd pushed him away for the umpteenth time, all of a sudden, he'd sat up straight and turned on the light.

'I'm sorry, I can't do this any longer, Stella,' he'd said dully. 'It's not a marriage any more. Your coldness is killing me. I'll find somewhere to rent. It's sad, I know, but these things happen. We'll be better off apart.'

Silence had descended and Stella thought he must have been able to hear the pounding of her heart.

At that point, she'd had a choice: she could have begged him to stay and promised to spend more time at home with him and the kids. But she didn't. She felt spent, with barely enough energy to put one foot in front of the other, let alone fight for her relationship.

'If that's what you want,' she'd said wearily, wiping away the tears that had started to trickle down her cheeks. 'You're probably right. I can't give you what you need. Perhaps it's for the best.'

'We'll speak to the kids tomorrow. I'll find a flat nearby with a spare room, so they can stay anytime. We'll make this work for their sakes.'

'You wish to buy?' The stallholder waved the bag of herbs in front of Stella's nose, making her snap out of her daydream.

'Or something else?' he went on. 'Some basil? Saffron? Cumin?'

Stella shivered. 'Not today, thanks.'

She looked round for Louise, who was on the other side of the street, holding up a beaded necklace, and put the money back in her purse before returning it to her bag.

'I might come back tomorrow, sorry,' she said, embarrassed, and she started to move away. 'Thanks again.'

As the women wandered on, they heard quite a bit of English being spoken, as well as German, French and Spanish. Louise's eye was caught by a leather shop, with a pair of gladiator-style Greek sandals in the window. There were also bags, belts, purses, glasses cases and wallets on display in a multitude of colours.

'Shall we go in?' she asked, and Stella nodded, following her friend into the dark room, which smelled of oil and wax, chemicals and perfume. It was a heady mix but Stella liked the scent; it reminded her of the favourite leather jacket her father wore when she was a child.

As her eyes adjusted to the dim light, she became aware of a very old man sitting behind the wooden counter. He had snow-white hair and a bushy white moustache. A jaunty red and white scarf was tied round his neck and knotted in front, like a cravat.

Stella nodded in greeting before asking if she and her friend could browse.

'Of course,' the man said with a charming smile, supporting himself with his hands on the counter top while he rose as gallantly as he could from his chair.

He was tall, extremely thin and deeply wrinkled. He had on a pale blue shirt rolled up at the sleeves, and the skin on his tanned arms looked as dry and fragile as parchment.

'What can I do for you two ladies?' Despite his advanced years, there was a definite twinkle in his eye. 'It's not often I see two beautiful women in my shop at the same time!'

The old devil! Stella laughed, but Louise wasn't easily flattered and announced crisply that she wished to try on a pair of the gladiator sandals.

The man produced a wooden stool from behind the counter for her to sit on, before rootling round in a room at the back of his shop for the right size.

On returning with a shoebox, he swayed from side to side like bamboo in a gale and Stella steeled herself to catch him. Luckily, there was no need. By extending his arms like windmill sails, he managed to balance long enough to hand the box to Louise, before tottering back to his seat and slumping down with a barely disguised sigh.

Surely he should be taking it easy, not working in a shop? Stella felt quite angry on his behalf, until she decided he must enjoy the job and it probably kept him young. His body was falling apart but there was certainly nothing the matter with his mind.

Louise loved the tan leather sandals, which strapped up the ankle and had a double buckle fastening.

'Do I look like an ancient Greek noblewoman in them?' she joked, admiring her feet from several angles.

'Like Aphrodite!' the old man replied with a wheezy smoker's chuckle. 'Or Hera, the queen of Olympus!'

'Not Maximus, anyway,' Stella commented wryly, meaning the Russell Crowe character from the Hollywood film, *Gladiator*. 'Your legs aren't hairy enough.'

After paying for the sandals, Louise was on the point of leaving when the old man mentioned his daughter, Marina.

'She's an artist, a painter. She's very good. You should take a look at her work. She sells it from her studio. It's right here, at the end of the street.'

Stella said they'd definitely pay a visit, which seemed to please him.

However, when he asked where they were staying and she told him, his expression changed.

'That place?' he said with a sneer, which took her aback. 'It shouldn't be rented to foreigners; it should be lived in by a person from this island, a local person or people. It's not right.'

'Oh,' Stella said, wide-eyed. 'I'm sorry, I didn't mean to offend you.'

The old man shook his head and waved his hand in the air dismissively.

'It's not your fault. *You've* done nothing wrong.'

Stella glanced at Louise, who appeared as mystified as she was.

'We haven't met the owner,' Stella went on. 'We've only had dealings with Mrs Papadakis.'

Secretly, she rather hoped at this point he'd let slip who the owners were, but on hearing the housekeeper's name, he sneered again.

'Her? Pah! That woman's nothing but trouble.'

'That was weird,' Stella commented when she and Louise finally left the shop and stepped out into the sunshine again. 'What a strange reaction!'

Louise nodded. 'He's obviously got some sort of grudge against Katerina. I wonder why.'

Intrigued, they decided to visit the old man's daughter's studio right away, but when they checked the time, they realised they'd already been gone a good few hours.

'We'd better get back. The kids are probably awake by now.'

As they strolled the other way up the high street, Stella's phone rang. It was Jon and she had that familiar sinking feeling again.

'Why did it have to be Harriet?' he blurted before he'd even said hello. There was a crack in his voice. 'She was a good person; she had so much more to give.'

Stella swallowed. He hadn't improved since yesterday, then. In fact, he sounded worse. She desperately wanted to help, but it was hard to find the right words.

'She was a wonderful person, a one-off,' she replied gently. 'Cancer's just so cruel. It doesn't discriminate.'

Louise stopped to look at some cheap sunglasses on a rotating display stand, giving Stella space to move a little way away and talk in private.

'I'm sorry I can't make things better,' she went on. 'I'm always here to support you.'

'I know you are.' He made a choking sound, which she felt deep down in her gut. 'I'm so lost without her. At least work's some sort of distraction. I don't know what to do with myself now it's the holidays.'

'Why don't you come and join us?' The words escaped from her lips before her brain had time to catch up. 'There's a spare room with a double bed and plenty of space. You can swim and go for walks and read. It'd be so good for you. You can hang out with us if you fancy and not if you don't. The flight's only four hours; it's easy.'

Jon hesitated. 'I'm not—'

'You don't need to decide now.' Stella was on a roll, swept along by her own idea. 'Have a think and talk to friends. We don't need much notice, or any, really. You can let us know the day before if you like.'

'It's a really kind offer, but—'

She was convinced he was going to say no. Maybe it was just as well. After all, she hadn't checked with Louise. Then again, surely she wouldn't mind. She knew how much Jon had suffered.

There was a pause and Stella wondered if he'd bring the conversation to a close. To her surprise, though, his voice came back louder and clearer than before.

'I'll give it some thought, I promise. I'll let you know asap.'

* * *

Seeing that the conversation was over, Louise re-joined Stella and the women continued their journey.

'All right?' Louise asked.

Stella nodded. 'Sort of.'

'What was it about?'

'The usual stuff. Why did Harriet have to die, how lonely he is. I feel useless a lot of the time. I mean, what can I say?'

'It sounds like he just wants you to listen,' Louise replied. 'You're doing all you can. I wish he'd occasionally give you a break, though, and talk to someone else instead.'

A group of young English women walked by, wearing skimpy tops and shorts and laughing loudly. They weren't looking where they were going and one bumped into Louise, who wobbled, almost knocking over a display of hats. Luckily, she managed to right herself just in time.

'Careful!' she said sharply. The woman paused briefly to apologise, but Louise scowled.

'Miserable cow,' one of the other girls muttered as they sauntered off. Her friends tittered. 'Looks like she's eaten a lemon.'

Stella had to agree. Louise *had* rather overreacted. What had got into her? After all, the woman had apologised. She decided she wouldn't mention her spur-of-the-moment invitation to Jon just now.

By the time they reached the end of the street, thankfully Louise had recovered her equanimity and stopped, pointing towards the bay. 'Look! An artist! I wonder if it's the leather shop man's daughter.'

The woman in question was perched on a little wooden stool at the water's edge in front of an easel, attached to which was a large white parasol. Her pink and red tie-dye dress looked startlingly bright in the morning light, set against a backdrop of cobalt-blue sky and sea.

She was wearing a big straw hat and her long, dark, wavy hair ran down her back like a waterfall. Stella thought she looked like a character from a play or film, too dramatic to be real.

They strolled in her direction and peered over her shoulder, careful to keep a respectful distance so she wouldn't feel crowded.

The big canvas on which she was working was half covered in thick splodges of oil paint in flamboyant pinks, yellows, oranges, blues and greens.

It was impossible to tell what the image depicted, but to Stella, it gave a rather dreamlike impression of sea and sky. It was a joyful, celebratory painting, like a fanfare. If you had it on your wall, it would make your heart sing.

Stella and Louise hadn't made any noise, but the woman must have sensed their presence because she turned and gave a wide, serene smile.

She wasn't as young as Stella had imagined. She was probably in her mid- to late-fifties but was still beautiful, in an unconventional way.

She was very slender with olive skin, a long, slim face and high cheekbones. Her nose, which was dead straight, seemed to spring from her forehead, and there was hardly a dent where glasses would normally sit.

Her dark-brown eyes were quite deep set, crinkled at the edges and framed by thick black lashes and smooth, arched brows. She wore little makeup, save black kohl, and had an air of quiet composure, as if it would take a lot to disturb her peace of mind.

'That's lovely,' Stella said, still staring at the painting. 'I really like the colours.'

'Thank you, you're very kind.'

The woman placed her palette on her knees, put down her brush and shifted round to give the strangers her full attention.

Her dress was full length and sleeveless. There was something relaxed and elegant about the way she straightened her lean, tanned arms, cupped her hands over her knees and neatly crossed her ankles. She wore a chunky silver bracelet round her wrist and another round her upper arm.

'Please don't let us interrupt you.' Louise sounded quite dismayed. 'We were just curious to see what you were doing.'

The woman shook her head. 'No, it's all right. It's getting a bit too hot now. I was thinking of packing up anyway.'

She couldn't rise without dropping her palette so she extended a hand from her seated position. Louise took it first, then Stella. The hand was surprisingly small and cool.

'I'm Marina, by the way,' she said. 'I live here. My studio's just up the road.'

She pointed in the general direction.

'Oh! I think we just met your father in the leather shop,' Louise said. 'He mentioned you. I bought a pair of his sandals.'

Marina gave a tuneful little laugh, like wind chimes tinkling in the breeze.

'He's always trying to push my work, bless him. He's my most ardent fan – my best promo guy!'

Stella grinned. 'Well, his efforts certainly paid off with us. We couldn't resist coming over. We'll definitely visit your studio.'

Marina uncrossed her feet and stretched out her legs. She was wearing leather sandals, quite like the ones Louise had just acquired, and her toenails were painted orange.

'Are you on holiday?' she asked, and both women nodded. 'Where are you staying? Here in Porto Liakáda?'

'We're renting Villa Ariadne,' Louise explained. 'Our children are here, too – we've got four between us. They're teenagers, though, so they don't get up early.' She raised her eyebrows and Marina smiled back, amused.

'Do you know it?' Louise went on. 'The villa, I mean? It's very beautiful.'

'Oh yes, I know it.'

'Who owns it?' Stella asked quickly. She was even more eager to find out now, after the old man's odd reaction in the shoe shop.

'Ah, you'll have to ask Mrs Papadakis that,' Marina replied, much to Stella's frustration.

She was about to say they *had* asked, but the housekeeper had ignored them. She didn't, though, fearing it might seem rude. She was beginning to think there must definitely be more to the villa and its owner or owners than met the eye. The mere mention of it round here seemed to stir up so many peculiar emotions.

Marina quickly changed the subject.

'I love your earrings.'

She was admiring Louise's array of gold studs and sleepers. The artist pushed away the thick curtain of hair on one side of her face to reveal her own ears, decorated with four silver hoops of differing sizes. 'You see! We think alike!'

A speck of dust flew into Stella's eye and she removed her sunglasses and tried to rub it away.

In an instant, Marina's focus switched again to her.

'Let me look at you properly.'

The woman was gazing intensely at Stella's face, which made her feel shy all of a sudden. She wanted to replace her shades, but didn't wish to be impolite.

'Is my mascara splodged?' she joked.

Marina didn't reply. 'You look sad,' she said instead, leaning forwards over her palette and frowning.

Stella shuffled uncomfortably. 'Do I? What makes you think that?'

Sensing Stella's unease, Louise sprang to her rescue. 'That's not a very nice thing to say. You don't know anything about her!'

Marina scarcely blinked, but she leaned back a little and softened her gaze. Her eyes, though, remained firmly on Stella.

'I'm sorry if I alarmed you. I didn't mean to speak out of turn. What I wanted to say was, I think you've suffered, but you'll soon be reunited with someone you love.'

All of a sudden, Stella felt herself wobble. She was surprised the stranger's words had had such an effect.

Louise must have noticed her friend sway, because she glowered at the artist and placed a protective arm round Stella's shoulders, drawing her in.

'How dare you upset her! You've no idea what she's been through.'

'Forgive me. I meant no offence.'

Marina's stillness was disarming. She glanced at her lap, where the palette was still resting, and didn't budge.

With a sigh, Louise gave Stella a gentle squeeze before turning her in the direction of the steps.

'C'mon, let's go home. I've had enough of Porto Liakáda for one morning.'

They didn't look back but were aware of Marina's eyes following them until they were out of sight.

Stella took deep breaths as they slowly ascended the steps. She felt winded, as if she'd been punched in the stomach.

'What the hell was she thinking?' Louise muttered, almost to herself. 'Stupid cow.'

Digging in her shorts pocket, she found a wodge of tissues, which she passed to Stella. 'Here, take these. Who the fuck does she think she is?'

They stopped for a moment while Stella blew her nose.

'What do you think she meant about being reunited with someone I love?' she asked, tucking the damp hankies in her back pocket.

'Absolutely nothing,' Louise said with a growl. 'Forget it.'

Despite being naturally sceptical about anything supposedly supernatural, Stella didn't feel entirely convinced. 'What if she meant Harriet? Does she mean I'm going to die too?'

'Don't be silly. She's just a weird woman who doesn't know what she's talking about.'

'She didn't seem weird.'

Louise paused for a moment. It was true, they'd both liked Marina straight away. She had warmth and style – and was clearly a talented artist. But that didn't mean she could predict the future. She wasn't the prophet Cassandra, for God's sake!

'Let's keep going,' Louise urged. Even her walking seemed angry. 'Look, I know it was unsettling back there. I wish it hadn't happened. Maybe she fancies herself as a fortune-teller. It must get pretty dull here in winter with no tourists. The locals probably need someone like her to liven things up.'

'D'you really think so?' Stella was still doubtful.

'Absolutely. Marina doesn't know about Harriet, remember. I reckon she was trying to intrigue you, to draw you in. P'raps it's the way she sells her paintings, getting tourists interested in her so they flock to her studio. Don't give her any more thought, she's not worth it.'

Stella was quiet after that, until they reached the cottage of Eleni Manousaki, the elderly woman with the chickens.

The door was open, though the owner was nowhere to be seen. A grey and white cat was lying on its side on the front step, enjoying the warm sun.

'Oh look, kittens!' Stella cried, pointing to three or four tiny balls of fluff nestling against their mother's tummy, half hidden in her fur.

She crouched down to look more closely. The kittens were all the same colour and very well camouflaged.

'They can't be more than a few days old. They're so sweet!'

The mother cat gazed languidly at the two women and didn't stir, but the tip of her tail twitched, warning them not to come any nearer.

Stella backed away, anxious not to upset her, but thanks to the distraction, she'd temporarily forgotten about Marina and managed to enjoy the last part of the journey, chatting with Louise about plans for the next two weeks.

'We must visit the palace at Knossos if we have time,' Stella said, 'and I'd like to do the Aradena Gorge. The photos look amazing.'

'Josh said we have to visit the caves at Matala. The Romans used to bury their dead there and apparently in the sixties, they were occupied by hippies.'

Josh was Louise's on-off partner. They didn't live together, and Stella had a feeling Louise wanted more commitment, perhaps marriage, even, but he didn't. She'd tried asking Louise about it, but she was too proud to admit it.

When things were going well, she and Josh seemed to have a lot of fun, but all too often, he became distant for no apparent reason and failed to call. At these times, she threw herself into her work and pretended not to care, but she wasn't herself and it was obvious she really minded very much indeed.

Stella was surprised her friend put up with her boyfriend's careless behaviour, especially when she was so strong in other ways. She felt a bit sorry for her in this regard, but couldn't offer help or advice unless Louise opened up and asked for it.

The women had almost reached the sandy track that led to the gates of the villa when Stella caught the toe of her boot on a tree root and fell to the ground.

She landed on her hands and knees and rolled onto her back, where she lay for several seconds, hugging herself into a ball.

'Ouch! That really hurt.'

Louise crouched down and looked anxiously at her friend. 'Are you okay?'

With help, Stella managed to sit up enough to examine her wounds. The palms of her hands were covered in grazes, and dark-red blood was trickling down her calf from the cut on her knee.

'More injuries,' she said gloomily, reaching in her back pocket for the wodge of tissues Louise had given her earlier and dabbing at the blood. 'I wasn't looking properly.'

'The cut isn't too deep,' Louise commented. 'I bet it's painful, though. D'you think you can walk back to the house?'

Stella leaned on Louise's shoulder as she hobbled and hopped towards the villa. The cut stung, there was a lot of blood down her lower leg and the big bruise on her other knee had turned deep purple.

'I wish I wasn't so clumsy. I don't feel as if I walk round with my eyes half shut, but maybe I do.'

'You *are* accident prone,' Louise agreed with a wry smile. 'Maybe you should start wearing protective gear when you go out. I'll get you a crash helmet and knee pads for Christmas.'

It was only a joke, but it reminded Stella of Marina's disturbing words about soon being reunited with someone she loved, and her face fell.

Louise, noticing, frowned. 'I'm sorry—'

'It's all right.' Stella pulled back her shoulders. She was smiling, but a shadow had passed over her and Louise cursed the artist yet again.

What Stella needed was a great big confidence boost, she was thinking. Not the strange mutterings of some crazy woman who thought she was the Oracle of bloody Delphi.

5

Back at the villa, Lily and Amelia were only just finishing breakfast and Will and Hector were still upstairs.

The table outside was covered in plates, bowls, used cutlery, crumbs and milk spills, but the girls' smiley, welcoming faces made everything all right.

'How was it?' Lily asked, rising and kissing her mother on the cheek.

She was wearing her pink and white checked bikini today, which knotted at the front. Amelia had the same one – they'd bought them together – but she was covered up now in an oversized green T-shirt.

'Good,' Stella replied, pulling out a chair and sitting down. 'It's a charming village. Lots of nice shops. You'll love it.'

She wasn't going to mention Marina; it would only make the girls worry.

'Great. We might walk down later. D'you mind if we go for a swim now?' Lily went on. 'Sorry, I know you've just arrived, but we're so hot.'

Her thoughtfulness warmed Stella's heart. 'Of course I don't mind. Go. I'll join you in a bit.'

She and Louise watched the girls saunter off to the pool, chit-chatting all the way.

'They never stop, do they?' Stella said, amused. 'Girls are so different from boys.'

'We were the same at that age,' Louise replied. 'Don't you remember? In fact, we're not that different now. Josh can't believe how long we spend on the phone. Just as he thinks we're about to hang up, he says we launch off into another great long topic of conversation about nothing in particular. He gets a bit annoyed, actually. He only uses the phone to make quick arrangements. Bish bosh and that's it, call over.'

Perhaps if he listened more carefully to Louise, Stella thought, he'd realise these conversations were as important to her as Stella, and not just about 'nothing in particular.' But she didn't say so.

There was a little coffee left, which they agreed to share.

'I wonder why Marina wouldn't tell us who the villa's owners are,' Stella mused as she poured cold milk into her mug. 'I can't think why it's such a mystery.'

Louise took a sip of her drink before raising her eyebrows. 'I think you should make it your mission to find out. You're good at that sort of thing.'

'What? You mean I'm nosy?'

Louise grinned. 'Well, you always seem to know an awful lot about everyone. It doesn't take you long to tease out someone's life story.'

'I'm just interested in people, that's all,' Stella protested.

'That's what I said. Nosy.'

It was the hottest part of the day now and both Stella and Louise were keen to swim. After getting changed, Stella did a few laps then lay in the shade for a while under a sweetly scented lemon tree.

It was several hours since she'd checked her messages and to her relief, there was nothing urgent. She was weary and could easily have fallen asleep, but Louise's words had struck home and before long, she found herself googling Villa Ariadne to see if she could discover anything more about its previous and current owners.

It wasn't listed on the usual travel agency sites; it had its own website which you had to book through. Stella had first stumbled across it when searching for a quiet villa to rent in Crete for six people, near the sea, with its own private swimming pool.

The website was pretty basic and must have been created quite some time ago. The pale-blue font looked old fashioned and the photographs were slightly grainy. However, as soon as she'd seen a picture of the outside of the house, with its grand yet welcoming façade and the avenue of ancient olive trees leading up to it, she'd known this was where she wanted to stay.

She'd become even more convinced after reading the unusual and rather charming blurb on the homepage, written by the housekeeper, which she now read again:

Eleni Papadakis welcomes you to the magic of Villa Ariadne and Porto Liakáda. No roads, no cars, no mopeds. You will arrive here by ferry from Chora Skafion, fifteen minutes away, and immediately feel as if you have left behind the stresses of the modern world.

Villa Ariadne is a historic jewel. Built by the Venetians, sections date back to the fifteenth century. Whilst retaining many traditional features, however, it has been lovingly updated to create a modern, luxurious yet laid back and uniquely calming home.

Everywhere you look, there is some piece of art, pottery or sculpture to delight tired eyes and soothe weary souls and senses. Everywhere you go, you will be able to lose yourself in nature, whether in the mountains, by the coast, in the azure Libyan sea or just at home in the villa's gardens, filled with aromatic flowers and trees.

The villa is set high up in the White Mountains overlooking Porto Liakáda, where discos and clubs don't exist, just a few quiet bars and restaurants by the beautiful bay. Night life is you, your conversation, your next drink, as you gaze up at the night sky and feel yourself start to heal...

It had seemed to Stella then, as it seemed now, that the piece had been written just for her. It was quite uncanny. It was almost as if Mrs Papadakis knew she was weary to her bones and sick with sadness. She needed far more than just a fun-filled beach holiday; she needed to convalesce and be reborn.

Once she'd finished re-reading the blurb, she went to the next page and scrolled through a gallery of pictures. On the third and final page, there was a lot of information about things to do and see in and around Porto Liakáda, but as she'd thought, nowhere was there any mention of the villa's owners, past or present. Strange. Curiously, there were no reviews either, which was surprising, considering Katerina had given the impression the villa was much sought after.

Stella could imagine the housekeeper wasn't very good with technology or marketing, but she'd have thought the owners would be more savvy. One thing was certain: they should definitely fork out on a brand new website. The current one might have appealed to Stella, but it was distinctly amateurish and could easily put others off.

After closing down the site, she wracked her brains to try to think of another way of finding the information she was after. She tried typing in the simple question – *Who owns Villa Ariadne, Porto Liakáda?* – and was excited when it seemed to yield results.

There was quite a bit of information about a villa with the same name above the ancient Minoan ruins of Knossos, Crete. Of much more interest, though, was an old newspaper article about Leo Skordyles, who'd died some twenty years ago and who'd been descended from a long line of Cretan nobles.

It seemed he'd bought Villa Ariadne back in the seventies and lived there with his wife, who'd outlived him. He was a well-known character, having been mayor of Sfakia for a number of years and also a generous patron of the arts.

Although he and his wife had no children, they'd also helped set up and fund a local private English-speaking international school, which was still open today. It followed the American curriculum and its students received accreditations that enabled them to study anywhere abroad.

Intrigued, Stella read on eagerly until she reached the final paragraph, convinced she was about to discover what had happened to the villa at last. Her hopes were soon dashed, however.

After Skordyles died, it seemed his wife had continued to live there until she, too, passed away in 2010. The piece ended with a brief description of the wife's traditional Greek Orthodox funeral, attended by 'many local figures as well as the current mayor of Sfakia.' It added:

> She is buried beside her husband in the Argoulide Cemetery in the regional unit of Chania.

Stella frowned. Now she'd got the bit between her teeth, she wasn't about to give up. There must be more information somewhere, even if she had to trawl through pages of dull, irrelevant documents to find it.

Her search came to an abrupt end, however, when her phone pinged. Jon. Again. She was tempted to ignore him, but couldn't.

'Hey!' he said, sounding much cheerier than he'd been this morning. 'Guess what? I've booked my flight. I'm arriving tomorrow at midday.'

Stella's heart fluttered. So soon! She wondered what had prompted his sudden reversal of mood. There was a pause while the information sank in.

'I hope that's okay?' he added, sensing her hesitation. 'You haven't changed your mind, have you?'

'Of course not. That's brilliant news!'

'I've got a flexible ticket – I was thinking I might return at the same time as you.'

Stella swallowed. 'Great!'

It had been her suggestion, of course, and a break was no doubt exactly what he needed. So why had her stomach clenched and her mouth gone dry?

'I'll meet you at the ferry,' she offered.

At that moment, Louise, who was on a nearby lounger, sat up straight and raised her eyebrows enquiringly.

Stella held up an index finger: *One moment.*

'It's very hot here,' she went on, returning to Jon. 'Pack light clothes – and don't forget sun cream.'

He wanted to hear about her trip to the village earlier and how the kids were settling in. He was clearly still at a loose end and fancied a chat. But Stella cut him short.

'Sorry, I've got to go. I look forward to seeing you tomorrow.'

'I can't wait.'

'What's he on about now?' Louise asked when the call had finally ended.

Stella swallowed again.

'He's going to join us tomorrow. You know he's not working, and he sounded so down earlier. It's not good for him to be on his own so I said he could use the empty bedroom here. I hope that's okay. I doubt we'll see much of him. He'll probably take himself off on long walks and things.'

To her dismay, Louise's eyebrows knitted together and angry red spots appeared on her cheeks.

'You could have asked me first.' She crossed her bare arms tightly.

'I'm sorry, I didn't think you'd mind.'

This wasn't true, of course; there was a reason why Stella hadn't mentioned her spur-of-the-moment invitation until now. Part of her had been hoping Jon would refuse, so she wouldn't ever have to. Louise was well within her rights to be annoyed; Stella would have been just as angry if she'd done the same to her.

'I mind a lot, actually,' Louise said sharply. 'An extra person will change the dynamics. Plus, he's bound to talk non-stop about Harriet. I thought you wanted to escape from that for a while, even though he's been calling you constantly since you arrived anyway.'

Stella tried to catch Louise's eye, to plead for forgiveness, but she was staring doggedly at her lap.

'I'm sorry,' Stella repeated. 'I-I did want to get away from it,' she added with a guilty stammer. 'It's just, I felt so bad for Jon. And I thought having all the children round would sort of dilute him. There'll be so much going on, he'll be too distracted to dwell on his woes.'

'I'm not convinced about that.'

'I thought you liked him?'

It was a cheap shot, but Stella was desperate to smooth things over and win Louise round.

'You know I do.' She still sounded angry, but her frown had started to lift. 'Look, we should have discussed this first, but it's done now. I know you asked him for the right reasons. It's not ideal, but we'll make the best of it and I'm sure it'll be good for Jon, as you say.'

Relief washed over Stella, and she felt a whoosh of gratitude. That was one thing about Louise: she spoke her mind and flared up fairly easily, but didn't bear grudges. She'd say her bit, then move on.

Stella was the one who tended to bottle things up and simmer away in silence. It had exasperated Al, especially after Harriet died.

'How can I know what I'm doing wrong if you won't tell me?' he'd say.

He'd had a point, of course, but it was the way she'd always been. And unfortunately, stress and upset had put her in no mood to work on herself and try to change. In fact, it had only made things worse.

* * *

'You've what?'

Hector scowled at his mother, who was still lying by the pool.

She'd broken the news of Jon's visit to all four children, who'd just had a late lunch of Katerina's leftover Greek salad and bread.

Will, in turquoise swimming trunks, and the girls, in their skimpy bikinis, had been sitting listening at the pool edge, dangling their feet in the water. It seemed it was only Hector who had a problem with Jon coming to stay.

'Why the fuck did you ask him? He's so fucking depressing. He just needs to open his mouth and I feel like slitting my wrists.'

Stella blinked and swallowed. She was used to Hector's rudeness, but this was taking things to another level. He knew she'd hurt herself this morning, though she hadn't told him about Marina's creepy comments, which had troubled her even more.

'Don't say things like that,' she said, sitting up straight, her eyes flashing. 'Don't you dare make jokes about people killing themselves.'

The cut on her knee had only just stopped bleeding and she couldn't bend the joint, for fear of breaking the newly formed scab. Her hands stung, too.

For once, Hector seemed to sense how close his mother was to the edge and backed down.

'Sorry.' He dug out his tobacco and cigarette papers from his jeans pocket and started to prepare a roll-up. 'It's a turn of phrase. I wasn't thinking.'

Stella took a deep breath. 'Okay.' She wasn't in the mood for a fight.

Hector was standing, barefoot and bare-chested, at the end of her lounger, casting a long shadow. He was pale and thin, but burned with anger.

'I don't understand why you asked him,' he went on, just a little more gently. 'None of us want him here.'

He glanced round for support, but the others had their heads down and were staring hard at the water.

Stella started to explain how Jon was lonely and a break would be good for him, but Hector wasn't having it.

'He should've booked his own holiday, not gate-crashed someone else's.'

At that moment, Louise, who'd been indoors clearing up the dishes, came out to join them. She seemed to have recovered from her earlier annoyance, and seeing her made Stella feel instantly lighter.

She settled next to Stella again on the sun lounger and spread herself out lazily on the yellow cushion, her legs stretched and arms tucked behind her head.

The tanned skin on her thighs and abdomen glistened with sun cream and her bronze bikini sparkled in the sun.

'Bliss,' she said, closing her eyes with a small, contented smile playing on her lips. 'I'm quite tired after our walk. I might have a little siesta.'

Stella glanced at Hector, who slunk away to light his fag near the villa, where there was more shelter. At least he had the decency not to continue the row in front of Louise.

Leaning against the wall, with one knee raised, foot resting on the whitewashed stone, he appeared lost in his own thoughts. But Stella sensed his every move was designed to rattle her.

He knew she disliked the way he held his fag between thumb and forefinger and blew ostentatious smoke rings. He was well aware she loathed him smoking, full stop, because it was so bad for his health.

He hadn't been in the pool once and was persisting in wearing thick, hot jeans as if to prove he wasn't really part of this vacation, he was merely suffering it.

His behaviour often made Stella fume, but the feeling never lasted long because deep down, she knew he was unhappy and that made her sad, too. She'd tried so hard to reach him, and failed.

In truth, it was only because of Al that he'd finally agreed to come to Crete. Stella had even promised to buy him a second-hand car if he passed his driving test, but he'd still refused.

In the cab going to the airport, she'd thanked him for showing up.

'It's only because Dad made me,' he'd replied nastily. 'Otherwise I wouldn't be here.'

Stella had no idea how Al had done it, but she was truly appreciative; he hadn't needed to make the effort. Now, though, she was beginning to wonder if it wouldn't have been better if Hector had stayed home after all.

'What do you fancy doing this afternoon?' she asked the girls, more to distract herself than anything. Will had slipped silently into the pool, perhaps to escape the tension.

Lily shrugged and glanced at Amelia. 'Hang out here? It's too hot to go anywhere now.'

Amelia nodded in agreement.

The girls' hair hung damply down their backs, Lily's dark brown and Amelia's fair. Amelia was a little bigger than Lily, with broader shoulders, but they looked very alike otherwise in their matching pink and white checked bikinis.

Even their body language was similar. They were sitting so close together, their sides touched, and every now and again, they'd shake with amusement at some secret joke.

It was as if they were in their own little world with a language just for them. Like Stella and Harriet, they'd been friends since babyhood and probably knew what the other was thinking without the need for words.

Stella's heart melted with love for her daughter and she hoped the girls' safe, cosy familiarity with each other would last.

All of a sudden, she felt Harriet's absence again so keenly, it was as if someone had chopped off a limb, or her stomach had developed a hole in it so big, it could never be filled.

Of course, Louise was a good mate, too. But she was a very different personality from Harriet and she and Stella had never had quite the same, deep understanding.

Stella doubted Harriet would have questioned her decision to invite Jon on holiday, for instance, if he'd been a different mate's grieving husband. And she'd totally get why Stella was still raw about everything that had happened; though Harriet could be tough at work, she was super giving, full of compassion and had the warmest heart.

Stella's knee hurt and she shifted slightly to change position, before bending down to pick up her phone in the bag beside her.

There were no new texts, just the unopened one from Al yesterday.

They'd decided to have a period of no contact because things had been getting out of hand before she'd left for Crete. For some reason, she and Al had started messaging each other more, mostly about the kids but sometimes about nothing in particular. Stella felt it wasn't healthy, given that they'd separated, and somewhat reluctantly, Al had agreed.

She could ignore his text; he'd phone in an emergency anyway. But curiosity got the better of her.

> Hope you have a great time. Just to let you know I'm away for a week from tomorrow. There won't be much reception but I'll check my phone when possible. Al.

> PS Hope Hector's behaving…

Resting the phone face down on her stomach, she stared into the distance. All of a sudden, everything looked strangely blurry: the girls, the pool, Hector still leaning against the wall, the villa itself and the trees beyond.

For a moment, she wondered if she were about to faint. Maybe the heat had got to her, combined with the difficult conversation she'd had with Louise and shock from the fall. There was a bottle of water on the ground at her feet, which she reached for groggily, and took a few sips.

She heard her daughter squeal in excitement and plunge in the pool, but her brain couldn't seem to focus. If she waited a while, with luck, the sensation would pass.

'Stella, what's the matter?'

Louise's voice brought her back to the here and now.

Stella glanced over and her friend was propped up on an elbow, staring at her. She'd thought she was asleep.

'Sorry, I felt dizzy all of a sudden. I think I'm all right now.'

'You should lie down somewhere cool.' Louise sounded very firm. 'Go to your bedroom for a bit. I'll bring you up a cup of that mountain tea, made from dried leaves and flowers. It's supposed to be very good for you.'

'I'll be fine, honestly.' The last thing Stella wanted was to be alone right now.

Louise's gaze fell on the phone, still resting on Stella's stomach, and she raised her eyebrows. Stella pretended not to notice.

She didn't want to talk about Al or Hector or Jon, for that matter. Al was perfectly entitled to a break, if that's what he was having.

He was probably there now, wherever *there* was. She didn't need to know. She hoped he was enjoying himself, alone or with someone else. It didn't matter either way; it was none of her business.

Lily might know, but Stella wouldn't quiz her. She'd asked Al to leave her be and he was doing exactly that.

Her mind flitted to the single lady who lived in the flat above his. She was a makeup artist called Sasha. Lily had mentioned her.

'She's worked on loads of different films and TV series, Mum,' she'd said. 'She did the makeup for *Sex Education*! She even offered to show me how to do my makeup sometime.'

'That's kind of her. Remember to say thank you from me.'

Having finished his cigarette, Hector sloped off indoors. Stella guessed they wouldn't see him again till supper. Will and the girls were still splashing around in the pool.

'I'll stroll into town at two-ish tomorrow to meet Jon off the ferry.'

Louise frowned.

'What about your knee?'

'It'll be okay by tomorrow. I'll take it slowly and leave plenty of time.'

She lifted her leg to examine the sterile dressing on her open cut.

Both women had brought essentials like ibuprofen, plasters and anti-septic cream, but only Louise had thought of adhesive bandages.

Some blood had soaked through the gauzy fabric but it had dried now. A cut knee wasn't going to hold her back.

Jon's imminent arrival suddenly seemed more appealing. Looking after him might take her mind off her own worries.

Maybe he'd know where Al was; she was aware the two kept in touch by phone. It seemed strange not having any idea even which country her husband was in. He'd mentioned the weak phone signal, so it had to be somewhere remote. Perhaps he was hiking in the mountains, or renting a cottage in the middle of nowhere.

He liked company, though. He was very sociable. Maybe he'd gone with his best mate, Danny, but he rarely took time off work. Al had told her he wasn't dating anyone; he said he wasn't interested. But perhaps that had changed since she'd insisted they stop speaking so often. He loved women and surely couldn't survive without female company for too long.

'I'm going to check on Jon's room,' she said, starting to rise. 'I can't remember if the bed's made up.'

It was a fib. She'd already checked and the room was immaculate, but she felt as if ants were crawling over her body and she couldn't sit still any longer.

'I'll do it; you stay where you are.'

'No, I need the loo anyway.'

Louise gave in and lay down again.

'You're an amazing support to him,' she said, closing her eyes. 'He's lucky to have you. I just pray he doesn't cause any trouble.'

* * *

At first, Stella didn't recognise the thin, grey man walking towards her, struggling under the weight of a big green holdall.

Jon used to be solidly built but like her, he'd lost a lot of weight when Harriet died. The last time Stella saw him, she was pleased he seemed to have regained a few pounds. Clearly, it hadn't lasted though, as he was thinner than ever now and looked much older.

He was wearing smart navy shorts, blue boat shoes and a white polo shirt, which was too big for him but appeared brand new. He was frowning but his face lit up when he spotted Stella and he removed his Panama hat and waved it at her.

'You made it!' Stella cried when he was close enough to hear. She held out her arms and he put down the holdall and walked into them, burying his face in her neck. She could feel his bony ribs and vertebrae when she hugged him and her neck felt damp. Was he crying?

His arms wove round her back, too, and he was much taller, but she seemed to be the one holding him up.

'Hey!' she said softly. 'It's good to see you.'

'I'm sorry,' he replied, retreating unsteadily and wiping his eyes with the bottom of his shirt. 'I... I just felt so emotional, seeing you there, waiting for me.' His breath came in judders.

'You don't need to apologise.' Stella gave an encouraging smile, hoping he wouldn't lose it completely. 'Come on, let's have coffee or a cold drink before we walk to the villa. I want to hear about your journey – and everything else.'

Bending down, she picked up one of his bag straps and he took the other, wordlessly. They settled in the same café where she and Louise had been the previous day. The waiter, a young man in jeans and a black T-shirt, arrived almost immediately. Before Stella had time to order, however, Jon jumped in.

'This calls for a celebration! Let's have a bottle of wine.'

His sudden jollity seemed out of place and she was taken aback. She was also thirsty and hadn't been planning to drink alcohol; she'd rather have had lemonade or Coke.

Jon's mind was made up, however, and he asked the waiter which local whites he'd recommend.

'Vidiano is very popular,' the young man replied. 'The grapes are grown in the Heraklion area of Crete. It is quite full-bodied. I think you will like it.'

When he returned with a bottle and two glasses, Jon insisted on doing the pouring himself.

'Here's to us,' he said, clinking glasses with Stella, whose eyes widened in surprise.

'I mean, here's to us having a great holiday – to everyone having a good one,' he added quickly, before taking a sip of wine. 'Delicious.'

Stella was relieved his mood had picked up so rapidly and she took a sip herself. The pale-yellow wine tasted rich and fruity. She'd better go easy or she'd be drunk in no time.

'How was your flight?' she asked, putting down her glass. He held the stem of his in both hands and played with it, twizzling it round a few times before drinking some more.

He told her the travelling was perfectly smooth and he'd had no problem finding a taxi to take him to the ferry.

'Much more importantly, how are you? Are you managing to unwind?'

They were under a parasol and Stella extended her legs so they'd be in the sun. She was wearing shorts again – white ones this time – and decided they'd look better on her if she had a tan.

She was about to reply when he noticed the bandage with dried blood on one knee and the large, bluish-purple bruise on the other.

'What on earth have you been doing to yourself?'

'I fell – twice, on two separate occasions. I'm very clumsy.' She smiled ruefully. 'It's okay, though; they're getting better.'

'Stella, that's terrible!'

Dragging his chair closer to hers, he leaned over to get a better look.

'Have you seen a doctor? There's quite a lot of blood.'

His concern made her laugh. Neither of her children was remotely worried on her behalf. Even Louise had forgotten to ask how her cut felt this morning.

'No need,' she said. 'I cleaned it carefully and put on antiseptic cream. It'll heal in a few days.'

'You might need stitches.'

'It's not deep enough.'

'Still, I think you should get it checked out, just in case. And that bruise looks horrendous. You must have gone down with an almighty bang.'

Glancing round, she noticed the whites of his eyes were bloodshot and his brow was a mass of wrinkles. His solicitude was touching, but it could start to get on her nerves.

'Thanks, but I'll let nature take its course. I'm sure sea water will help it heal, too.'

Straightening up, he set his Panama on the table and ran his hands through the tufts of grey-brown hair on either side of his bald patch.

'You look after everyone else, but no one looks after you.' He reached for the wine bottle and topped up both their glasses. 'I wish you'd let me take care of you for once.'

'I don't need to be looked after. Anyway, I'd rather talk about *you*.'

He grimaced, before picking up his glass and draining it. When he tried to top her up again, she shook her head.

'I feel a bit fuzzy; I'd better stop.'

Nodding, he emptied what was left in the bottle into his own glass, took another swig and stared into the distance.

His broad, flat nose was shiny and there were beads of sweat on his upper lip.

'I've been doing a lot of thinking since you invited me here.'

Stella swallowed. 'Oh yes?'

'It's time I moved on from Harriet. She's gone and nothing's going to bring her back. I accept that now. I've done enough wallowing. I need to start a new chapter.'

The skin on Stella's arms prickled and her mouth felt dry. This was good news, surely? It just wasn't what she'd expected. She'd imagined she might have to stop him going on about Harriet all the time, because it would pull everyone down.

Her head itched; in fact, everything itched. She wasn't sure where to scratch first. He had a right to look to the future now, for his daughter's sake as well as his own. He couldn't go on mourning forever. Even so, she couldn't help but feel wounded on Harriet's behalf, as if she'd been jilted.

'That's great,' she said without conviction. 'I'm really pleased for you.'

He turned to her. 'Are you? Really?'

'Well, yes. I mean, you deserve to be happy. It's what Harriet would have wanted, I'm sure.'

'That's wonderful!' He drained his glass again and replaced it on the table. 'Thank you.'

Stella wasn't quite sure what he was thanking her for, but he certainly seemed relieved. Did he plan to dip a toe in the dating game and wanted her blessing? If so, he had it; she just didn't need details.

A sudden memory made her stomach turn over. It was a Wednesday morning, just a month or so before Harriet's death. She lived close to a giant wholesale store and Stella had decided to pop in, as usual, on her way to buy food for a forthcoming catering event.

They'd sat at the breakfast bar laughing and drinking coffee. Harriet was pale and painfully thin but remarkably bright and chatty, given the circumstances – right up until the time Stella said she needed to go.

'Must you?' Out of the blue, her friend's face had crumpled.

Stella had looked properly at Harriet and could still recall that jolt she'd felt, like an electric shock. Harriet's eyes were frightened, terrified, even. She was like a small child, alone and completely lost.

For a few moments, Stella had hesitated, thinking she mustn't leave; she should stay and keep her friend company. But then she'd remembered the catering event at the weekend and all the work she had to do beforehand.

She told herself Harriet could cope until Amanda arrived after lunch to do the next shift. She was a local friend and very supportive.

'What time is Jon back?' Stella had asked next, and she'd been relieved by Harriet's response:

'Early. I'll be okay,' she'd added, no doubt sensing Stella's concern. 'I've got a casserole in the freezer for supper, a ready-made one from that great shop that sells food which is almost as good as homemade.'

Stella nodded. She knew the store well. It had sorted her out on numerous occasions since Harriet had been diagnosed.

'Marvellous place!'

'What would we do without it?' Harriet had agreed with a smile. 'Jemima's got netball practice but she should be home by seven-ish.'

By Stella's calculations, this meant Harriet would only be alone for an
hour or so before and after Amanda's visit, which wasn't too bad.

'Good. Look after yourself. I'll ring later.'

How she wished she'd listened to her instincts! They were screaming
at her, telling her Harriet was feeling scared stiff and needed Stella to stay
with her at this moment more than ever. But several times in those final
few weeks, she'd allowed work to get in the way – and now Harriet was
dead and didn't need her any more anyway. And Jon wanted to find
someone new.

'Stella?' His voice brought her back. The wine had started to take
effect and he'd become louder and a bit flushed.

She noticed his glass was empty again.

'Here, you have this,' she said, tipping her remains into it and
watching him swallow. 'We should probably make a move. The others
will be wondering where we've got to.'

They talked about many things on the walk but her focus was elsewhere. She was thinking that before Harriet died, she hadn't spent much,
if any, time with Jon alone. She knew him mainly from weekend dinner
parties, Sunday lunches and holidays, mostly with the two families.

Grief had brought them together, along with her determination to
help him and Jemima as best she could, for her friend's sake. If he'd
truly resolved to 'move on', however, she wasn't sure she could remain as
close. She might feel as if she were betraying Harriet, however silly that
sounded. Stella herself hadn't moved on and didn't think she ever
would.

When they let themselves in through the big black gates and reached
Villa Ariadne, Jon stood still for a moment, looking up, and whistled.

'It's enormous! Stunning. I had no idea!'

'I told you it was beautiful.'

'Yes, but I imagined something much less grand. This is like a palace!'

Once inside, he dumped his bag in the hall and followed Stella into
the yellow and white kitchen. Louise, in her bronze bikini, was bent over,
fetching a bottle of chilled water from the giant American-style fridge.

'Hey! You're here!' She straightened up and set the bottle down on the
worktop.

Stella noticed her do a double take when she clocked Jon's gaunt appearance, but she quickly disguised her dismay with a warm smile.

Her hair was wet from the pool and she'd turned golden brown after a day in the sun. If she were embarrassed about being half naked, she didn't show it, but walked straight up to Jon and gave him a hug. 'Welcome!'

Bursts of laughter were coming from the garden so Louise and Stella led him outside. Amelia, Lily and Will were messing around in the swimming pool with a plastic orange ball, splashing water everywhere.

Hector, with a white towel on his head, was watching them from a sun lounger. He was in jeans and a black T-shirt and the sun was beating down on him, but he didn't seem to care.

When Jon called hello, one by one the swimmers heaved themselves out of the water and came to greet him. Meanwhile, Hector remained stubbornly supine.

Unperturbed, Jon strolled over to him, while Louise offered to bring a tray of drinks.

'The girls will give you a hand,' Stella said, but Louise insisted she'd do it on her own.

After pulling up more strollers and chairs, the group sat next to Hector. He started to pull the towel over his face, but Stella whipped it away.

'You having a good time?' Jon asked, and Hector shrugged before scratching his stubbly cheek with dirty nails that were almost bitten to the quick.

'Your mum's got a terrible cut on her knee,' Jon went on, rather pointedly.

'Yeah, I know.'

'We need to look after her. She mustn't do too much till it heals.'

'She should be more careful.'

'Shall I get you another bandage?' Amelia piped up, wanting to ease the tension, but Stella said she'd have a swim first.

'I've got to cool off; I'm so hot after that walk.'

'You must dry it really carefully,' Jon insisted, coming over all concerned again.

'I will.'

'How are you feeling about Harriet? Any better?'

Hector's question came out of the blue and the air turned frosty. His comment sounded innocent enough, but his lip had a sarcastic curl.

'A-a bit better, yes, thank you,' Jon said with a stammer. 'It's taken a long time, you know, these things do. It takes a bit of getting used to, being single. I think I'm starting to get there...'

Hector was quiet for a moment, perhaps trying to construct a suitable response. He didn't get the chance, however, as Louise appeared with a tray of glasses, a jug of iced water, a bottle of cordial and a bowl of peanuts, which she set on the end of the lounger Will was sharing with the girls.

'I need you to walk to Porto Liakáda in a bit and get us something for supper,' she told all three. 'It's cooler now. The supermarket's open till ten.'

Amelia groaned. 'It's so far!'

'Come on, you haven't exactly done much today.'

Amelia made a face, but Lily nudged her in the ribs.

'We can look round the shops and have a few drinks.'

'Just one,' Louise said firmly. 'Otherwise we won't eat till midnight.'

She filled the glasses with water and asked who wanted cordial. When she started to pass Stella her drink, she straightened up, wincing, and tried to bend her sore knee, which had stiffened.

In a flash, Jon had risen to his feet. 'Don't move. I'll get it for you.'

Louise glanced at him oddly; Stella wondered what she was making of him.

A short time later, Will and the girls set off for Porto Liakáda, leaving Louise, Stella and Jon in the garden with Hector.

'Okay, I really am going in the pool now.' Stella peeled off her shorts and top to reveal a navy swimsuit underneath.

Jon hurried into the house and reappeared in a pair of yellow trunks.

When he saw Stella limping towards the steps, he tried to help by tucking an arm under hers.

He was much taller and it was all a bit awkward, but she didn't want to hurt his feelings by pushing him away.

'Take your hands off my mum!'

They both turned to look at Hector, whose expression hadn't changed. He hadn't moved either.

Louise laughed as if it were a joke, but Stella wasn't sure. She wriggled out of Jon's embrace and his arm fell to his side.

Once in the water, she launched into a slow breaststroke and headed for the deep end, relieved to leave him behind.

But when she'd done a few lengths and returned to the steps, Jon was still standing there, waiting for her.

6

Will and the girls returned from Porto Liakáda at around 10 p.m., by
which time the others were extremely hungry and had started to worry.

'We used the torches on our phones,' Amelia said in response to her
mother's comment about it being pitch black outside. 'We were fine.'

Her eyes sparkled and her cheeks were rosy. Will and Lily kept
bursting into giggles for no apparent reason. They'd clearly had more
than one drink but they'd remembered to buy pizzas, salad and a sweet,
sticky tart, which had got crushed on the journey.

Stella and Louise were too famished to take them to task for being
late and after reheating the pizza in the oven for a few minutes and fixing
a salad, they sat down to eat on the terrace.

Stella lit two citronella candles to ward off the mosquitoes, and set
one on the wall beside them and another in the centre of the table.

As she ate, her eyes were repeatedly drawn to the yellow flames flickering mysteriously in the large, glass, hurricane candleholders.

Jon's were, too. She was at one end of the table and he at the other.
Once, their gazes met in the middle and when she glanced up, she
realised he was staring at her. Puzzled and a bit embarrassed, she gave a
small smile before looking away.

The girls were in high spirits, as was Will. He told a story about a 'mad Englishwoman' with blonde hair, who was chasing round the tables at the bar where they were sitting, trying to catch two children in night-clothes: a girl and a boy aged about six or seven.

'She was ranting and raving and threatening to ground them for weeks, but they completely ignored her and just carried on racing round, with her running after them. They seemed to think it was funny. To be honest, it was funny. Everyone was laughing, until the little girl fell over and started crying and the mother picked her up and marched them both home.'

'That sounds like April,' said Stella. 'I don't think she's got much control over her kids. She's from Leeds originally. She's very friendly.'

'A bit *too* friendly,' Louise added wryly, her gold earrings glinting in the half-light.

Lily leaned across the table and helped herself to another slice of pizza. She'd caught the sun and her shoulders had turned pink.

'Oh, and some weird lady came up and talked to us.'

She bit into her food and tomato sauce dribbled down her chin. Amelia pulled a mock-disgusted face and passed her some kitchen roll.

Freckles had sprung up on Lily's cheeks and nose and her topknot was lopsided, with bits of hair sticking out all over the place.

'What weird lady?' Stella asked, only half listening. She was smiling inwardly, thinking her daughter had no idea how young and sweet she looked.

'She had really long hair and was wearing all these droopy, colourful clothes. She asked if you and I were related.'

Stella's ears pricked up. 'Marina?'

Lily shrugged. 'She didn't say her name.'

'How did she know you had anything to do with me?'

Amelia chipped in now. 'She just guessed. She said Lily looked like you.'

'Oh!'

The fear in Stella's voice alarmed Lily, who put down her slice of pizza.

'Is something wrong?'

Stella checked herself; she mustn't frighten the girls.

'No.' She fiddled with the wedding ring she still wore, thinking it was probably time to take it off, though she couldn't quite bear to.

'She's an artist. We bumped into her the day before yesterday and she said a few odd things. Best to steer clear. She's just a bit strange, that's all.'

'What odd things?' Jon's speech was slightly slurred. He was bending forwards, his elbows on the table, helping to prop him up.

There was an almost empty bottle of red wine in front of him, which he'd had to himself, as the others were drinking white wine, lager or Coke.

Stella shook her head. 'It's not worth repeating; it was nothing.'

The last thing she wanted was to stir him up – or the children, for that matter. She'd rather make light of the incident.

Jon wasn't going to let it go, though. He opened his mouth to speak, but Louise interrupted.

'We stopped by the bay to look at a painting she was doing. She made a couple of stupid comments about our appearance, that was all. I don't think she meant any harm, but we were keen to get away.'

She turned to Amelia. 'Can you clear the plates and bring out the dessert, please? I've put some bowls on the countertop. We can use those.'

'Great,' Hector muttered. 'A lunatic in our midst.'

Louise shot him a look which made him shut up, and he rose reluctantly to help Will and the girls with the plates.

While the others were in the kitchen, Louise asked after Jon's daughter, Jemima. He confirmed she was still enjoying university and had a new boyfriend, Ahmed.

'Have you met him?' Louise wanted to know.

He shook his head. 'Not yet. Maybe she'll bring him home in the summer. She's talking about going to Thailand and Cambodia with him.'

'Gosh! That's adventurous. How do you feel about it?'

Jon flapped an arm clumsily in front of his face, knocking over his empty glass, which he left on its side.

'It's fine, you know, they've got to grow up.' His speech was slow and deliberate. 'I told Stella earlier, it's time I moved on from Harriet. Jemima should, too.'

His gaze fell on Stella, who stared at her plate and wished he'd have the sense to call it a night.

'Oh!' Louise's eyebrows shot up. 'Well, that's good, I guess...'

She was sitting beside Stella and reached out to touch her hand.

'You okay?' she whispered.

Stella nodded uncertainly. 'Ish. I mean, it's difficult for me to hear, as you can imagine, but I'm sure it's the right thing.'

Louise and the girls devoured the sticky tart but the others didn't want any. Jon cast around for more wine, but Stella had screwed the top firmly on the bottle of white and hidden it by her feet.

'I'd better go to bed,' Jon said at last, rising unsteadily and grabbing the back of his chair for support.

Lily giggled and at his mother's behest, Will leaped up to offer help.

'Nah, I'll be okay.' Jon flapped his arm again dismissively before staggering towards the door.

'Sleep well,' Stella called after him, and he gave a drunken thumbs up before stumbling on the first step. Luckily, he managed to right himself just in time.

Once he'd gone, Stella and Louise exchanged glances.

'He's very drunk, isn't he?' Lily sounded in awe. She'd sobered up completely, having been allowed soft drinks only since returning from Porto Liakáda, and she looked happy but exhausted.

Hector laughed nastily. 'Absolutely rat arsed.'

Amelia couldn't stop yawning and had black bags under her eyes. Louise said she and Stella would clear up.

'You all go to bed. Thanks for getting the pizza.'

While the two women were bent over, loading the dishwasher, Stella felt the need to apologise for Jon's behaviour.

'He drank practically a whole bottle of wine in Porto Liakáda before we even got here. I really didn't want any but he was dead keen. With luck, he'll have calmed down by tomorrow and won't get so carried away.'

'I hope so.' Louise stood up and leaned against the worktop, crossing her arms. She was wearing a batik midi dress, predominantly blue, with slim gold chains for straps. Stella recognised it; Louise had had it for years and it was still fabulous on her.

'He looks terrible, really unwell. I reckon he's been hitting the bottle big time.'

'Do you?' Stella scratched angrily at a mosquito bite on her thigh, which started to bleed. 'Oh dear. Maybe he'll cut back now he's here.'

'He'd better.' Louise frowned. 'It's not good for the kids to see him like that and he could be a liability. I thought he was going to fall off his chair at one point, and he could hardly make it indoors.'

'I'm sorry,' Stella repeated, managing to squeeze one more bowl into the very full machine.

'Stop apologising.' The tetchiness in Louise's voice took Stella aback and made her wince. 'It's done now.'

Louise found a box of cleaning powder under the sink and turned on the dishwasher, which made a comforting swishing sound.

'I just don't want us having to keep an eye on him the whole time. This is supposed to be a holiday for us all, you know.'

* * *

Jon was already up and making coffee in the kitchen when Stella went downstairs at around 8 a.m.

'I slept like a baby,' he said with a cheerful smile that belied his pasty complexion and bloodshot eyes. 'My bed's really comfortable and it's so quiet here.'

If he were at all embarrassed about last night, he didn't show it. Perhaps he didn't realise how drunk he'd been.

He was wearing his yellow bathing trunks from yesterday, with leather flip-flops and a loose navy T-shirt. His neck looked thin and exposed and his legs scrawny.

Harriet would have been so worried about him. Stella found herself pondering over how best to fatten him up. Lots of those pastries Katerina had made might do the trick, or the ones she and Louise had eaten on their first full day.

After pouring coffee for himself and Stella, he said he was going for a swim and took his mug into the garden.

Instead of following, Stella strolled into one of the little anterooms off the main hall and settled into a dark-red leather armchair to start some different online research.

She wanted to do something active today, to *go* somewhere. It would be good for Jon, if he decided to come; for them all, in fact. And if he chose to stay behind, at least they'd have a break from him, which Louise, especially, would no doubt welcome.

The walk to Sweetwater Beach looked challenging but manageable, and not too far. Her knee still hurt, but she'd take a painkiller before they left.

When Louise appeared some ten minutes later, she was in favour of the idea and even offered to rouse the kids, a job that Stella wanted to avoid at all costs.

Hector refused point blank to join them, but the others were up for it and Jon was, too. It took a while for them all to muster and when they finally set off, with swimming togs and backpacks, it was almost 11 a.m.

It was another beautiful sunny day and the sky was breathtakingly blue. The rough, stony coastal path would lead them all the way to their destination, and they took their time, taking care not to stumble on loose rocks and stopping frequently to admire the view.

From their vantage point high up on the cliffs, the sea looked extremely inviting. It was crystal clear, deep blue and turquoise at the edge where the water was shallower. The colours were so bright, they looked almost cartoonish and reminded Stella of certain Disney movies.

They were all in shorts, T-shirts and walking boots, even Lily, who'd initially refused to put hers on, insisting she'd be fine in sandals.

Luckily, Will had told her not to be silly. 'It'll ruin the holiday if you break your ankle.'

She wasn't as fearless as Amelia and at one stage, the path became very narrow and she almost lost her nerve.

'I can't do it,' she said, glancing at the slim, stony, winding track before her, and the sheer drop to her right.

Stella, who was ahead, having already navigated the scary bit, turned round.

'Yes, you can. Hold on to the rocks and don't look down. It's not as bad as you think.'

A bit further on, they came to a steep, uphill section covered in precarious scree, which they had to pick their way over.

When Stella tripped and almost fell, Jon reached back to offer his hand, but she shook her head.

'I'm all right, thanks. I wasn't looking properly.'

They had to stop twice to allow a young couple and a group of middle-aged foreigners to pass by in the opposite direction, but otherwise, they had the mountain to themselves.

It was hot and there wasn't a scrap of shade. Stella was pleased she'd worn her navy baseball cap. Jon had been forced to remove his Panama because it kept blowing off. He'd slathered his bald patch in thick factor fifty, which gleamed white in the bright morning light, making him look rather peculiar.

Stella found herself thinking she was relieved Al still had a good head of hair, until she remembered they weren't together any more.

Her pace slowed and her feet started to drag. Before the final split, Al had kept complaining she was pushing him away. Husbands and wives were supposed to share their feelings and support each other, he'd said.

'I know you're grieving, but how can I help when you won't talk to me?'

They were in the kitchen. The kids had just left for school and Stella was clearing away the breakfast things. Harriet had been gone six weeks and now the funeral was over, Jemima had returned to her classes. Jon, meanwhile, was technically back at work, but there were days when he simply couldn't function properly. Today being one of them, Stella had promised to go for a long walk with him instead.

She could ill afford the time. The cupboards were bare at home and she desperately needed to do a supermarket trip. Plus, she had two quite lucrative dinner party bookings coming up which she might have to cancel if she couldn't devote enough time to the preparations. This was weighing on her mind.

'Stella?' Al nudged her because he could tell her thoughts was elsewhere. 'I need you to talk to me.'

She wanted to scream at him to go away and leave her alone; she couldn't face a discussion now.

'What do you want me to say?' she'd replied instead in a sullen voice, opening the dishwasher and deliberately stacking it noisily with cutlery, bowls and mugs. 'You know how stretched I am. It must be boring listening to me repeating myself.'

Al rose from the sofa, where he'd been carefully watching her, and started to put away the cereal packets on the table.

'What can I do to make things easier for you?' he'd asked again.

It was a genuine question, but her nerves were even more frayed than usual.

'Can you go to the supermarket and make supper and organise the catering for the two parties I've got coming up and spend time with Jon, who's in a bad way today? Oh, and meet Jemima after school to talk about uni options, and think about meals for her and Jon, too, and make sure the washing's up to date?'

He was in a clean white shirt and navy trousers, ready for the office. She knew full well he wouldn't be able to do half those things.

'No,' he'd said with a sigh, 'I can't take time off, sorry. But I can shop for us after work and make supper, and do you really need to see Jon? Isn't there someone else who could keep him company today?'

She turned and glared at her husband with flashing eyes.

'There's no one else; you know that perfectly well.'

'Could you get someone in to help you with the catering? Just as a temporary measure, I mean?'

'Who? Good chefs don't grow on trees. Besides, I don't make enough to justify paying someone else as well.'

Realising he was on a losing wicket and she'd bat everything he suggested straight back, he tried another tack.

'Hasn't Lily got a hockey match after school?'

'Yes, and I've told her I can't go.'

'That's a shame. You enjoy watching her. She'll be sorry you're not there.'

Stella stuck her hands on her hips.

'Don't guilt-trip me. Why don't you go instead?'

'I wish I could, but I can't.'

She snorted meanly. 'Hah! Well then, get off my back.'

He seemed to sway a little, and there was uncertainty in his eyes.

'Stella?' he said, holding out his arms, wanting her to walk in and make everything better, but tears pricked her eyes and she shook her head.

'I can't, Al. I'm sorry.'

Turning back to the dishwasher, she heard him give a deep sigh before leaving the room. A few moments later, he slammed the front door behind him and was gone.

Looking back, she could see how difficult she'd been to live with – bad-tempered and martyrish. Her excuse was, she'd been so unhappy and consumed with grief, she couldn't really think about anyone or anything, other than Harriet, Jon and Jemima. If only Al had let her be for a while. Ironically, it was his insistence on trying to be a good husband and get close to her that had driven her away.

Louise, who was ahead of Stella on the walk, stopped for a drink of water, making her refocus and stop, too. Louise looked like a seasoned hiker in her sturdy brown leather boots, thick socks, tan shorts, white T-shirt and khaki cotton hat with a wide brim.

She'd brought walking poles as well. Amelia had teased her about them before they set off, but was using them now, much to the amusement of Lily and Will. She said they were especially useful going downhill.

They'd been hiking for well over an hour when Louise clambered onto a flat rock and pointed.

'I can see the path down to the beach. We're almost there.'

They stood on tiptoe and peered round the side of her. The wide, crescent-shaped bay was clearly visible now and almost empty, save for a few rows of blue and white umbrellas in certain places.

The sea was so clear, you could spot the rocks and stones beneath. Stella couldn't wait to explore underwater in her snorkelling gear.

Not for the first time that morning, she thought of Hector and greyness descended once more. It was sad he wasn't with them. He used to love snorkelling, too. When he was about ten, they'd been on a family holiday to the Red Sea in Egypt and he'd spent practically the whole two weeks underwater with Stella, checking out the astonishing, multi-coloured sea life. Their fingers and toes were permanently like prunes. She was sure he'd have enjoyed the walk, too, if he'd only given himself permission to come.

A familiar anxiety nibbled at her insides. What was he doing now? Probably lying in bed in the dark, smoking roll-ups and getting more depressed.

Worry and a recurring sense of failure were grinding her down, leaving her feeling permanently exhausted. She tried to bat away the negative feelings by focusing harder on the view.

Their pace quickened as they began the steep descent and Lily started talking about lunch.

'D'you think they'll do proper food, not just sandwiches?'

They'd already decided to eat at The Mermaid Island Taverna, which stood on rocks a little way from the shore and could be reached via a wooden jetty.

'They do all sorts of things,' Stella replied. 'Lots of fresh fish.'

When they finally stepped onto the white shingly beach and found a good spot to park their bags, Will immediately threw off his clothes and ran into the waves.

After putting on his bathing trunks, Jon spread out his towel next to Stella's and sat for a few moments, staring out to sea.

They were just beyond the taverna, which looked charmingly rustic with its wooden sides and grassy canopy. Some people were eating and drinking in the outside dining area, but the place didn't appear to be full.

'I read it's called Sweetwater Beach because there's spring water just below the surface of the pebbles,' Stella said, picking up a small, smooth, greyish stone and stroking it between her fingers. 'You can dig for it. It comes from underground mountain springs and apparently you can drink it. Isn't that amazing? No wonder the sea's so clear.'

'Mm.' Jon nodded but she sensed he wasn't really listening. He seemed a bit agitated, for some reason, tapping his fingers on his knee as if playing the piano.

'Coming in?' he said at last, rising and extending a hand.

He had an apprehensive frown, as if he feared she'd reject his offer. Not wishing to disappoint, she accepted his hand and allowed him to pull her up.

'You go ahead,' she said, once she was on her feet. 'My swimsuit's in the bag. I won't be long.'

She hoped Louise and the girls would join them, but they were flat on their backs with their eyes closed and didn't appear to have any intention of moving.

Will was still out there, swimming parallel to the beach, practising his manly crawl, but he'd probably have had enough soon.

Once she'd changed and pulled out her mask and snorkel, she padded gingerly over the pebbles to the water and tested the temperature with her toes. It was surprisingly chilly.

Jon was floating on his back a little way out, his feet facing the shore. As soon as he spotted her, he righted himself and gave a big wave.

'It's beautiful once you're in,' he called. 'I've warmed up already.'

She felt a shiver of annoyance, but quickly checked herself. She must never forget what he'd suffered and how much he still needed support. It was a miracle she'd persuaded him to come on holiday at all. She hoped Harriet, wherever she might be, was looking down on them and smiling.

Will started swimming in Stella's direction and she waded out to meet him. His feet soon touched the ground and he began to emerge, soaking wet, with a cheeky grin on his face.

Stella read his mind. 'Don't you dare splash! I'll kill you!'

He laughed and teasingly flicked water at her before running to join the others. She braced herself. She was up to her hips now and there was no point delaying any longer.

A little way in front was a small wave, not much more than a ripple, really. Taking a deep breath, she plunged in headfirst, still hanging onto her mask and snorkel.

The cold made her go numb and her heart raced, but it was exhilarating, too. She came up, gasping for air and almost crashed into Jon.

'Oh! You made me jump!'

'Sorry.' He was waist deep in the water and standing rather stiffly, his eyes darting this way and that.

'It's cold but lovely,' she said, wondering what was making him so nervous. She began to put on her mask. 'I'm going on a fish safari.'

'Wait!'

Startled by his tone, she stopped in her tracks.

'Come with me,' he commanded.

Before she had time to ask why, he took hold of her upper arm and started to pull her away from the beach.

'Where are we going?'

'There.' He pointed with his other hand to a rocky area at the edge of the bay. 'There'll be plenty of fish round those boulders.'

Now she knew what he was planning, she felt more comfortable, though his manner disturbed her. She was relieved when he released his grip and they started to half swim, half wade in silence past the taverna towards the cliff edge, well away from the others, who became nothing more than distant pinpricks.

After a while, he led them into a patch of deeper water where they could no longer touch the bottom and had to swim. He seemed to know exactly where he was aiming.

'We'll head for that big rock just ahead. It looks like a good one to sit on.'

She felt like saying she wanted to explore, not sit around, but feared sounding curt and hurting his feelings. Besides, he was so focused on reaching his destination, she doubted he'd even hear her.

When they were just a few feet from the rock, she put the snorkel in her mouth and started to pull down her mask. Once again, he stopped her.

'Wait a minute – please. I need to talk to you.'

There were deep wrinkles on his forehead and he kept blinking, as if he'd developed a nervous tic or had something in his eye.

Stella's heart pitter-pattered. 'What about?'

When he didn't reply, she was gripped by a powerful urge to swim back to shore. She could pretend she felt sick, but he'd know she was lying. She'd have to hear him out or risk causing serious offence.

He started to scramble up the side of the boulder, covered in bits of vegetation and crusty-looking barnacles.

She followed as quickly as she could and in the process, nicked her calf on something spiky. It was only a small scratch but looking down, she could see it was bleeding profusely. Damn. Another injury to add to her ever-growing list.

As soon as he was standing on top of the rock, he bent down to help her and reluctantly, she let him grip her by the wrists and haul her up. She felt a bit like a piece of furniture, but he was stronger than he looked and it was all over quickly.

At first, she couldn't find a comfortable place to sit. The rock looked reasonably flat, but on closer inspection, there were lots of hard, spiky bumps on the surface. After shuffling back a bit and sweeping off some loose stones, however, she managed to find a smooth enough patch on which to settle.

Her calf and foot were covered in blood, washed to a pale, pinkish red by the water. Jon's frown was so deep, she might as well have broken her leg in several places.

'I'm sorry. I shouldn't have made you climb up. It was stupid of me.'

'Don't be silly, it's nothing. It's just a tiny scrape. There's only so much blood because I've been in the sea.'

The silence that followed felt laden with a meaning Stella couldn't begin to decode. After a few minutes, unable to bear the tension any longer, she screwed up all her courage and seized the initiative.

'What did you want to talk about?' Her voice sounded smaller than she'd intended.

Jon gave a big sigh.

'There's no easy way to say this.' His tone was so grave and portentous, it made the hairs on the back of Stella's neck stand up, and her stomach lurched. 'I'm in love with you, Stella. I've been in love with you for a long time, since well before Harriet—'

A nervous laugh bubbled up in her throat and shot out before she could stop it. 'Sorry,' she said, covering her mouth with a hand. 'I couldn't help—'

'Stella, I'm not kidding—'

She stared at him and her jaw dropped as reality sank in: he was deadly serious.

'Stop!'

She raised her hand, palm open and facing forward. 'Don't say anything else. You don't mean it. You're not thinking straight; you're still grieving. I never heard what you just said. It never happened.'

While she spoke, he shook his head from side to side, slowly and deliberately. It made her want to slap him and bring him to his senses.

His statement was so absurd, she couldn't believe what she'd just heard. Of course it wasn't true, it couldn't be. But if it was... She shivered, though she wasn't cold, and squeezed her eyes tightly shut.

'Please, just hear me out.'

The crack in his voice forced her to open her eyes again and pay attention. His own eyes were heavy and the corners of his mouth sagged.

She felt confused, both sorry for him and angry with him for putting her in this extremely uncomfortable position.

'Please?' he repeated.

She hugged her arms tightly round her body.

'Okay, if you really want to. But you're not in your right mind. I'm worried you'll regret it.'

At this, he drew up his knees, widened his legs and folded himself between them, as if for protection. His arms were long and stiff and his hands grasped each other tightly.

'It's all true, Stella,' he said slowly. 'I mean every word. I think I must have always loved you, but when Harriet was alive, I didn't allow myself to go there. I put you in a box, so to speak, and kept the lid firmly shut.'

A sudden, horrible thought made Stella gasp. She felt as if her head might explode.

'Did Harriet know?' Her voice sounded shrill and piercing.

'No. Absolutely not.'

This was something, at least. She took a deep breath.

'How do you know?' she said more gently.

'Because I never gave her any reason to suspect. I loved her. I'd never have done anything to hurt her. What I want to say is...' He cleared his throat and she felt a renewed sense of dread. 'Now Harriet's gone and Al's left,' he went on, falteringly, 'I'd like to think you and I could maybe, you know, well, make a go of things. We've got so much in common. I know we could be happy. What do you think?'

At first his head was bowed, so she couldn't read his expression. But then he straightened up and gave her a penetrating stare.

She felt invaded, violated, even, as if he were probing into her soul, trying to uncover its innermost secrets. Gripped with revulsion, she had to stop herself from jumping in the water to wash herself clean.

As far as she was concerned, he was still Harriet's husband and always would be. To have a relationship with him was unthinkable. It would be the ultimate betrayal. It would almost feel like incest. Added to this, she wasn't attracted to him. She didn't even think she liked him much any more.

Her first instinct was to tell him the bitter truth, but then she remembered Harriet. When she'd sat in the funeral parlour beside her friend's coffin, with tears streaming down her cheeks, she'd solemnly promised again to look after Jon and Jemima for her, come what may.

No matter how misguided Jon was, she couldn't turn her back on him. Somehow, she had to find a way to put him off without destroying their friendship.

There was no time to mull over the best way to put it all into words, however. He was watching her, waiting for her answer.

'I'm really touched,' she said hesitantly, stretching out her legs, her gaze fixed firmly on the hands in her lap. 'Sorry for sounding angry; I was just so surprised—'

'It's okay, I understand. You weren't expecting it.'

Her swimsuit was almost dry and the sun was beating down on her back and shoulders. The blood on her foot and calf had turned rusty brown.

'I'm honoured you think so highly of me and you know I'm very fond of you...'

There was a sharp intake of breath; he didn't like that word, 'fond.'

'But the truth is, I can't ever have a relationship with you. It wouldn't seem right, because of Harriet. I'd feel I was being disloyal to her memory.'

Jon made a strange sound, a cross between a cry and a groan.

'Disloyal?' he repeated. 'I profoundly disagree. I think it would be a great tribute to her. If I hadn't loved her with all my heart when she was alive, I'd hardly want a relationship with her closest friend, would I?'

Stella frowned.

'What about Jemima? It would be awful for her to think of us together. Imagine trying to explain it to her friends. They might assume something was going on before Harriet died.'

'Rubbish.' Jon's body had tensed up. 'Jemima adores you. She'd love me to be happy. She'd rather I was with you than some strange woman she mightn't get on with.'

Stella's shoulders drooped and she picked savagely at some peeling skin on the side of her thumbnail. It seemed he had an answer for everything.

'Could you love me, if there weren't these objections?' he asked tentatively.

Her head ached and there was a throbbing pain behind her eyes. How could she give him the honest answer, but kindly? She didn't dare look at him for fear of giving herself away.

For a moment, she pictured Al standing right in front of her, frowning with exasperation and running a hand through his thick, silver-flecked hair.

Why are you beating about the bush, Stella? Just tell him the truth, for God's sake. Stop trying to people please. It doesn't work. Give him a clear, direct message. It's the kindest way. You don't fancy him, that's all there is to it. He'll be upset, of course, but he's a big boy. He'll get over it.

If only she could guarantee Jon wouldn't fall apart!

But there was no certainty, and Stella knew she couldn't bear to inflict more pain by being so frank. Stumped, she cast around desperately for a suitable response and almost cried with relief when a fresh idea sprang to mind.

'There's another thing,' she said, sensing Jon stiffen again. 'I'm not over Al. I thought I was but I'm not. I miss him a lot. I keep thinking about him, especially here, for some reason. I know initially I was the one who wanted the separation, but I'm beginning to think I've made a mistake.'

'Really?' Jon's disbelief was palpable. 'Not long ago, you told me you were completely over him. What's changed?'

Stella felt a prickle of annoyance. She shouldn't have to justify her feelings to him; to anyone, in fact.

'I don't know. Maybe it's being here, in such a beautiful place. It reminds me of all the happy times we had together. It wasn't all bad, by any means. We worked really well together for a long time. It was only towards the end things began to fall apart, and I'm sure that was my fault as much as his. In fact, it was probably mostly my fault because I was so sad about Harriet. I'm wondering if we should try again.'

She didn't like lying and the fib had come so easily, she'd surprised herself. But she took some comfort in knowing her words weren't totally false. She *had* been thinking about Al more than usual and in a more positive way. All she'd done now was exaggerate the truth.

Jon stood up and started pacing to and fro across the rock.

'I can't believe I'm hearing this,' he said accusingly. 'You told me a few minutes ago I wasn't in my right mind. Well actually, I think that applies to you. Have you forgotten what you said about Al? His selfishness? The way he was always trying to force himself on you?'

He stared at her with blazing eyes.

'You're wrong, Stella. You shouldn't be with Al. You did the right thing, splitting up. You should be with *me*.'

Stella swallowed. She'd once told Jon on the phone about Al's frequent requests for sex, and bitterly regretted it. Jon made it all sound much worse than it really had been.

She and Al used to have a great love life, but she'd gone off physical contact completely when Harriet died, and he simply couldn't under-stand. In his eyes, sex and love were the same thing and the more she turned him down, the more desperate and needy he became. He wasn't an ogre, though, and he certainly never hurt her physically.

Thinking she couldn't take much more of the conversation, she rose and brushed the bits of shingle off her bottom and thighs.

'There's no point talking about this any longer. We've both said how we feel. We need to put it behind us.'

Jon, looking pained, opened his mouth to say something else, but she pulled the mask down firmly over her eyes and nose.

'I'm off to find some fish.' She walked to the edge of the rock and prepared to jump. 'Feel free to go to the restaurant with the others. Don't wait for me. I'll catch up with you later.'

7
———————

It was a huge relief to turn her back and plunge into the crystal-clear, greenish-blue sea. On reaching the surface again, she trod water for a few minutes while she adjusted her mask and snorkel.

Aware that Jon was watching her, she didn't look behind once. She could feel his presence casting a big, black shadow and couldn't wait to put some distance between them.

The water seemed to have warmed up and didn't take much getting used to. She swam fast for a while then stopped and floated on her stomach, gazing down at the seabed.

At first, all she could see was sand, rocks, spiky urchins and seaweed, but then a small, olive-green turtle cruised slowly past, using its front flippers like paddles to propel itself along.

It was alone and appeared to know exactly where it was going. It didn't seem remotely bothered by her presence until she had to kick her legs quite hard to stay afloat. Immediately, it shot off towards the rocks, leaving her marvelling at how fast it could shift when it wanted to.

Now that she was far enough away from Jon, it seemed unlikely he'd catch her up any time soon, so she headed back towards the shoreline where she hoped to spot more sea life.

A shoal of graceful, red and green striped fish passed by and she paused to admire them, holding her breath and diving below the surface to get a better look.

The silence helped her mind and body relax. When she surfaced again, all she could hear was the steady, high-pitched sound of air flowing through her snorkel, which was curiously comforting.

A little later, her eye was caught by a strange, brownish lump on one of the rocks below her feet.

Its surface appeared slightly different from the rest of the boulder – smoother and shinier. Intrigued, she watched for a while and was amazed when long, sinewy tentacles appeared from underneath the lump and it began to move.

An octopus! She smiled in wonder at its clever, stealthy crawling motion. She fancied the creature was grinning to itself, believing it had played a smart trick and hadn't been spotted.

Not wishing to frighten it, she tried to stay completely still. Something must have startled it, however, because all of a sudden, it made a jet-propelled leap off the rock and scooted to a nearby boulder, trailing its tentacles behind. Once there, it drew them in and anchored itself to the surface with suckers, making itself blend in again and become quite inconspicuous.

Stella gurgled with laughter. She'd never observed an octopus up close like this and hadn't realised the creatures were such brilliant masters of disguise.

A little further on she saw a pale, delicate seahorse, hiding in a clump of swaying reeds. There were also brightly coloured corals, eels, scuttling crabs and spectacular round, yellowish-brown jellyfish, which looked like bouquets of flowers from the side.

Mesmerised, she circled round some of the rocks several times before holding her breath to dive down again and peek in a small, underwater cave.

She was so absorbed, she totally forgot about the others, until it occurred to her she'd been out here so long, Jon must surely have overtaken her and reached the shore by now.

The mere thought of him gave her a sick feeling in her stomach. She was convinced, as she'd told him, that his 'love' for her was nothing more than a confused manifestation of grief and loneliness.

The point, though, was he believed it was real. She could only pray her comments about Al had done the trick and destroyed any false hope he'd been harbouring.

Leaving the rocky area behind, she struck out now into deeper water, thinking all the while about what had happened. She realised Jon's harsh words about Al had made her angry, even though he'd really only repeated some of the things she'd said to him.

What's more, she'd had to stop herself leaping to Al's defence. What was that about? She prayed it had nothing to do with her inkling that he might be seeing someone else. God forbid she should turn into one of those nasty, jealous creatures who didn't want their ex, but didn't want anyone else to have him either.

As she came closer to the beach, she could see it had filled up quite a bit in the time she'd been gone. There was no sign of Louise, Jon or the others, but she spotted their towels on the sand and guessed they'd taken her suggestion and gone to the restaurant.

Dreading seeing Jon again, she was tempted to swerve lunch and sunbathe instead. She knew she should eat, however; and besides, she'd only be putting off the inevitable. She'd have to face him soon enough and do her best to act as if nothing had happened.

After struggling out of her bathing suit and into her clothes, she strolled barefoot to the taverna, which gave off an inviting, laid-back, bohemian vibe. It was painted yellow, with leaping blue dolphins on the side. The outside tables were all shaded by the rustic blue, grassy awning.

As soon as she'd walked up the gangplank, she spotted her group sitting at a rough wooden table at the far end of the restaurant, looking out to sea.

Louise waved at her while Jon, who was facing the other way, turned briefly and gave a small nod of acknowledgment.

There were plates of food in front of them and several large sharing bowls in the middle.

'Come and join us,' Louise called when Stella was close enough to hear. 'We've saved you some food but you'll have to hurry!'

There was an empty chair for Stella at one end, next to Lily and Amelia. As she settled down, she was grateful to notice Jon was focusing intently on his plate, not her.

'Fancy a glass of wine?' Louise asked, reaching across the table and picking up a bottle of white, which was three quarters empty. Stella shook her head.

'I'm really thirsty. Is there any water?'

Amelia passed along a half empty jug with chunks of ice and fresh lime. Stella filled her glass right up to the top and drank the lot in one go.

'I needed that.' She wiped her mouth with the back of a hand and topped herself up again.

Meanwhile, Jon stretched over, grabbed the wine bottle and poured what was left into his own glass. Stella and Louise exchanged glances.

Louise wasn't a big drinker and Stella suspected he'd had the lion's share of the bottle to himself. This didn't bode well for the rest of the afternoon and evening; Louise wouldn't be impressed if he got stupidly drunk again.

The group had ordered a variety of dishes and Stella helped herself to a soft, rice-stuffed tomato with aromatic mint, some creamy courgette fritters, a portion of freshly caught sea bream and a serving of the most delicious-looking Greek salad, with crumbly feta, crisp cucumber, green peppers, red onion and tangy black olives.

Louise wanted to hear about the snorkelling and Stella described the clever octopus. Lily's eyes were wide with excitement.

'Can I borrow your snorkel?' she pleaded. 'Amelia, you can have a go, too.'

Once everyone had finished and the bill had been paid, the girls scuttled off, soon to be followed by Will.

'I guess I should have a swim.' Louise wiped her mouth on her table napkin and left it, crumpled up, by her empty plate. 'I'm feeling so lazy.'

She rose, taking her black bum bag from the back of the chair and fastening it round her waist. Appalled at the thought of being left behind with Jon, Stella quickly stood up as well.

'I'm coming.' She cleared her throat and tried to sound nonchalant. 'Jon, what about you?'

'No. I think I'll have some coffee first.'

Stella glanced at him and immediately wished she hadn't. His reproachful stare made her feel guilty, angry, trapped and tearful, all at the same time.

It was over in a few seconds, but Louise must have noticed because she nudged Stella on the way out.

'What was *that* about? He looked like someone on death row.'

Stella desperately wanted to unburden herself, but it wasn't the right time.

'I'll tell you later – when we're on our own.'

She couldn't disguise the catch in her voice.

'You all right?' Louise asked, studying her friend's face anxiously.

'Sort of – well, not really. Just when I thought things were getting a bit easier, the house starts falling down.'

* * *

After spending a couple more hours on the beach, they took a small taxi boat back to Porto Liakáda, a journey of only about fifteen minutes. Will was the first to spot the rising and falling footpath they'd walked along earlier, which appeared to be clinging to the mountainside as if for dear life.

To the left were miles of deep blue sea and in the far distance, the outline of an island. The skipper informed them it was called Gavdos, which sat on the very edge of Europe.

Jon was silent on the trip, staring out to sea with a haunted, melancholy expression. It was getting on for 6 p.m. and as the boat approached the harbour, they could see the bars and restaurants were already filling up.

'We'd better stop at the supermarket and buy something for supper,' Louise said.

Stella suggested they eat in one of the restaurants instead, but Lily and Amelia were tired and grumpy and wanted to shower and chill at home.

They were appalled at the prospect of having to walk back to the villa, and Stella didn't fancy listening to them moaning all the way either. So it was agreed the girls would go on ahead while the women, plus Jon and Will, stocked up on provisions.

'That's not fair,' Will said with uncharacteristic belligerence. Louise fixed a pair of gimlet eyes on him, which did the trick.

It was dark in April's supermarket. Stella's eyes took a few moments to adjust and she stumbled straight away on something just inside the door and almost fell.

All at once, the object let out a bloodcurdling shriek, which made her heart pound so violently, for a moment she thought she was having a heart attack.

'Oh my God! It's a baby!' she screamed, looking down at her feet, finally able to focus.

A round, red, scrunched-up, tear-stained face stared back at her, holding its chubby arms aloft as if it wanted to be picked up and comforted.

Stella's heart turned into a buttery mess and she bent down, scooped up the infant and squished it into her bosom.

'Shh, shh, I'm so sorry, sweetie,' she said, rocking the baby in her arms and kissing the top of its soft head. 'Are you all right?'

The baby was too young to reply but thankfully, it stopped shrieking and emitted a few sad little whimpers instead. Stella cast round desperately for April and asked the others to look for her as well.

Not before time, she appeared from the back of the shop and Stella quickly passed her the child, explaining what had happened with an uneasy sense of déjà vu. Stamping on April's children seemed to be becoming a bit of a habit.

'He's all right, aren't you, Nikos?' April said, clutching him to her chest and stroking his mop of black hair. 'I only left him behind the counter for a second, but he's just started crawling, the little imp. I didn't realise he could move so fast!'

She was in a strappy turquoise sundress with lots of tanned flesh on display. Nikos made a grab for one of her big gold hoop earrings, but she pulled back her head in the nick of time so the jewellery was out of reach.

At that moment, Meaty came bursting through the door, panting heavily. Everyone, even the baby, turned to stare.

'It's Zenobia!' Meaty cried, looking panic-stricken. He bent over, hands on knees, while he tried to catch his breath. 'He's stolen her!'

'Who's stolen her?' April asked, frowning. 'What are you talking about?'

'The shoe shop man! He's tied her up with rope! He said he's calling the police!'

Stella's mouth dropped open. Poor Zenobia! She had no idea who she was or what she'd done, but no one deserved such appalling treatment.

'You can't tie people up,' she blurted. 'It's illegal!'

April gave her a funny look. 'Zenobia's the dog, our dog,' she said slowly, as if Stella was a bit slow.

Then, turning back to Meaty, she asked suspiciously: 'Why did he tie her up? What's she done? What did *you* do?'

Nikos, the baby, had forgotten all about his accident and was clawing at the top of his mother's dress, wanting milk, but she ignored him.

When Meaty's breathing finally went back to normal, he was able to fill them in properly.

'She grabbed a whole cooked chicken from this lady's bag outside his shop and ate it,' he explained, very matter-of-fact. 'I tried to stop her but she sank her teeth into it and growled so fiercely, I was scared. The lady had only been looking in the shop window, and soon there were bits of chicken and bones everywhere. Then another dog came along, a little one, and it tried to scoff the bits that were left and Zenobia snarled and the lady screamed and I thought there was going to be a fight.'

Stella's and April's eyes widened simultaneously. 'Oh my lord,' April said, putting a hand to her mouth.

A strange snuffling noise made Stella glance down, and another dog – an enormous black furry thing – had seemingly sprung from nowhere and was hovering at April's side.

'Basket, Violet!' April said fiercely, but Violet remained resolutely still. Behind her was a pretty, dark-haired, dark-eyed girl of about ten, holding the hand of a younger girl of about three. They looked so alike, they were obviously sisters.

'Take her upstairs,' April commanded, and the older girl obediently grabbed the dog's collar and dragged her off, still clutching on to her sibling.

April raised her heavily pencilled-in eyebrows. 'Bloody hell!'

Stella didn't know whether to laugh or commiserate.

'Where's Georgios when I need him?' April added with a sigh.

It was true, her husband was nowhere to be seen, and Stella found herself thinking she'd definitely lose track of the kids and dogs if she had to manage all this on her own.

'Can I help?' It was Jon. Stella had temporarily forgotten about him. She quickly introduced him to April, who looked him up and down.

'That's very kind of you, I must say.' She sounded rather doubtful. 'That man, the one who owns the shoe shop, he can be a right pain in the arse. He's dead proud of his store but it's a shithole, if you ask me. Everything looks nice but it's badly made and overpriced. I wouldn't buy from there if you paid me.'

'He's stubborn as hell, too. Zenobia's soft as anything, she wouldn't hurt a fly, but whatever happens, he won't give her up without a fight. He might be ninety-five but he's hard as stone.'

'Ninety-five?' Stella said, astonished.

'Well, maybe not quite that old, but getting on for it.'

Louise looked slightly sheepish, perhaps because she'd succumbed to temptation and bought some of the old man's sandals. She omitted to mention this to April.

'Would you like me to have a word with him?' Jon asked. 'Have you got a dustpan and brush?'

April nodded.

'Give me a mop and bucket as well. And warm water and bleach. And a bin bag. I'm sure he'll give the dog back if the chicken mess is cleaned up properly.'

Thrilled to be able to delegate such an unpleasant task, April dug into her pocket and swiftly produced a black plastic bag for starters.

'He's Mr Makris, for your information,' she said, passing the bag across. 'He reckons he's above everyone else, on account of his daughter.'

Jon raised his eyebrows.

'Marina,' April explained. 'The artist. She's a weird one, if you ask me, but everyone else round here seems to think she's marvellous. They reckon she's got special powers.' She tapped her nose. 'They say she can see things others can't.'

Jon looked sceptical, but April pressed on regardless.

'They say she was born with the gift. Personally, I think it's all a load of nonsense, but Mr Makris loves boasting about her.'

Stella shivered, remembering the artist's strange comments. Despite having little time for mystic hocus pocus, one thing was certain: she didn't wish to hear any more of Marina's 'insights', whether there was any truth in them or not.

After April had scurried upstairs to dig out an assortment of cleaning items, Jon heroically headed off to the scene of the crime, accompanied by Meaty.

They'd only been gone about five minutes when April, who wasn't very patient, plonked the baby back in Stella's arms and stuck her head round the door to see what was happening.

'They're on their hands and knees, scrubbing,' she said, half excited, half outraged. 'They've got wire brushes. The old fool's just standing there, watching them slave away.'

The baby, Nikos, started whimpering and clawing at Stella's neckline now, desperate to be fed, but April was oblivious.

'He's got my Zenobia on such a tight leash, she's probably choking, the poor lamb,' she went on. 'And now that old crone, Mrs Papadakis, is getting stuck in. What does she want? It's got nothing to do with her.'

At the mention of the housekeeper's name, Stella's ears pricked up.

'I hope it wasn't her chicken that was stolen,' she mused. 'She wouldn't be at all impressed.'

April sniffed, before giving a mean chuckle. 'Lady Muck!' Then, leaning further out, 'She's having a right go at Mr Makris. Looks like he's backing off. Ooh! And Meaty and your friend are standing up. And the old fool's handing Zenobia over!'

'Thank God,' said Louise, and Stella gave an inward cheer.

At that moment, the baby finally succeeded in pulling the neck of

Stella's T-shirt down so far, her boob popped out. Luckily, she was wearing a bra.

'I'm sorry, sweetie, I don't have what you want,' Stella cooed, making herself decent again as quickly as possible. 'You'll have to ask Mummy. Here—'

She thrust him into his mother's arms.

April sniffed again, before yanking down one of her sundress straps, whopping out her enormous breast and latching the infant on. Then she jiggled him to and fro on the spot while he made contented slurping sounds.

Stella didn't dare look at Will, who was hovering by his mother. He was probably mortified.

It wasn't long before Jon and Meaty returned with the dog, who was thirsty but otherwise none the worse for wear despite her ordeal.

Jon plonked the mop and bucket on the floor of the supermarket and wiped his sweaty brow with the back of an arm.

Meanwhile, Meaty couldn't wait to tell them how Mrs Papadakis, who hadn't lost the chicken but just happened to be passing when Zenobia grabbed it from the other woman, had spotted him and Jon on the ground and kicked up a real stink of her own.

'She called Mr Makris a "lazy sod" for making us do all the work.' He sounded thrilled. 'And she shouted "mingebag" at him. What does that mean?'

April glanced at Stella, who shrugged. Louise and Will were in the dark, too.

'And what did Mr Makris make of her insults?' April wanted to know. 'Was he furious?'

Meaty's eyes widened. 'Oh no! He was really scared! He kept saying sorry. He even thanked us for cleaning up!'

Now the drama was over and had reached a satisfactory conclusion, Louise and Stella whipped round the supermarket aisles, picking out food for supper: ready-cooked lamb skewers from a smart electric roller grill in the corner of the store, which were still slightly warm, fresh oregano, salad, fruit and crusty bread.

As Stella selected four large, round, ripe peaches from a pile and placed them carefully in the wire basket, she found herself speculating on the relationship between Mr Makris and the housekeeper.

Unless Katerina make a habit of rounding on anyone who happened to annoy her, it seemed likely she knew the old man quite well – well enough to feel she could harangue him, anyway.

While Stella paid the bill, she couldn't resist asking April about the elderly pair.

'Did they both grow up here in Porto Liakáda?'

'Just Mrs Papadakis,' April said. 'Mr Makris is from Viron originally, near Athens. I think he came here for work when he was a young man and never left.'

'Are he and Mrs Papadakis friends? Or were they, before this happened?'

April nodded, before correcting herself. 'Well, sort of. It's a bit of a love-hate relationship, to be honest. She was mainly friends with his wife, Cora. She got cancer, the poor woman. She was gone within six months. Must be about ten years ago now. How time flies!

'She and Katerina used to meet for coffee sometimes here in town. She was so sweet and gentle, Cora. Everyone warmed to her. Not like that husband of hers with a wandering eye. I can't think why she put up with him. If it wasn't for their daughter, I reckon she'd have thrown him out years before. She adored Marina; they both did. I gather she thought she couldn't have children; she had loads of miscarriages, then one day – bam! She got pregnant in her late thirties. Apparently, she went away to stay with her parents while she was expecting and she came back with a baby girl.

'Marina was a strange little thing, by all accounts, not like other children. Obsessed with books. The art came later. She didn't play with toys or other kids her age; she was always reading. My friend Sofia – she runs the restaurant up the road, Odyssey – her mum told her Mrs Papadakis lent Marina books from the big house, where you're staying. The two of them used to read together on one of the benches looking out to sea. Cora wasn't a reader, you see, but Mrs Papadakis was. She and Marina had that in common.'

Stella paused for a moment, reflecting on what she'd just heard, before picking up the bags of shopping from the counter and handing them round.

The high street was buzzing with people when she, Louise, Jon and Will left the supermarket having said their goodbyes.

Most of the tables in the restaurants and bars were full and there was a steady hum of voices punctured with the occasional burst of laughter.

Stella glanced anxiously to her right but fortunately, Mr Makris was nowhere to be seen, though his shop door was still open. Katerina had vanished, too.

'You did a really good thing, cleaning up that mess for April,' she told Jon, who was just behind her. She sounded rather stilted, despite her best efforts, and he grunted some sort of reply. This 'acting normal' business wasn't going to be easy.

They were at the foot of the concrete steps, about to begin the long, arduous ascent to the top, when someone called out Stella's name.

Surprised, she spun round and was dismayed to see Marina, in a long, flappy, purple and white dress, waving wildly at her from across the road.

From the enthusiasm of her greeting, you'd have thought she and Stella were long-lost friends, not virtual strangers whose last encounter had ended frostily.

Stella gave a cool nod of acknowledgment before turning back to the steps, and Louise grabbed her upper arm.

'C'mon, quick! Let's get out of here.'

They rushed up three or four steps, followed by Jon and Will. Marina, however, was too fast for them.

'Wait!' she cried.

'I don't believe it! She's running after us,' hissed Louise. 'Bloody woman.'

Stella's heart was racing and in her panic, she dropped her shopping bag. Several items of food rolled out including the ripe peaches, which splattered all over the place.

'Shit!'

Bending down to retrieve a bottle of sparkling water and a carton of milk, she was gripped with a sense of foreboding. Marina was determined to address her again and Stella, trapped, was doomed to have to listen.

Sure enough, after stuffing the water and milk back in the bag, she glanced up and the artist was on the bottom step, staring at her.

'What do you want?' Stella heard Louise say icily. 'Can't you leave us alone?'

'I need to speak to Stella,' Marina replied calmly. 'It'll only take a minute.'

'Don't—'

'It's okay, I can handle this.'

Stella rose and touched Louise lightly on the shoulder.

Slowly, she started to descend, past Will and Jon, who had their backs pinned to the wall. She felt as if she were being pulled by invisible strings.

On reaching the final step, Marina made way for her and they stood face to face on the ground. Marina's intense, deep-set eyes were like bottomless wells, filled with strange meanings.

She seemed older today, with heavy frown lines and dark circles. Her olive complexion had lost its glossy sheen and appeared thin and dry.

All of a sudden, Stella no longer felt frightened. Marina was just a woman, for God's sake. And she looked like she was in need of a good night's sleep.

'Hi.' Stella gave a half-smile, neither friendly nor hostile but somewhere in the middle. 'Did you want to say something?'

Marina nodded. 'Thank you for waiting.' She sounded relieved. 'I'm sorry but I must give you a warning.'

'Oh for fuck's sake!' Louise, who'd followed Stella down, wasn't one to mince her words. 'This is getting ridiculous. Can you please leave my friend alone? She doesn't want to hear your stupid warning or anything else you've got to say. She's absolutely fine, thank you very much.'

Marina blinked a few times, but her gaze remained fixed on Stella and her expression didn't change.

Despite the fact that her heart was pitter-pattering, Stella felt curiously composed.

'Tell me,' she said softly, her eyes glued to Marina's.

'No!' cried Louise, but Marina nodded almost imperceptibly.

'You must be careful of the sea,' she began. 'I sense danger.'

'What? Drowning?' Stella said shrilly.

Marina shook her head. 'I don't know. Possibly. Or some other peril. I urge you to be watchful. Keep an eye on those around you – and be careful yourself.'

Louise gave a derisive laugh. 'What great advice! You're on a beach holiday but don't go in the water or let anyone else, for that matter, because of some supposed danger that doesn't even exist. What are we meant to do? Stay indoors for two weeks? How absurd!'

'I didn't say that,' Marina replied patiently. 'I just said be careful. Take sensible precautions – and make sure your loved ones do, too.'

Louise snorted again. 'Can you be more specific? I mean, which one of us is doomed? It would be useful to be told.'

'I don't know,' Marina said earnestly. 'It's not clear. But my intuitions are normally right.'

Jon coughed and everyone turned to look.

'May I ask, where did you get your special powers from?' he asked in a formal voice, feigning professorial-style interest. 'Is there a course you can go on? Can we all sign up?'

He was being sarcastic, of course, but Marina took him at face value. 'I was born with them, I think. I started having premonitions when I was a little girl. I soon worked out what they were and realised they were mostly accurate.'

'Mostly?' Jon added. 'It must be a bit annoying for people if you tell them something's going to happen, then it doesn't. It can't do your reputation much good.'

Marina shrugged. 'I don't care about my reputation. Not in the least. If someone chooses to ignore me because I've made the odd mistake, that's their business. All I can do is report what I've seen.'

'Well, thank you for your report; now we need to get home,' Louise said, slightly less angrily. 'Stella, you go first; we'll follow.'

Stella breathed heavily as she trudged up, and her mind was filled with disturbing images.

Everyone said Marina was a complete fraud, and they were no doubt right. So how come she couldn't put her words out of her head?

8

When they finally arrived back at the villa, it was a big surprise to find Hector by the pool in the garden, chatting to none other than Katerina.

They were perched side by side on sun loungers and he looked more animated than Stella had seen him in a long while. What's more, he was smiling! He quickly wiped the smile from his face when he spotted his mother, though.

'I dropped by to make sure everything is in order,' Katerina explained, rising and smoothing down her tailored navy trousers. 'Hector seemed to think you have all you need? He said the girls are upstairs.'

Stella nodded. 'Everything's perfect, thank you.' She was secretly marvelling at how quickly the old woman managed to get here. She can't have left the village much before they did. She was like a mountain goat.

Stella was also in awe of Katerina's ability to make Hector talk. What on earth could they have been chatting about? She'd love to know.

'I gather you managed to rescue my friend, Jon, and Zenobia the dog from the man who runs the shoe shop?' she said to the housekeeper with a grin. 'Thank you.'

Katerina frowned. 'Yiannis? Pah! He's a silly old fool. He goes way over the top. He was talking about calling the police. Imagine! Because the dog was doing what dogs do when they smell food. They'd have laughed in his face.'

'It must have been annoying for the poor woman who lost her chicken, though,' Stella observed. 'I hope she won't have to go without supper.'

'Very annoying,' Katerina conceded. 'It was right that Mrs Vasilakis' son cleared up the mess. But you can't go kidnapping other people's pets. Yiannis went way too far!' She clicked her tongue. 'He always does.'

When Katerina left, Stella took her place by Hector's side. She could hear Louise on the phone to someone in the kitchen. Her voice sounded different and she was laughing a lot and rather self-consciously, Stella thought. Josh, no doubt.

'How long was Mrs Papadakis here?' Stella asked, turning to Hector, hoping to draw him out.

He shrugged. 'Not long.'

'She's nice, isn't she?'

'She's okay.'

'Did you have a good day?' Stella persisted. 'What did you get up to?'

He was twitching with irritation. She could sense it.

'Nothing much.' He rose quickly. 'See ya later.'

'Where are you going?' Stella asked desperately, watching as he loped towards the door, his skinny black jeans hanging loosely from his hips, despite the studded leather belt that was supposed to hold them up.

Her whole body felt heavy and weary. Nowadays, he always had this effect on her.

'My room. Too much fresh air. I'm a vampire.' He laughed nastily and made a silly hissing noise. 'I prefer the dark.'

A lump appeared in her throat and she felt like getting down on her knees and begging him to be nice, but what good would that do? He'd just say she was being over-dramatic and he hadn't wanted to come on holiday in the first place.

Thank God for Louise, she thought as she got up and walked slowly towards the house. She was the only person Stella could talk openly to, even though she could be a bit too blunt at times.

Louise was still on the phone in the kitchen when Stella entered, and she disappeared upstairs to finish her chat. Meanwhile, Stella started to fetch plates and cutlery for supper and prepare a salad.

It was after 8.30 p.m. and a long time since they'd had lunch in the taverna. The children must be ravenous, she thought. Even she felt hungry for once.

Glancing out of the kitchen window now and again, she watched the sun slowly turning from golden to orange, then pink to fiery red.

Apart from the rhythmical tz tz of the cicadas, the silence outside was so complete, she fancied she could hear herself think. It had been quite a day, what with Jon's declaration of love, the stealthy octopus, the dog incident and Marina's deadly warning. She'd be glad when it was over and she could go to sleep.

Louise returned while Stella was mixing a vinaigrette dressing for the salad.

'Sorry, that was Josh.' Surprise surprise. 'He was in an unusually chatty mood.'

'How is he?' Stella wanted to know.

'Fine. Going to the gym a lot. I think he's missing me. He said he was, anyway.'

'Good. Keep him on his toes,' Stella said wryly. But she'd clocked the uncertainty in Louise's voice. 'Have you two got any holiday plans, with or without the children?'

They'd been on a few glamorous-sounding trips in the past, just the pair of them.

Louise shuffled her feet. 'We might go to Mallorca in August, when the kids are away with their dad. It depends on Josh's work. He says he can't commit to anything till he's finished his current job.'

'That's a pain. Remind me what the job is?'

'This brand-new housing development in Camberwell, which he's project managing. There have been loads of hiccups, mainly with the suppliers.'

Stella frowned. 'Isn't that par for the course? Surely he can take a week off to go away with you?'

'I hope so,' Louise replied with a shrug. 'It's difficult when you can't plan anything till the last minute. I expect we'll manage something.'

'Fingers crossed. How do the children get on with him now?'

Stella knew this had been a problem in the past. Josh had no children of his own and didn't seem particularly interested in Will or Amelia or make much of an effort. Not surprisingly, they weren't that keen on him, either.

'Oh, it's fine now. Things are much easier on that score,' Louise replied, a little too quickly. 'They don't see a lot of each other, to be honest. I mean, everyone's so busy.'

Stella raised her eyebrows and was about to probe further, but Louise shut her down.

'Anyway, they've got a dad. They don't need another one. It's simpler keeping the two sides of my life separate. Everyone's happier.'

After that, they briefly discussed Marina again, and Stella promised not to ruminate. She had to cross her fingers behind her back, though.

Once Louise had confirmed that Jon was in his room, Stella quickly filled her in on his extraordinary outburst this morning. She knew he and the others might be down soon, so she wouldn't have long.

Stella expected Louise to be shocked, but hadn't predicted how furious she'd be, too.

'How dare he put that on you when he knows how fragile you still are?' she said hotly. 'It's incredibly selfish of him. It's not fair on you or Jemima, for that matter. What if she finds out? And what about your kids? It would be so confusing for them. Their mum's dead best friend's husband? Horrific! Besides, you and Al aren't even divorced yet.'

'I keep thinking about him,' Stella admitted, changing direction for a moment. 'I know I only said that to Jon to put him off, but it's actually the truth. I think I'd be a teeny bit jealous if I found out Al was seeing another woman.'

Louise frowned. 'I'm sure that's normal. You were together such a long time, after all. But for God's sake, don't do any toing and froing. It wouldn't be fair on Al or the kids. You've got to stick to your guns and see this thing through. You'll feel so much better once the divorce is sorted.'

Stella was doubtful, but didn't say so. She could imagine how annoying it would be for Louise, who'd given her so much support through the separation, if she suddenly turned round and said she and Al were giving their marriage another try.

Besides, she didn't think Al would be up for it. He seemed to be moving on.

'Let's have some music.' Louise turned on the radio and they listened to some Greek folk songs while she divided up the lamb skewers.

The sharp, metallic, slightly nasal sound of the bouzouki instruments grated on Stella's nerves, but she didn't complain. Louise was jigging to the music and enjoying herself.

'Do you want a drink?'

They both jumped at the sound of Jon's voice. If he'd appeared five minutes earlier, he'd have overheard their conversation.

'Good idea.' Stella turned down the volume and tried to act casual. 'There's a bottle of rosé in the fridge. Shall we open that?'

He fetched three glasses from a cupboard and pulled out the bottle of rosé. While he unscrewed the lid and poured the wine, Stella noticed his hands were trembling.

'*Yamas!*' she said fake-cheerfully once they all had a drink. She'd heard locals using the word when they chinked glasses.

After taking a sip, she glanced up to find Jon staring at her with damp, mournful eyes.

'I'll set the table,' she said hurriedly, picking up the wooden tray she'd laid with cutlery, glasses and plates. She couldn't wait to get away. He was making it hard for her to breathe.

'I'll help,' he said, quick as a flash.

Her heart sank, but what could she do? She didn't want to make a scene. Jon started to follow her outside.

'Me too!' Louise said, trailing after them both with a jug of iced water.

Stella was grateful to her friend for saving her from another awkward encounter, but wondered how long they could keep this up. Louise couldn't be her minder for the rest of the trip. They'd just have to hope Jon would see sense.

Supper in fact turned out to be quite a jolly affair. Surrounded by people, Jon couldn't moon after Stella or make reproachful digs. Instead, he sat quietly, playing around with his food and drinking more than his fair share of the wine.

Having recovered from the walk back to the villa, the girls talked animatedly about their daytrip and the snorkelling.

'Can we go to a different beach tomorrow?' Lily asked. 'It's so fun exploring new places.'

Louise suggested having a quiet day round the pool to recuperate instead, and visiting a gorge the day after.

'It's called the Aradena Gorge and it's supposed to be stunning. There's a beach at the end of the walk and a taverna. I suggest we set off early and have lunch there. It's quite a tough hike – very steep in places. It'll take us three to four hours.' She looked pointedly at Hector. 'I hope you'll come this time? It'll be worth it, I promise.'

He picked something out of a tooth, which he examined, before putting it back in his mouth.

Stella winced but managed not to comment.

'Dunno. Maybe,' he said.

'Great!'

Unlike Stella, Louise didn't get angry or frustrated with him. Stella wished she could be as cool headed. His behaviour wound her up so much and left her utterly humiliated.

The others all agreed with Louise's plan and the girls and Will decided to wake up early tomorrow and look round the shops in Porto Liakáda.

'I want a hat,' Lily announced. 'A straw one. I saw a stall selling them.'

'Will you be all right, Will?' Louise asked with an amused smile. 'Trailing round with the girls while they try on endless stuff?'

He grinned. 'Yeah. I'll probably end up sitting in a café. I need to call some people. I'll be fine.'

Everyone helped clear the table. Even Hector carried out more than just his own plate and glass.

As Stella crouched down to stack the dishwasher, she was aware of Jon standing close behind her, just that bit too close for comfort. She almost stepped on him when she stood up and he backed away wordlessly.

He followed her again when she went outside to shake the tablecloth and blow out the candles. It was like having a tiresome puppy at her heels.

While he hovered nearby as she folded up the covering, she prayed he wouldn't say anything. They were alone and she desperately wanted someone to join them.

Without any warning, he suddenly stepped forward and put his hand on hers, pinning it to the table.

She jumped – 'Oh!' – and her heart flew into her mouth.

'Can we talk somewhere in private?' He nodded at a shadowy area to their left with olive trees and bushy shrubs.

'I don't think—' she began feebly, but she didn't get to finish as a noise behind made them both turn and stare.

Hector had left the kitchen and was striding towards them. He glanced quickly at them and spotted Jon's hand on Stella's just before it was whipped away.

Stella's stomach turned over and her legs felt wobbly.

'What's going on?' Hector sounded angry and uncertain in equal measure. 'Have I interrupted something?'

The air seemed to turn cold and he gave a fake laugh, which made it even chillier.

'Not at all.' Stella forced herself to straighten up and she clutched the tablecloth to her chest. 'I was just going to put this in the washing machine.'

She knew she looked guilty, and Jon did nothing to help her out.

'Goodnight, Stella,' he said in a stiff, stern voice. 'We'll speak about this another time.'

And with that, he walked swiftly back to the villa, leaving an even frostier atmosphere behind.

Stella's guts twisted and she wished the ground would open up and swallow her whole. The last thing she'd wanted was for Hector to find out about Jon's infatuation. She'd hoped to protect both her children from that.

More to the point, Hector always thought the worst of her and would undoubtedly jump to the conclusion that this was somehow her fault.

Whichever way she looked at it, her relationship with her son would become more difficult still.

'What was that about?' he asked coldly before she'd managed to gather her thoughts and think of an appropriate explanation.

She hesitated before speaking. 'Jon's in a really bad way.'

'I know that.'

'He wants to move on from Harriet's death but doesn't know how.'

Hector's face warped into an ugly snarl.

'So he's hitting on you? He thinks you'll mend his broken heart?'

Stella swallowed. She could deny it, but her son was so sharp, he'd know she was lying.

She racked her brains to come up with a palatable response. 'He's completely deluded,' she replied at last. 'I think it must be because of the trauma he's gone through. I've told him there's no way I'd ever have a relationship with him. It's not going to happen. Hopefully, he'll get the message soon.'

'Jeez.' Hector crossed his arms and gripped his biceps tightly, as if for self-protection.

The garden was only partially illuminated by lights from the house, and half his face was in shadows.

As Stella glanced at him warily, she thought he looked as if he were wearing a mask. The side that was showing was angry and inscrutable. But if you flipped the mask over, you'd see the full range of his emotions.

His brow was furrowed and his mouth was set in a grim, hard line. Behind the anger, however, she was sure sadness lurked, hidden from view.

'What are you thinking?' she asked gently. 'You do believe me?'

He rubbed his eyes. Was he crying? She wanted to give him a hug but didn't dare.

'Dad...' He started to speak but stopped again almost immediately.

'Dad what?' Stella asked encouragingly. 'What about him?'

For a moment, it seemed Hector was going to tell her something, but he must have thought better of it and clamped his mouth shut.

'Nothing,' he said bitterly. 'It doesn't matter. Go and fuck Jon if you want; I don't care.'

Her jaw dropped and tears of fury, hurt and disbelief pooled in her eyes.

'Don't speak to me like that!' she cried, her face and neck bursting into flames. 'I'm your mother! Maybe that doesn't mean anything to you any more. I've told you, nothing's happened with Jon and never will.'

Hector pushed his face into Stella's, making her recoil, and his dark eyes flashed in the gloom.

'You lost the right to be my mum when you kicked my dad out. You almost broke him. How do you think that makes me feel?'

His cheeks were burning, too, and his body trembled with rage.

She let out a sob and buried her face in her hands. 'I can't stand it. I can't cope with your hate any more.'

Her legs buckled and she felt close to collapse. She was about to try to stagger indoors when Hector spoke again, but gently this time.

'Mum?' Was that concern in his voice?

She peeked at him timidly through her fingers and, behind the mask, she thought she spied a faint glimmer of the Hector she used to know: kind, caring, loving, thoughtful Hector. The one who used to give her the best hugs.

A seed of hope buried itself deep in her chest.

'Yes?' she said cautiously.

He hesitated, swaying to and fro for a moment, before shaking his head. 'Nothing.'

The seed dislodged itself and her heart froze over.

He turned on his heel and was gone.

* * *

Back in the house, Stella didn't want to talk about what had just taken place, but it was obvious she'd been crying and she felt she owed Louise some sort of explanation.

'Hector and I had a row. He said some terrible things,' she whispered when the others were out of hearing.

Jon and Hector had gone to their rooms while the girls and Will were playing cards at the grand marble dining table next door.

Louise led her outside again and suggested a stroll round the moonlit garden. The cicadas' singing was quieter now the air was cool. They were at their noisiest in the hottest part of the day.

A distant, low hoot, which seemed to echo round the mountain, made them stop in their tracks.

'An owl,' Louise observed. 'What a lovely sound!'

Stella glanced up to Jon's bedroom on the second floor. His shutters were closed but the light was on, and she guessed the window was open.

'This way,' Louise said, nodding in the direction of a narrow, paved path that led away from the villa to the edge of the property. Most of the fruit trees had been planted here against the wall, where they'd be somewhat sheltered from the strong Cretan wind that could suddenly whip up and take you by surprise.

Louise shook her head in disgust when Stella told her about Jon's ambush, and then again when she repeated some of the language Hector had used.

'He shouldn't speak to you like that,' she muttered. 'Whatever happened to "Honour thy father and thy mother"?'

'But what can I do about it? He's an adult now; I can't stop his pocket money or ground him.'

Louise paused for a moment. 'It must have been a huge shock for him, seeing you and Jon like that. I can understand why he jumped to the wrong conclusion.'

'Yes, but what I don't get is why he wouldn't believe me when I told him the truth.'

Louise took a deep breath. 'I think he's extremely lost and confused. Obviously, Harriet's death was traumatic for him, too. On top of that, he's had to cope with your low moods as well as his dad's misery. And it can't be easy for him, with you spending so much time with Jon and Jemima. I imagine he feels rather abandoned and left to his own devices.'

Stella was stung. She knew Louise could be direct, but implying she was falling short as a mother was a step too far. It hurt like hell.

'I've asked him loads of times if he wants counselling,' she said defensively. 'Obviously, I'd pay. But he insists he doesn't need it. I don't know what else I can do for him. And clearly, I have to look after Jon and Jemima...'

'You could ask Jon to leave?'

Both women pulled up short and Louise's words seemed to hang, suspended in the air between them.

It was Stella who broke the silence.

'Are you serious?'

Louise nodded. 'It would send a strong message to Hector about how you really feel about Jon. To be honest, it'd be a relief for the rest of us as well. He's not exactly good company. No one wanted him to come except you.'

Stella's pulse started racing and her head hurt.

'I can't possibly send him home.'

'Why not?'

'It might tip him over the edge. I promised Harriet I'd look after him.'

Louise made a clicking sound with her tongue, which made Stella's teeth jangle.

'Always Harriet,' she said. 'Nothing's changed, has it? You hero-worshipped her when she was alive, and she's still running your life now she's dead. When are you going to grow up and stand on your own two feet?'

'What?' Stella could hardly believe her ears. This sudden, inexplicable burst of malice took her breath away. 'I didn't hero-worship her,' she said hotly. 'I don't know why you think that. She was a dear friend. We'd grown up together, remember. We were like sisters. We *understood* each other,' she added pointedly. 'She'd do anything for me and vice-versa.'

Even in the darkness, she could sense Louise's skin prickling with annoyance.

'Really? I know you'd do anything for *her*. You've shown that a hundred times over. But what about the other way round?'

'What do you mean?' Stella was stunned.

'Well, where was Harriet when Robin died, for instance? And I don't remember her looking after Hector much when you were trying to get your business off the ground.'

It was true, Harriet hadn't been there when Stella had heard the news about Hector's real dad; she'd been away on a work trip. She'd kept in touch by phone, though. And Louise was between jobs and didn't have children when Stella had been setting up Deliciously Yours, whereas Harriet was working full-time with a two-year-old.

'I was really grateful for your help; you were amazing,' Stella said quietly, as it slowly dawned on her Louise must have disliked Harriet far more than she'd ever realised. 'Were you jealous of Harriet?' she asked suddenly, genuinely wanting to understand where the anger was coming from.

'Not in the least.' Louise gave a humourless laugh, which made Stella think she must have hit a raw nerve. 'Why would I be jealous of *her*?'

A real nastiness had crept into her tone, which made Stella's pulse race. It was as if a switch had been flipped and she suddenly saw red.

'I think you were. I think you envied our closeness,' she blurted. Now she'd started, she couldn't stop. 'You've always been critical of her. You never made much effort to be friends. I often wondered why. I was quite surprised you didn't do more to help when she was dying, actually. I didn't say anything at the time, but I noticed you didn't visit much; you were always too busy. And now you're telling me to do less for her family. At last, I understand why.'

There was a silence again for a moment and the atmosphere surrounding the two women felt heavy and sinister. Even the air they were breathing seemed toxic.

Stella could hear her heart hammering and her fists were clenched. She squeezed her eyes closed, gearing up for another verbal onslaught, but instead, Louise inhaled deeply.

'Look, there's no point arguing like this. We're both upset and we'll only say things we'll regret. I do think you need focus more on Hector and Lily, though. They need you just as much – probably even more than Jemima and Jon.'

Heat rose up through Stella's body and her cheeks caught fire for the second time that evening.

'Do you think I don't know what my kids have been through? They're my main priority. Their needs are always uppermost in my mind.'

'Hey!' Louise touched Stella lightly on the arm, which made her jump and instinctively pull back.

'I'm sorry for what I said. I know you loved Harriet and I didn't not like her, if you see what I mean. And you're a good mum. I just think Jon's affecting the atmosphere, especially now he's told you he's in love with you. It must be really awkward for you, too.'

They'd reached the perimeter wall and began to skirt round the edge of the garden. It was a clear night and the way was lit by the silvery moon and stars.

This sudden, surprise apology made Stella cool down a bit. She wasn't wearing shoes and the grass felt pleasantly chilly beneath her feet.

It was clear Louise wanted to smooth things over, which wasn't a bad thing. It was late and Stella needed a decent night's sleep, not more of an ugly, deeply upsetting confrontation. She couldn't forget Louise's words, though. Out of the blue, she'd gone for the jugular, and it really hurt.

'I've taken on board your comments about Jon,' Stella said carefully, after pondering for a few moments. 'I do understand where you're coming from, but I can't do what you ask. I'll see what he's like tomorrow. If he's still acting weird around me, I'll tell him he's making everyone uncomfortable and it's got to stop.'

'Fine.' Louise sounded frustrated, but resigned.

'Thanks,' said Stella, scratching a bite on her arm with her fingernails. Relief from the itching only came when the bite started to bleed.

By now, they'd circled round the whole villa and come back to their original spot. A burst of laughter came from inside; the girls and Will were probably still playing cards.

Stella glanced up to Jon's window again and saw light still shining through the shutters. She shivered, and hoped Harriet would appreciate what she was doing for him; Harriet wouldn't want Stella turning her back on Jon, no matter what. It had put her in a very difficult position, though.

'Just so you know, I'm going to keep my distance from Jon as much as possible tomorrow,' Louise said firmly.

Stella nodded, wishing she could do the same.

Goosebumps ran up and down her arms when she remembered his

hand on hers, him standing so close to her at times, there was barely a sliver of breathing space between them.

'Good idea. Me too,' she added without conviction.

9

'Who's your dad gone on holiday with?'

Stella hoped her question would sound innocent, but Lily's eyes narrowed suspiciously.

'Why d'you want to know?'

'No reason,' Stella replied nonchalantly, popping a spoonful of thick Greek yoghurt drizzled with honey in her mouth. It was delicious. 'I just wondered, that's all. He said he probably wouldn't be able to call as there'd be no signal. He must be somewhere remote.'

'He's in *Cornwall*,' Lily said crossly. She seemed to think her mother had no right to ask anything about Al now they were separated.

'How nice!'

Lily poured herself some orange juice. There was only a little left in the carton, which she scrunched up and pushed irritably away.

'We need to do a shop,' Stella observed. 'Maybe you and Amelia and Will could pick up some things when you go into town?'

'Yeah,' Lily replied, before swigging back the inch or so of juice in one go.

The pair were having breakfast together in the garden, having woken up earlier than the others. It was a relief for Stella to spend time alone with her daughter, who usually managed to lift her mood.

The row with Louise the previous night had deeply unsettled her. What had been said couldn't be unsaid, and she feared their relationship would never be the same again.

She'd resolved to do her best to be as amicable as possible for now, so as not to let a hostile atmosphere spoil things for everyone else. But she was resigned to the bitter fact that for her, the holiday wasn't going to be the relaxing break she'd hoped for, but a painful ordeal instead.

She and Lily talked about all manner of things, including Lily's hair, which she mentioned often.

'D'you think I should get a fringe?' Lily asked, pulling some hair over her forehead to show what it might look like.

A few days earlier, she and Amelia had discussed having bobs, or choppy layers.

Stella smiled. She loved these chats and knew how important hairstyles were to girls of that age, as well as nail polish, boys and whether or not to have their ears pierced.

'Maybe,' she replied, cocking her head to one side to prove she was giving the matter serious thought. 'It's lovely as it is, but it's up to you. The only problem is, if you don't like it, it'll take a long time to grow out.'

Lily pondered this for a moment with a frown. 'Mm. You're right.' Her eyes lit up. 'Maybe I could get just a bit cut off, like half a fringe. To about here.'

She indicated to a point just below her cheekbones.

'Good plan. It needs to be long enough to tuck behind your ears, though. Otherwise it could get in your eyes and be quite annoying.'

'But then it wouldn't be like having a fringe at all,' Lily retorted. 'I want it to look *different*.'

After this, Stella couldn't help steering the subject back on to her husband.

'Have *you* managed to get hold of Dad?' she ventured, crossing her fingers under the table. She knew she was pushing it but couldn't seem to stop herself. She hoped Lily wouldn't blow.

'Yes.'

'Oh! That's good. How is he?'

'He's fine, Mum. Stop talking about him. He's just going on lots of long walks, like he does.'

'On his own?'

Lily glared at her mother across the table. 'None of your business.'

'Sorry.' Stella leaned back, hands raised and flattened palms facing out. 'What do you want to buy today, other than a straw hat?' she said, quickly changing tack. 'I saw some nice little sun dresses hanging up in one of the stalls.'

They were soon joined by Will and Amelia, who'd both turned a lovely shade of light brown. Lily was tanned, too, but her nose had started to peel and the skin underneath was baby pink, much to her disgust. She hadn't been conscientious enough with the sunscreen, but would never admit it.

Stella went quiet, watching the three of them pouring out bowls of cereal and buttering chunks of white crusty bread. She was thinking about Al and trying to work out whether Lily's responses gave any clue as to whether or not he had company on holiday.

All of a sudden, Lily's voice rose above the others.

'Sasha said you shouldn't ever pluck your own eyebrows; it's too hard. You should always go to a salon.'

'What if you can't afford it?' Amelia piped up.

Stella's heart missed a beat. Sasha was the name of the makeup lady who lived in the flat above Al's. Why had *she* crept into the conversation?

Without pausing to think, she launched herself headlong into the chat.

'Sasha's right,' she said. 'I plucked mine when I was young and ended up with half an eyebrow. It looked terrible.'

Everyone laughed, including Lily. Encouraged, Stella tentatively cast another Mayfly.

'Did Sasha give you any other tips you can pass on? Like the best brands of makeup to use? I could do with some advice.'

Lily shook her head. 'Not really. I think she uses lots of different brands.'

'I'd love to find a really good mascara that doesn't clog,' Stella persisted. 'Can you ask her advice?'

She was hoping Lily would take the bait and agree to have a word with Sasha next time she was on the phone to her dad. That way, Stella would know for sure that they were together. But her plan failed.

'I doubt I'll remember,' Lily replied casually, slathering apricot jam over the slice of buttered bread on her plate before glancing up at Amelia and Will. 'Let's leave straight after breakfast? Agreed? Otherwise it'll get too hot.'

As soon as they'd gone, Stella went to find Louise, who was in her bedroom having just come out of the shower.

'How did you sleep?' Stella asked warily, studying Louise's expression in an effort to gauge her mood.

'Fine,' Louise replied, rubbing her hair dry with one of her white towels. She'd wrapped the other tightly round her body and tucked the overlapping bit in front to hold it up. 'You?'

'Okay, too, thanks.'

'Good.'

It was an awkward, stilted sort of exchange, but to Stella's relief, Louise seemed just as keen as she was to paper over their nasty argument, at least for now.

'Any sign of Jon?' she asked fake-casually, as if his presence wasn't the major problem they'd argued over last night.

Stella, sounding just as nonchalant, said she hadn't seen him but almost straightaway, they heard him opening his bedroom door.

They both started. Louise's door was ajar and she tiptoed over to close it as quietly as possible. Moments later, she spotted him out of the window in his bathing trunks, with a towel slung over his shoulder.

'I think he's going for a swim,' she observed, darting away from the window in case he looked up.

'I'll read for a bit indoors,' said Stella. 'I don't feel like talking to him if I can help it.'

She lay on her bed for a couple of hours, immersed in a novel. When her eyes grew tired, she texted Louise to ask if she knew of Jon's whereabouts now. Apparently, he was asleep by the pool.

Stella's eyes narrowed into slits and she cursed under her breath. Why was she the one who had to make herself scarce? He should have the nous to realise he'd upset her and take himself off somewhere, preferably for the whole day. Didn't he understand she wanted to enjoy the pool and read her book in peace?

He was being incredibly selfish, but she wouldn't call him up on it; she was determined to get through the holiday without another row. The one with Louise had been bad enough. She'd only beat herself up if she and Jon argued, and feel horribly guilty.

To avoid any risk of contact, she decided to forgo a swim just now and stay indoors to explore the house. She'd scarcely been in the rooms downstairs yet, save the kitchen, and was sure there'd be some interesting artefacts to look at.

Paintings adorned the walls of every room, small and large, and she stopped to admire the ones that took her eye. Quite a few depicted scenes from the ancient Greek myths, including Jason with his Argonauts, Atlas bearing the world on his shoulders and a gory one of Perseus slaying the gorgon, Medusa.

There were also a number of portraits, including several of the same woman at different stages of life. In one, she was young and attractive, perching coquettishly on a garden table in a silk floral dress, with a nipped-in waist and pussy bow. Dark curls peeked out from beneath her felt hat, set at a jaunty angle, and her red mouth curved upwards in a teasing little smile.

Next door, there was another painting of her in middle age, and a third when she was much older. Her hair, though still curly, was now white. Deep wrinkles encircled her eyes and she had sagging skin on her neck, around which hung a string of pearls.

She was wearing a pale-yellow twinset, typical of the 1950s, when Stella guessed the portrait had been done.

This time, however, there was no smile. The woman looked composed but tired, perhaps even a little bit sad. She had an air of quiet resignation, as if life had dealt her a disappointing hand, but she was determined to endure it with dignity.

Stella suspected she was the former lady of the house, though she couldn't confirm it. Elsewhere, she noticed two paintings, clearly done by the same artist, of a handsome, distinguished-looking man, who was probably the woman's husband. From his confident, upright, commanding demeanour, she guessed this was Leo Skordyles, the former mayor of Sfakia.

To her surprise, hanging in a prominent position on one of the walls, there was also a portrait of a young Katerina, who'd evidently been quite a beauty. Stella wondered who'd commissioned the painting and why. It struck her as unusual to have a picture of a servant on display. The previous owners must have been very fond of the housekeeper.

They had also amassed quite a collection of pots, including a strange terracotta vase in the form of a bull's head, which sat on top of the piano.

Another of the anterooms was filled from floor to ceiling with books. Stella couldn't read the Greek titles, but stopped to look at some of the covers.

Her gaze fell on a large, handsome hardback, which she pulled out.

She blew on the spine several times to clear away the dust, which went everywhere, including up her nose, making it itch. Her eyes watered, too, and she wiped them with the back of her arm.

The tome was very heavy and had a picture of an eagle on the front and a handwritten inscription on the first page. Her interest piqued, she settled on a red leather chair and quickly flicked to the middle section, which was filled with black and white photographs.

Soon, she was poring over images of Crete in years gone by: two elderly men with big, twirling moustaches sipping coffee outside an old-fashioned café, enjoying the passing scene; a peasant woman in a white headscarf on a donkey, with a baby in her arms and an older child behind, trudging into town, laden with baskets.

Although Crete had obviously changed enormously since those times, Stella couldn't help thinking life for folk like Katerina and her neighbour, Eleni, the old woman who kept the chickens, perhaps wasn't so very different.

After all, there weren't any trains or buses, let alone cars, and they both had to walk up and down the steep mountain to fetch food, or keep livestock and cultivate their land so they could feed themselves.

Likewise, there were no cinemas or theatres nearby and socialising mostly took place, as it always had, in local cafés or people's homes.

On turning to the next page, Stella noticed a small, loose, black and white photo, which she picked up. It must have been placed there for a reason, she mused, examining it with curiosity.

It was quite a casual-looking snap of two women.

There was nothing written on the back to identify who they were but that didn't matter, as Stella recognised them instantly anyway.

The lady in the paintings she'd just seen was sitting on a garden bench smiling, her head resting comfortably on Katerina's bosom.

Although the housekeeper was considerably younger, the way she was posing gave the impression that she was the mother, with an arm round the other woman's shoulders, giving her a protective hug.

How Stella wished Katerina would appear right now and tell her the story behind the image! She popped the photo in an empty vase on the little table beside her, telling herself it would be quite safe there. She'd show it to the housekeeper next time they met, before returning it to its original hiding place.

Having seen enough of the books, she rose and strolled into the study area. Small and dark, it contained a mahogany bureau with a folding lid and brass handles, more chairs and an antique wooden table with a chessboard on top.

Intrigued by her photograph find, she walked straight over to the desk and opened the lid. A furtive glance over her shoulder confirmed no one was watching, so she eagerly turned her attention to what was inside. Anticipation soon turned to disappointment, however. The six pigeon-holes were empty, as were the drawers beneath.

If the desk had once been in use, it had clearly been emptied and was now there just for show. It even smelled of lavender polish, rather than the slightly musty scent she associated with workspaces piled high with old books, pens and stacks of paper.

Closing the lid, she turned away in disgust. She'd done enough investigating for the day. Jon or no Jon, she wanted a swim, some lunch and a couple of hours in the sun. She deserved it; she'd paid for it, after all.

Her swimsuit and beach towel were on the back of one of the garden chairs, where she'd hung them last night to dry. As no one was about, she dodged behind a bush to change, plonking her clothes on the table to pick up later.

It was almost 2 p.m. and the heat was so intense, she found herself hopping along the path leading to the pool to stop the baking flagstones from burning her bare feet.

Louise had moved her lounger into the shade under a tree and was reading a magazine. Meanwhile, Jon was spread-eagled on his seat by the water's edge, still apparently sleeping after all this time.

'D'you think he's okay?' Stella whispered to Louise when she was close enough to be heard. 'I hope he's wearing sunscreen.'

Louise put down her magazine and glanced at Jon disapprovingly.

'He's probably had enough sun,' she said with a sniff. 'He's been out here for ages. Which one of us is going to tell him?'

Stella pulled a face.

'All right,' Louise said tetchily. 'I'll do it.'

Stella watched while her friend walked over to where Jon was lying and said his name. When he failed to respond, she poked him in the side and repeated 'Jon', much louder this time.

His leg twitched and he grunted something unintelligible before sitting bolt upright and staring round in confusion.

He was in such a daze, he clearly had absolutely no idea where he was. Before long, his eyelids started drooping and he shut his eyes again, as if intending to block everything out and go back to sleep.

Louise was having none of it.

'YOU NEED TO GET IN THE SHADE,' she shouted, shaking him roughly by the shoulder. 'You could get heatstroke.'

Slowly, Jon started to rise from his chair and stagger towards the shade. Once his focus became clear, he spotted Stella, standing close by, watching, and an expression of fear and recognition crossed his features.

The skin on his face, chest, arms and thighs looked red, tight and burning. He swayed slightly and Stella thought he might faint.

'Oh my God!' she said, running over and grabbing him round the back with both arms. 'Help! Louise! He's going to fall.'

Louise rushed to his side and together, they helped him struggle to the lounger in the shade, where he flopped down.

Grabbing a bottle of water lying on the grass, Louise shoved it in his hands.

'Drink this. All of it.'

She sounded cold, hard and angry. She'd come to his rescue out of a sense of moral duty, but it was obvious that as far as she was concerned, he was nothing but a pain in the neck. Her lack of sheer human sympathy made Stella cringe.

They both watched while he greedily glugged the water.

'What an idiot,' Louise muttered, before glaring at Stella. 'Sunstroke can be really dangerous, you know. We've got to cool him down.'

Stella clenched her jaw and narrowed her lips to stop herself from lashing out and saying something she might regret. Louise intended to make her feel stupid, too, as if this was somehow all her fault. She supposed it was, in as much as she was the one who'd invited Jon. But Louise should have woken him earlier, instead of thoughtlessly leaving him to fry. She herself was far from blameless.

When he'd finished all the water in the bottle, he took a deep breath and scratched his head. He was already looking more normal.

'I'll get in the pool,' he said. 'That'll sort me out.'

It seemed like a sensible plan. The women kept a close watch while he walked slowly, unaided, to the edge of the pool and sat down before launching himself in.

'D'you think he'll be okay?' Stella asked as he bobbed beneath the surface and managed to swim a few strokes. 'Should I find a doctor?'

Louise made a sucking in sound at the back of her throat, like a low growl.

'No. He doesn't need one. His skin's going to hurt like hell, though. I should care, but I really don't. He's a bloody liability.'

Stella glanced at her friend, who was scowling. She looked angrier than Stella had ever seen her.

'Hey?' she said, hoping to go some way towards placating her, but she shook her head.

'Don't. Say. Anything,' she muttered, extending her arm and placing her hand, face up, between them, like a barrier. 'You want him to stay?

You look after him. He's your responsibility. I wash my hands of the whole affair.'

* * *

So much for trying to smooth things over with Louise. Her savage words about Jon had an air of finality that Stella couldn't ignore and made her wonder if, after the holiday, their friendship would survive at all.

The last thing Stella wanted was to be Jon's nursemaid, but as no one else was willing to care for him, least of all Louise, it was down to her.

After he came out of the pool, she followed him upstairs and went to fetch a bottle of aloe vera lotion from her bathroom.

She waited while he took a cool shower to remove the chlorine from his skin and told him to call her when he'd finished.

He was sitting on the end of the bed, wearing white boxer shorts and a black T-shirt, when she entered his room.

'You'd better take off your top and lie on your front,' she said, trying to sound matter-of-fact. 'I'll do your back. You can do the rest.'

'Thanks so much.' Obediently, he pulled off his T-shirt, turned round and lay face down on the crumpled white quilt. 'I'm sorry for causing all this trouble.'

She didn't reply; she was too focused on the task ahead. In the intimate setting of the bedroom, his nakedness made her shudder. She didn't want to have to touch him and was afraid of giving him the wrong message, but the job couldn't be avoided.

After squeezing some of the clear lotion onto her hand, she stood over him and began smoothing it into his back and shoulders. Despite the shower, his skin felt hot to the touch and she could already see painful little white, fluid-filled blisters starting to form.

'How bad is it?' he asked, lying perfectly still, with his head on one side.

'Um, pretty bad,' she replied truthfully.

He must have been in some pain because he winced a few times. But otherwise, he seemed relaxed, his arms at right angles, elbows bent and fingers spread wide.

A small cluster of cappuccino-coloured moles beneath his right shoulder blade caught her eye, along with a patch of soft, pale-brown hair on the base of his spine, just above his boxers.

Al's back was quite different – much broader and he hadn't any moles, or very few, anyway. Only a tiny brown birthmark above his right hip.

Had Sasha seen it? Stella tensed. She didn't want to think about it. Come to that, she didn't want to think about Jon's moles or his patch of hair either. It felt wrong, like betraying Harriet. She wished she hadn't noticed.

Jon shifted slightly, bringing her back to the here and now. She warned him he'd have to stay out of the sun for several days and might need painkillers until the redness subsided.

'Uh huh,' he murmured lazily. She realised his eyes were closed and a small, contented smile was playing on his lips. He'd forgotten to be angry and upset with her; he was enjoying her attention.

'Right, that's it,' she said quickly, rubbing the last of the lotion onto his lower back and snapping the lid of the bottle shut. 'You can do the backs of your legs and arms and your front. I'll leave the lotion here.'

Rolling over with a sigh, he sat up.

'That was wonderfully soothing, thank you.'

He tried to catch her eye but she avoided his gaze, wiping her hands briskly on the white towel beside him.

'How often do I need to apply this?' He'd picked up the bottle and was pretending to scan the instructions. She knew he was hoping to detain her; he was playing for time.

'Several times a day.'

'Will you do my back again later?' He sounded wheedling and needy.

Frowning, she resolved not to go into his bedroom again; he might start to like it too much.

'Bring the bottle downstairs and I'll do it after supper.'

Her words obviously annoyed him. His face clouded over and she could swear his bottom lip stuck out, like a sulky child's.

'I'm feeling sick. I won't want supper.'

'Oh dear.'

'I doubt I'll be well enough to come on the walk tomorrow either.'

Was he trying to make her feel sorry for him? Or perhaps he hoped she'd beg him to join them?

'That's a shame.'

She secretly thought it would be a big relief if he stayed behind, but then guilt got the better of her and she berated herself for being mean.

'I'll bring you a glass of water,' she said, more kindly. 'They say you should drink lots if you have sunburn.'

Her newly conciliatory tone instantly perked him up.

'Thank you for looking after me so well.'

He reached out and took her hand, giving it an unwelcome squeeze.

Goose bumps ran up and down her back and arms. She glanced at him sharply before snatching her hand away.

'I'll be back in a moment,' she said, turning on her heel and hurrying to the door.

Hector was in the kitchen, making himself a sandwich. It was the first time she'd seen him today. He looked as if he'd just got out of bed with knotty hair, a scraggy beard and bare chest. Down below, he was in the black jeans he'd worn all week and she wondered if he ever took them off.

He grunted when she said hello but didn't look up.

He seemed to have removed the entire contents of the fridge and sprayed crumbs all over the worktop and floor, but she didn't comment.

'Pass me the water, will you?' she asked, and he handed over the bottle. After filling a glass, she went back upstairs and put it on the table by Jon's bed.

'I'm going for a swim,' she said, giving him no opportunity to respond. 'I haven't had one yet. And by the way, I won't be around for the rest of the afternoon. I need some peace and quiet. I'm off to read my book by the pool.'

10

Lily, Amelia and Will didn't return from Porto Liakáda until almost 5 p.m. and until then, Stella was alone. She decided to take herself off to the plunge pool, tucked away in its private stone courtyard, where she lay in the water for a long time with her arms outstretched and resting on the side, her back against the cool blue and white mosaic tiles, gazing up at the lush green plants and trees above.

Whatever the future held in terms of her friendship with Louise, she thought, kicking her legs out lazily in front to stay afloat, she hoped she'd have calmed down and recovered her equilibrium by suppertime. And although Stella was still angry and deeply hurt, she resolved to make a special pasta sauce for supper that she knew Louise would like, as a sort of peace offering.

But as soon as Louise appeared at the table that night, Stella could tell she was still furious. She sat down without a word and refused to look at her or address her in person, concentrating only on her food.

Even the fact Jon didn't emerge from his room failed to lift her mood. When Stella asked Lily to take him up a small plate of pasta, prompting a brief discussion about the perils of sunburn, only Louise stayed schtum.

'Will his skin all peel off?' Amelia wanted to know.

Her mother didn't answer, so Stella stepped in.

'I think so, yes. And the skin underneath will be pink and tender.'

'Like my nose?' said Lily, wrinkling it. 'Yeeuch!'

'That'll teach him,' Hector said nastily, and Will laughed.

'If it had been one of us, you'd have killed us, Mum.'

Will glanced at his mother, but she didn't look up from her plate.

'What's got into her?' he said with a frown, but when no one commented, he lost interest and started playing with a blob of soft candle wax that had dropped onto the table.

It was Stella who assumed the role of tour guide for the following day's excursion. They'd have to leave at 7 a.m., she insisted, to avoid walking in the midday sun.

When she tried again to persuade Hector to join them, for once, Louise didn't back her up.

'You can't force me,' Hector said angrily, throwing down his napkin, pushing back his chair and standing up.

Out of habit, Stella shot Louise a desperate look, but her friend's face was tight and closed.

'All right then, have it your way,' Stella said finally, her shoulders slumping. 'We'll miss you.'

* * *

At six thirty the next morning, she tapped lightly on Jon's door and called his name. She was almost positive he wouldn't want to do the hike and expected him to be asleep still, or at least snoozing.

To her dismay, however, he came quickly to the door and flung it open. He was already dressed in a pale-blue shirt, rolled up at the sleeves, and tan hiking trousers. Over his shoulder, she could see his black backpack on the bed, stuffed with items for the walk.

'I guessed you'd be leaving pretty sharpish,' he said with a grin. 'I feel much better after a good night's sleep. Almost myself again.'

'Great.' She hoped he wouldn't detect her barely disguised lack of enthusiasm. 'I thought you'd want to rest today. It's amazing you've recovered so well.'

Downstairs in the kitchen, Louise was filling up her water bottle.

'Jon's coming,' Stella said heavily.

'That's nice. You can talk to him all day and put on his sun cream for him.'

Sarcasm dripped from every syllable, and Stella felt as if she'd been stabbed in the gut. Part of her wanted to make peace with Louise and say the bad atmosphere was killing her and please could they be friends again? But the other part was screaming Louise wasn't the person she'd thought she knew.

She had a mean, hard, jealous streak, which was probably why a lot of Stella's other friends, including Harriet, for that matter, hadn't warmed to her. How come Stella seemed to be the only one who hadn't noticed?

In any case, it was as if Louise had built a Berlin Wall around herself and Stella couldn't get through to her even if she wanted to.

Lily was annoyed at having to get up so early and snapped at her mother, who decided to give her a wide berth for a while.

Jon walked beside Stella as she led the way along a well-marked, zigzag path up the steep mountainside, while the others trailed behind. Mostly, the group remained quiet, lost in their own thoughts, the silence only occasionally broken by the girls' voices or the jangling of goat bells.

The air was fairly cool and they needed their sweatshirts. However, the layers soon started to come off as they continued their climb through stony desert, past crippled old trees and wildflowers humming with bees collecting pollen.

After about an hour and a half, they came to an abandoned village with an ancient white church, which Stella had read about in her guidebook. It was built in the form of a crucifix with a hexagonal dome, and sat right on the edge of the canyon.

From here, it wasn't too far to the famous, wooden-planked Aradena Bridge, which spanned the entire width of the yawning gorge. Stella didn't dare glance into the seemingly bottomless void, fearing she might faint.

Up to now, they hadn't seen another soul, but they spotted a few folk ahead when they began the slow descent into the canyon.

At first, the slope was fairly gentle, but before long, the ground shelved steeply, with slippery rocks underfoot. Stella had to keep her wits about her.

At times, she clung to small bushes for support, or slid on her bottom down boulders before clambering up the other side.

Soon, they were in complete shade, amidst towering walls of red stone. A golden eagle circled above them in the slim patch of sky visible overhead, before it landed on the craggy mountainside.

It remained there for quite some time, looking down on them haughtily from its throne-like perch. When Stella tried to take a picture, however, it flew off like a stroppy celebrity, tired of its irritating fans.

She was concentrating so hard on not falling, for quite some time, she forgot about Jon, who was a little way ahead. She was enjoying the physical challenge and her brain felt sharp and clear.

The fog of confusion rapidly descended again, though, when he stopped to wait for her. Glancing back, she could see the others were quite far behind and would take a while to catch up.

'Wow! It's pretty demanding,' she said when she reached him. She was desperate to keep the conversation light. She took the water bottle out of her backpack and had a drink. 'The scenery's stunning. I thought it would be much more crowded but there's hardly anyone else here.'

He didn't reply and she noticed he no longer looked cheery, as he had first thing this morning, but intense and serious.

Her heart fluttered and she quickly replaced the water bottle and tried to walk past him, but he stood in her way.

'Stella?' he said with an urgency she couldn't ignore.

'Yes?'

'Have you thought any more about what I said?'

The flutter in her chest became a wild beating of wings.

'I meant it, you know. Every word. It's torture, seeing you like this every day and not being able to show how I feel.'

Suddenly, Stella felt very alone. She glanced back again and the gap between her and the others had narrowed, but they were still too far away to be of any use.

Black vultures circled ominously above and she noticed a dead goat lying on the ground a little way ahead. Others were perched precariously on the mountainside; it wasn't surprising if they sometimes fell off.

She remembered Louise, and realised she wouldn't help anyway. Jon was Stella's problem. Louise had made it quite clear.

'Look,' Stella said, her mouth turning dry, 'I've told you I'm not interested. You've got to stop this. You mustn't talk about it any more.'

Jon dropped the backpack he was holding and sank to the ground.

'I can't bear it.' There was a catch in his voice and he shook his head desolately.

Her natural instinct was to reach out with a hug to anyone in pain, but she stopped herself.

'You'll get over it. Truly.'

'I won't.'

Stella's eyes pricked and a hard lump, like a pebble, stuck in her throat. She tried to push past him again but he grabbed her arm and hot tears started to trickle down her cheeks.

'Let me go,' she said, roughly shaking him off. 'Can't you see I've had enough?'

He released his grip and his arm fell to his side. She would have liked to run away but couldn't, because of the boulders blocking her path.

It seemed to take an age to find a route through, either by shinning over the rocks or seeking out the narrow cracks and shimmying between them. She didn't look back once and had no idea if Jon were following, so it was a surprise when she heard her name being called.

'Mum!'

Turning round, she saw Lily hurrying to catch up. She wasn't with Louise, Amelia or Will. Or Jon, come to that.

'Are you all right?'

Stella was touched by her daughter's concern and waited for her. When Lily made it to the top of the same rock, they sat down on a flattish shelf, side by side.

'What happened?' Lily wanted to know. 'I saw him grab you.'

She didn't use his name. She was clearly outraged.

Stella paused for a moment, wondering how much to give away.

'Nothing,' she replied at last. 'I'm fine, honestly.'

Lily scowled. 'Mum, I know you're lying. Tell me the truth. Everyone's behaving weirdly. Louise, him, you. I'm not stupid. What's going on?'

Stella had pulled up her knees and was gazing down at the rough, grey stone by her legs. Lily cupped a hand under her mother's chin and gently but firmly twisted her head round so she could see her face.

'And you've been crying,' she said, staring accusingly into her mother's eyes.

Stella sniffed. She hadn't realised it was that obvious.

'We had a bit of a disagreement, that's all.'

Lily's eyes widened. 'You and Jon? Why?'

Picking up a small, flat stone, Stella proceeded to roll it between her palms. It helped to distract from the sickening swooping in her chest.

'He's got a silly crush on me,' she explained hoarsely. 'I didn't want to tell you; I didn't think you needed to know. It's not real; it's all to do with Harriet. I can't explain. He'll get over it, but it's made things awkward between us.'

'Oh God.' Lily flung both arms round Stella's shoulders and pulled her close. 'Poor Mum. You don't need this.'

Warmth flowed through Stella's body, making her want to cry again, but this time with gratitude.

The temporary mother-daughter role reversal reminded her momentarily of the black and white photograph of Katerina, hugging the older woman. Had she felt comforted in the same way?

'It'll be all right,' she said, not sounding particularly convincing.

'I hate him,' Lily muttered through gritted teeth.

Stella sighed. 'No you don't. He's not a bad person; he's confused, that's all.'

'Well, he shouldn't make you suffer. It was so kind of you to ask him on holiday and now he's just making you miserable. I wish he'd never come.'

There was a shout and when they looked up, Amelia and Will were standing on the brow of the nearby rocky hill, waving.

'Let's keep going,' Stella said, waving back and doing a thumbs up. She was afraid Jon and Louise would appear at any moment and she wanted to stay ahead.

To her surprise, Lily agreed. Stella thought she'd insist on waiting for her friend.

'We must be halfway by now, surely?' Stella said, trying to negotiate a particularly sheer drop. On reaching the bottom safely, she noticed several new cuts on her knees and shins and a fresh array of bumps, which would no doubt turn into ugly bruises. She was going to return home looking like a prize fighter.

As they walked on, through a path lined with glorious pink Bougainvillea trees, Lily asked more questions about Jon. She seemed protective, wanting to be sure her mother wasn't afraid of him.

Stella tried to reassure her there was no threat.

'He's got this idea in his head I'll change my mind. I've told him I won't. He's stubborn but he'll see sense eventually.'

'I wish Hector would punch him,' Lily said savagely. 'He'd love to. He hates his guts.'

'Oh no,' Stella said quickly. 'That wouldn't help at all.'

After some while, the steep descent started to level off and the path became less rocky. Bit by bit, the sliver of light, where the rocky walls came to an end, expanded into a wide gash. Then all of a sudden, there, in front of them, was the sparkling sea.

Stella's heart skipped. 'We've almost made it!'

In fact, there was still some way to walk but in what seemed like no time, they were standing on shingly sand, staring at the wide, welcoming, blue-green water.

'I need a swim *now*,' said Stella, whipping off her backpack and clothes and pulling on her swimsuit.

There weren't many others on the beach but Lily was shy and took longer to change, hiding behind her small towel. Once she was ready, they left their things and gingerly made their way, hand in hand, over the pebbles and into the swell, giggling as the waves splashed up and around them.

After such a long, strenuous hike, the water felt cool, soothing and delicious. Stella floated on her back for a few moments, staring up at the deep blue sky.

Turning her head slightly to the left, she saw the tavern she'd read about, with a grass roof, perched high on a hill overlooking the bay.

The wooden tables were shaded by scrubby olive trees and there were steps down to the turquoise water. It really was an idyllic location and she hoped they'd manage to get a table.

Gazing up at the sky once more, she breathed in and out deeply, imagining she could see Harriet's beautiful familiar features in the wispy white clouds. She was smiling, which made Stella smile, too, until she noticed her friend's happiness gradually change to hollow-eyed despair.

Stella's heart suddenly hurt and her limbs felt heavy, as if someone had attached weights to them.

'I miss you so much,' she whispered, quickly closing her eyes to block out the vision. 'I'm so sorry you got cancer. I wish you were still here.'

'Look, they've arrived!'

Lily's voice cut through the air, scattering Stella's thoughts. She righted herself and found she could just about touch the bottom on tiptoes.

Amelia, Will and Louise were on the shoreline, blinking in the bright sunshine, while Jon remained near the cavern's exit, lurking in the shadows.

'Come in!' cried Lily. 'It's gorgeous!'

Amelia and Will stripped off straightaway and rushed in to join her, but Louise turned and stepped a few paces away from the shoreline.

After choosing a spot, she dropped her backpack on the shingle, sat down, shielding her eyes from the sun, and stared glumly at the horizon.

Meanwhile, Jon plonked himself on the place where he'd been standing, his back against some rocks near the mouth of the canyon and his legs stretched in front.

He seemed to be firmly fixed on Stella, who could sense his accusing gaze boring into her, even when she looked away.

All the pleasure she'd felt earlier had now gone. She left the water quickly and collected her things, before taking them over to where Louise was.

'Are you going in?' she asked, wrapping the towel round her shoulders and settling down. 'That was an amazing walk.'

Louise, unmoved by the attempt to break the ice, remained stony faced.

'I'll see if I can get a table in the taverna,' Louise said dully, rising and brushing the shingle off the backs of her thighs. 'Tell the others to join me, unless I have to come back because it's fully booked.'

'Okay.' Stella lowered her head and hugged her knees. It was bad enough having to deal with Jon and Hector. Losing Louise's support now, too, felt almost unbearable.

Overcome with emotion all of a sudden, she wanted to stamp her feet and scream. She was trying to do her best in a very difficult situation. Why had everything gone so wrong?

Tears stung her eyes and she clenched her fists to stop them coming, digging her nails into the palms of her hands.

By the time the others left the water, she'd managed to compose herself enough to speak.

'Lunchtime!' she said, pinning on a fake smile. 'Hopefully Louise has found us a table.'

At her request, Will ran over to tell Jon what was happening. Stella didn't turn round, but was aware he was following as they strolled towards the restaurant.

Louise was on a bench seat behind a wooden table to the left of the taverna when they walked in, with a bottle of white wine in an ice bucket beside her. She was sipping from her glass, idly watching a man in white overalls collecting supplies from his boat, moored at the jetty below.

Every table was full and the atmosphere was buzzing, with cheerful-looking waiters scurrying back and forth, carrying trays of delicious-smelling food.

Amelia and Will said they were ravenous and Louise took charge of the menu. This was normally Stella's job, because she was the one who really knew about food, but in truth, she was quite relieved not to have the responsibility today.

Louise ordered large plates of grilled shrimp, fried calamari, lamb slow cooked in olive oil, wine and herbs, and bowlfuls of chips. They also tried a rich, typically Cretan dish of *Staka*, made with creamy goat's milk and fried eggs.

Stella was hungry, too, and began to help herself. There was such a wide variety of different dishes to choose from, she hardly knew where to start.

Her mouth had started watering the moment she entered the restaurant, but when she began to eat, she found it difficult to chew. The food tasted oddly bland and got stuck in her mouth. She had to take sips of her drink to make it go down.

'Is everything all right?' one of the waiters asked when he saw how much was left on her plate at the end.

'Delicious,' she replied, anxious not to offend. 'I've got a slight headache, that's all. Please give our compliments to the chef.'

They took another taxi boat back to Porto Liakáda and plodded slowly up the mountain, carrying more bags of groceries they'd picked up from April's supermarket.

Stella found herself thinking a lot about Hector on the walk and wishing he'd come, too, instead of spending another day on his own.

As soon as they reached the villa, she went to find him. He wasn't in his bedroom or by the pool, and she thoroughly checked the whole place upstairs and down without success.

Feeling uneasy, she rang his mobile but it was turned off. She skirted round the garden next, calling his name, with Marina's warning words about the sea playing loudly in her ears. Telling herself she shouldn't listen and was being silly didn't seem to work.

The garden felt eerily empty as the sun began to fade. When she couldn't find Hector here either, her nagging apprehension turned into a silent scream. What if something had happened to him? What if Marina really did have special powers and had foreseen some disaster?

Without bothering to tell anyone where she was going, Stella grabbed her bum bag and hurried back down the mountain to the town. She was tired, aching and thirsty, but her mind was in turmoil and she couldn't rest until she'd seen her son.

Her first stop was the harbour, where she scanned round, hoping he might be looking at boats or having a drink by the water's edge.

She even checked far out to sea, cursing herself for giving Marina's words any credence at all. Thankfully, there was nothing but more boats, bright white buoys and seagulls.

Her heart still thumping, she scouted round the nearby cafés after that, before heading into the supermarket. April was in a flowery apron, trying to mop the floor, with the baby at her feet, getting in the way.

'Will you stop doing that, Nikos?' she said, picking him up and plonking him to one side, away from the bucket of water.

He immediately crawled back to the wet patch she'd made and tried to grab the end of the soggy mop.

'Jesus Christ!' she muttered, before looking up and spotting Stella near the door. She wiped away some strands of hair on her hot, damp forehead and her face broke into a grin.

'Hello! You back again already? Am I going mad? Didn't I see you here about an hour ago?'

Ignoring the question, Stella asked if she'd seen Hector, but April shook her head.

'He's probably gone for a walk,' she said reassuringly, placing both hands on top of the upright mop. 'Mine are always wandering off. I can never find 'em when I want 'em and the little buggers never come when I call.'

The baby, who was still on the floor, screeched and held out his arms, wanting Stella to pick him up, but she was distracted and failed to notice.

'Thanks! See you,' she called over her shoulder as she hurried from the shop, scarcely hearing the furious shrieks from Nikos that followed her.

Looking left and right as she walked the length of the high street, she kept hoping to spot Hector at one of the stalls or in a café. It was about 7 p.m. now and the place had filled up with diners and people just having evening drinks.

She would have popped into the old man's shoe shop to ask if he'd seen her son, but she feared bumping into Marina.

Instead, she stopped a few times to ask different groups of folk sitting at tables, as well as a couple of friendly looking waiters. No one seemed to have noticed a tall, thin young man with unkempt brown hair and a goatee beard. Stella felt increasingly sick.

Her phone rang, making her jump. It was Lily, wanting to know where she was.

'Louise is making supper. When will you be back?'

'Have you seen Hector?' Stella asked urgently. 'Can you check if he's in his room?'

Lily took the phone upstairs with her and had a look round.

'He's not here. I don't know where he is. He's probably sulking somewhere. He'll be fine, Mum. Stop worrying.'

Stella had come to the end of the main street now. Beyond was a small strip of pebbly beach, dotted with neatly stacked rows of sun loungers and folded-up umbrellas.

On first sight, the place appeared to be deserted, but then at the far end, she spotted one lounger set apart from the rest, close to the water's edge.

The chair was white with no cushions, which had evidently been tidied away, and someone was stretched out on it, staring at the horizon.

It was a melancholy sight and as Stella hurried towards the lone figure, her pulse started to race. The closer she came, the more familiar the person seemed until she knew for certain.

'Hector!'

She upped her pace and started to run towards him as fast as she could. 'Thank God I've found you!'

On hearing her cry, Hector sat up, staring, his thin arms crossed over his chest.

'What are you doing here?' he asked suspiciously when she finally reached him and stopped abruptly.

'I didn't know where you were,' she said breathlessly. 'I was worried about you.'

He shrugged. 'I wanted a walk. I'd been inside most of the day. You didn't need to get all worked up.'

Stella indicated she'd like to sit down and he shuffled along to make room. Now she was beside him, his body close to hers, her pulse began to settle.

'You could've left me a note or sent a text or something,' she said resentfully.

She was about to make another dig but stopped herself when she noticed his face. It was red and blotchy and his eyes were puffy. He'd been crying.

'Oh! What is it, my darling?' she said with a crack in her voice. Instinctively, her arm wound round his back and she hugged him close, resting her head on his shoulder. She was grateful he didn't move but let it stay there.

They remained like that for some minutes, huddled together, listening to the lapping waves and gulls' cries, as well as each other's steady breathing. It was the first time in a long while Stella had been allowed to hold her son. She didn't want to break the spell by speaking.

It was Hector who ended the silence.

'I've fucked up my life,' he said, hanging his head.

Stella paused. 'What do you mean?'

'Quitting uni, mainly. I wasn't coping very well, because of everything happening at home. But I should've stayed.'

'You can always reapply.'

'Dad said the same thing. He was going to help me write a new personal statement. There's no point now.'

'Why not?' He sounded so hopeless. Stella was genuinely baffled.

Hector's body tensed and he pushed his mother away, leaving a cold space between them. Her arm dropped limply to her side.

'Because you guys are getting divorced.' He was frowning and really angry. 'You won't be able to afford for me to go to uni now.'

Stella's eyes widened in astonishment. She didn't understand.

'Who told you that?'

'No one, but it's obvious, isn't it?'

She hesitated again for a moment, absorbing his words, and her cheeks flushed red with shame as the truth sank in: her only son had felt unable to talk either to her or his father. He'd been labouring under a crushing misconception – and it was all their fault.

'Look at me,' she said passionately, swinging round to face him. He did as he was told. 'I don't know where you got that idea from, but of *course* we can afford it. We have enough money, but even if we didn't, we'd find it. Your dad and I, both of us, we'll do anything we can to help. That's great if you want to go back to uni. Whatever you choose to do is fine by us. We just want you to be happy and fulfilled.'

Having had her say, she fell silent, watching him carefully while she waited for his response.

Gradually, the resentful, bored, cynical expression she'd become so used to appeared to melt away and the light came back into his eyes.

'I didn't know,' he said sheepishly. 'I assumed it wasn't possible now, with Dad paying for the flat and everything.'

A flush spread across Stella's cheeks and she reached out and rumpled his hair.

'Well, you do now. Thank God we've had this talk and set you straight.'

It was dark by the time they rose and started to walk back. Stella bought a torch from one of the stalls and gave it to Hector.

'You lead the way.'

At the bottom of the steps, she glimpsed something moving in the shadows. Thinking it might be a cat, she glanced to her left and saw the outline of a woman, hurrying away in the direction of the shops.

Where she'd sprung from, Stella had no idea. There was nothing nearby except the moonlit water and bobbing boats.

Before long, the woman darted into a stall and disappeared, but not before Stella had realised who she was.

Her long, dark, wavy hair and flowing dress, as well as her height and slimness, gave her away: Marina.

Stella inhaled sharply. What was she doing here? Had she been watching them? Her stomach clenched, then she remembered Hector was safe. She could put Marina and her nasty, fake prophecies right out of mind.

As Stella followed her son up the winding mountain path, she noticed a new lightness in his step, as if he'd shed a heavy burden.

How could she have misunderstood him so badly? She'd thought the sole cause of his anger was her split from Al. In fact, as much as anything, it was the devastating consequence he believed it would have on his future. How he must have suffered!

The thought made her shudder and she desperately wanted to talk to

Al. He'd be just as appalled by the way they'd failed Hector, and anxious to try to put things right.

Like her, he'd probably conclude they'd been so caught up in their own problems, they'd lost sight of what really mattered: the health and wellbeing of their only son.

An idea flashed through her mind and her body started to tingle. Maybe getting back together was the answer. They used to work well as a team. They could do so again, if they both wanted it enough. Two heads were better than one and they could figure out how best to repair the damage they'd caused and help their son.

Her stomach fluttered and she resolved to ring Al tonight. There was no point delaying. If he didn't pick up, she'd keep trying or ask him to call her back.

She was so caught up in her enthusiasm, it wasn't until they'd almost reached the top step that she remembered her husband was on holiday in remote Cornwall. Perhaps with Sasha.

Blackness descended again and the air seemed to seep from her lungs, leaving them painful and compressed.

No, Al was out of the picture and she'd have to find another way to make it up to Hector. She was on her own.

11

'I heard about Hector,' Louise said coldly when Stella came down for breakfast the next morning.

The two women hadn't seen each other since last night, before Stella left the villa to find Hector. By the time they'd returned, Louise had already gone to bed and Jon was in his room, too.

'Yes. I was so relieved when I saw him on the beach,' Stella replied, settling down at the garden table, which was covered with a yellow linen cloth, and helping herself to a mug of coffee from the cafetière.

She glanced round at all the empty places. 'Where are the others? No sign yet?'

'Still asleep.' Louise took a sip of her own coffee before removing her big, round sunglasses and eyeing Stella strangely.

'It's lucky you found him. Anything could have happened.'

'What do you mean?'

The accusing tone wasn't lost on Stella, who slapped down her mug harder than she'd intended, slopping coffee on the surface. Yesterday, her friend wasn't speaking to her. Today, resuming conversation with her could prove to be even worse.

'I was afraid something like this would happen,' Louise went on through narrowed eyes. 'He's so unhappy and confused and Jon's made it considerably harder for him.'

That old chestnut. Blood rose to Stella's cheeks. Who was this icy woman with pursed lips sitting in judgement opposite her? She felt she didn't know her any more. Perhaps she never really had.

Jerking back in her chair, Stella glared at Louise, crossing her arms defensively. 'We had a really good talk, actually. We cleared up lots of things.'

'Great.' She didn't sound convinced.

'He was worried we wouldn't be able to afford for him to go to university. I explained it wasn't the case at all.'

'Poor Hector.' Louise shook her head, making Stella's chest tighten and her neck tense.

'His world's turned upside down and he probably feels he's got no control over you guys.'

'Over me and Jon, or me and Al? Which one are you referring to?'

'Both.'

Stella felt herself grow larger; she was expanding with rage and upset. Unable to take any more, she leaped from her seat.

'I thought you supported me,' she said in a loud, high-pitched tone. 'I'm incredibly hurt by your criticism. I don't think I deserve it. You don't understand Hector, either. I know I've made mistakes, but I'm doing the best I can. It's not been easy, you know, without Al—'

Louise didn't let her finish. 'I was waiting for you to bring him into it. *You* wanted him to leave, remember? You can't turn round now and complain he's not there to help you with Hector.'

Stella saw red. 'Actually, he is there for me, especially when it comes to the children. We've got a very good relationship in that sense. Not like you and Josh, who's so unreliable, he won't even commit to a holiday with you, let alone move in with you. You run round after him all the time and bend over backwards but as far as I can see, you get nothing in return. It's sad.'

The words tumbled out with such ferocity, Stella shocked herself. Louise's face crumpled and she lowered her gaze and seemed to focus hard on some crumbs on the table.

'That's so unkind.'

Her shoulders drooped and she had an uncharacteristic air of defeat. Stella felt a stab of guilt, but it quickly passed. 'Well, you've been incredibly unkind to me.'

Glancing up again, Louise caught Stella's eye and her own eyes seemed to plead for a truce. She reached an arm across the table. 'Stella, I—'

But Stella wasn't listening. With a burning face and throbbing head, she marched indoors to find her bag, water bottle and shoes.

She was wearing a short, pink sundress, which didn't really go with walking boots, but she pulled them on anyway. Then she took out her phone and texted Hector and Lily.

Gone for a hike. Be back later xx

With that, she left through the front entrance, so she wouldn't bump into Louise, and banged the door shut behind her.

It seemed almost unbelievable she'd fallen out so spectacularly with her once dear friend, she thought as she set off down the mountain, with no clue where she was going.

In hindsight, of course she shouldn't have invited Jon, but it was done with good intentions and it wasn't her fault he'd become infatuated with her.

Deep down, she reckoned Louise must have been jealous and critical of her for a long time, and hidden it. She'd seemed to back Stella's decision to break up with Al, but perhaps she'd never really approved of any of her choices.

Her hurtful behaviour cast into doubt everything she'd said in recent months, every piece of advice she'd given. Stella now wondered if Louise had ever really even liked her. Maybe she'd just been faking.

About halfway down the mountain, she noticed a small, slight figure walking purposefully towards her, carrying two big brown bags.

They must have been heavy because the woman was arching forwards, her arms stretching down so far, they almost touched the ground. It looked quite painful.

Stella soon recognised Katerina and started to wave, but quickly stopped herself, realising the old woman would have to put down her bags to return the greeting.

'Good morning, Mrs Johnston,' Katerina said politely when she drew up close, still holding the bags. 'It's another beautiful day.'

Stella smiled. 'Yes, gorgeous.'

It seemed for a moment as if Katerina would continue on her way without stopping. Stella was relieved. After the fallout with Louise, she wasn't in the mood for small talk.

But there must have been something in her expression that made the housekeeper hesitate.

'Is everything all right?' she asked, plonking down her load at last. A juicy-looking fat orange rolled out and Stella stooped to pick it up.

'Fine.'

'Are you sure?'

Katerina fixed two sharp black eyes on Stella, who felt herself buckle under the scrutiny.

'Not really,' she admitted, her shoulders drooping.

'Whatever's happened?'

She didn't intend to tell Katerina much of her sorry story, but somehow she couldn't help herself.

When the housekeeper pointed to a grassy mound and they sat down, side by side, the words gushed from Stella's mouth like water from a burst pipe.

Katerina was a sympathetic listener and before she knew it, Stella was explaining all about Harriet, the marriage split, Jon's infatuation, Hector's unhappiness and Louise's fury.

'I came here to give the kids a treat. I thought they deserved it – well, Lily anyway. I also hoped I'd be able to relax and recover a bit from the last couple of horrible years, but now things are worse than ever. I don't know what to do.'

Her nose and eyes were dribbling and she sniffed noisily; she couldn't help it. Katerina patted her knee gently before leaving a small hand there to rest. To Stella's surprise, this felt comforting and entirely natural.

'I knew you had troubles,' Katerina said softly in her pronounced

Greek accent. 'You have suffered a great deal, but you've come to the right place. You will heal; you just have to be patient.'

Stella wished she had such faith. She desperately wanted to believe in the old woman's reassurances, but couldn't.

'But what about Jon?' she said croakily. 'I don't know how to handle the situation. Whatever I say seems to make it worse. And Louise? I've already lost my best friend, Harriet. Now Louise has gone as well.'

Katerina removed her hand and placed them both on her lap, her knees lightly touching. She was neat all over, in a straw hat, short-sleeved white blouse, black skirt and brown leather sandals. Her skin was tanned in the places where it showed, and her arms were thin and wiry.

She made a clicking sound with her tongue and shook her head.

'You can't force these things,' she said. 'You have to wait for the clouds to part. Only then will the way become clear.'

Stella frowned. This sounded like wishful thinking to her, but she was slightly afraid of the doughty housekeeper and didn't fancy challenging her.

'Would you like some water?' she asked, pulling a plastic bottle from her bag.

'I have some, thank you.'

Katerina fetched her own from one of the shopping bags and poured a few inches into a see-through cup, which she'd clearly brought with her.

She took a few ladylike sips before dabbing her mouth with a clean white handkerchief from her pocket. After that, Stella felt slightly embarrassed swigging straight from the container.

'Where are you going now? Into Porto Liakáda?' Katerina asked, replacing her cup in the carrier bag and smoothing some invisible creases on the front of her skirt.

She noticed Stella looking at the two gold rings on Katerina's left finger, one with three small round diamonds in the centre. Katerina's knuckles had swollen with age and it was doubtful the rings would ever come off, even if she wanted them to.

'My husband was a good man,' she said wistfully, holding up her hand and gazing at the jewels, too. 'But he died so young – before he even reached his thirtieth birthday. He was a fisherman. The boat capsized in a storm and all were lost.' She sighed. 'It was a tragedy for the wives and families, but you have to pick yourself up and keep going.'

Stella swallowed, feeling guilty for moaning on about her own problems.

'That must have been so hard,' she said, bending almost double and resting her elbows on her knees. 'How on earth did you cope?'

Katerina shrugged. 'I was lucky, really. I had a good job.' She nodded in the direction of Villa Ariadne. 'The owners looked after me. They were very kind.'

Stella's ears pricked. An opening at last! She seized her chance. 'Who were they? I read something about Leo Skordyles, who was the mayor of Sfakia. Did you work for him and his wife? And who took over the villa after they died?'

Glancing at Katerina out of the corner of an eye, she could tell the old woman was frowning and seemed lost in thought.

'Come with me!' Katerina said suddenly, as if inspiration had just struck. She rose and rubbed her creaky lower back. 'Help me carry my bags home and I'll explain some things you want to know.'

It was an opportunity not to be missed and perfect timing, as Stella had no other plans. She hadn't particularly relished the idea of another long walk; she'd just needed to escape from Louise.

'All right,' she said, rising as well and picking up one of the bags of shopping. It weighed a lot and she wondered how on earth Katerina had managed to lug the two of them.

The prospect of trudging even further up the mountain wasn't exactly appealing, but she was intrigued to see where Katerina lived and to hear about her life.

'I found a black and white photograph of you inside a book in the villa,' she said tentatively as they set off, with Katerina taking the lead. 'And there's a painting of you on the wall.'

There was no dawdling. Katerina set such a cracking pace, Stella had difficulty keeping up.

'Ah yes,' the housekeeper replied, pumping her legs and her loose arm. The weight of the bag in the other arm made her stoop, but she wasn't even breathless. 'My lady wanted it. I was honoured, but I didn't like sitting for so long. The artist complained about my fidgeting!'

'He painted your female employer too, right?'

Katerina nodded. 'Several times. And her husband.'

'How long did you work for them?' Stella asked next.

'I started as a maid when I was fourteen years old and I'm still there all these years on. I was very ignorant when I arrived, just a silly, naïve little girl. My lady was the one who taught me to read and write, and speak English. She let me borrow all the books in her library and passed on her love of literature. I owe her a great deal.'

'I read she'd sadly died a while ago, and her husband, too. So who's taken over?'

The old woman was shrewd, and she must have picked up on Stella's eagerness to discover the truth. She paused, before turning briefly to look at Stella over her shoulder.

'They are dead, yes. They've been gone some years, as you know. That is all I wish to say on the subject, if you don't mind.'

She was polite but firm, and Stella felt deflated, knowing there was no point pressing because she wouldn't get anywhere. She fell into silence while they resumed walking, speculating again on why the villa's new incumbents were such a secret.

Perhaps they were tycoons or famous actors, anxious to preserve their privacy. Such news usually got out eventually, though, and the fact no one seemed to have any clue as to their identity was a real mystery.

Furthermore, would a very wealthy person or a star really choose to rent the villa out to ordinary people like her? There didn't seem to be much security round the place, so it was possible they'd bought it as an investment only and had never actually stayed there themselves.

The two women were almost at Villa Ariadne now and Stella's heart started to pitter-patter. She was concerned about bumping into Louise or Jon, but Katerina seemed to be aware of this and skirted round on the other side of the trees, where they wouldn't be seen.

Soon, the mountain steepened sharply, and Stella couldn't have spoken if she'd wanted to because she was so short of breath.

Still, the housekeeper kept to the same speed, only stopping once to put down her bag and pick it up with the other hand.

There was no one else about and after a while, Stella began to wonder if this was all a trick and they'd never actually reach their destination.

Before long, however, she spotted an isolated, higgledy-piggledy old stone cottage, which seemed to spring from the mountain as if it had grown there rather than been built.

Though rough and basic looking, it was obviously well maintained, with neat wooden shutters, a tiled roof and terracotta awnings over the small windows.

An extra concrete floor seemed to have been added at some point, which was painted white, and purple bougainvillea frothed around the front door, creating a welcome explosion of colour.

'Is this yours?' Stella exclaimed. 'It's charming!'

She was hot and sweaty and it was a relief when Katerina pushed open the door, which wasn't locked, and led her into the cool, dark interior.

'It's only small, but it suits me,' she said, setting down her shopping bag on the stone floor and placing her straw hat on top.

Glancing round, Stella could see they'd walked straight into a sparsely furnished kitchen, in the centre of which was a rough wooden table, surrounded by four chairs.

Resting on the table was an open laptop with a blank, staring screen, which seemed strangely out of place in these rustic surroundings.

The kitchen area itself consisted of a sink, a rickety-looking gas cooker and stone worktops, which could have been hewn from the rocks. There was no sign of a washing machine, dishwasher or even a fridge. The main storage space seemed to be wooden shelves of various sizes, laden with pans, mugs, glasses, jars and tins, labelled with Greek words Stella couldn't read.

'I'll make us a pot of mountain tea,' Katerina announced, proceeding to fill one of her saucepans with cold water.

Stella sat and watched in amazement as she placed the pan on the gas cooker and lit the ring with a match. The only time she'd ever done this herself was on camping trips.

While the water heated up, Katerina washed her hands in the sink, put on a flowery apron and bustled about unpacking her shopping and putting cups, spoons and plates on a little wooden tray.

Now that her eyes had fully adjusted, Stella noticed vases of wild-flowers and pots of herbs on the windowsill. On one wall was a smallish, wooden-framed picture of three beautiful, smiling, bejewelled Minoan women in richly coloured clothes, with intricately coiled black hair, set against a vivid-blue background.

'I love that,' she commented, pointing to the image.

'It's from a fresco at Knossos. It's known as the *Ladies in Blue*. They look happy, don't you think? It makes me smile, too.'

Once the water had heated up, Katerina took a plain, brown, ceramic teapot from the shelf. Then she picked some dried stems, complete with flowers and leaves, from a glass jar, stuffed them in the pot, filled it up with water and left it to steep.

Next, she produced a large, chipped red tin which, when opened, contained six or seven small, round, golden pastries. They smelled deli-cious, and Stella's mouth watered.

'Have some *Kalitsounia*,' Katerina offered, popping one on a plate and passing it to her guest. 'I make mine with *myzithra* cheese, as well as eggs, flour, yoghurt, sugar, orange juice, lemon zest and a pinch of cinnamon. They can be savoury too, with herbs, but I prefer the sweet variety. I usually add a drizzle of honey. They're quite addictive.'

Reaching up to the top shelf, she brought down the biggest jar of honey Stella had ever seen and opened the lid.

'It's from the local farmer,' Katerina announced proudly, placing the jar on a saucer and setting a spoon alongside, as well as two pressed white linen table napkins. 'Now, eat! The tea should be ready. I don't like it too strong.'

The long wait had been agony and Stella was longing to try the pastry. The others had scoffed all the ones Katerina had left for them at the villa.

After spooning on a little of the honey, she picked up the pie in her fingers and nibbled off a corner before taking a proper bite, and another, until it was almost gone.

All the while, Katerina watched keenly, relishing her visitor's evident enjoyment.

'Delicious!' Stella muttered at last, licking her fingers and sighing.

Katerina smiled widely. She still hadn't touched her pastry and Stella had deliberately left a tiny bit so as not to appear greedy.

Now, the old woman took hold of the teapot and poured the tea through a strainer into two cups, before passing one to Stella.

'Be careful, it's hot.'

The brew smelled aromatic and slightly sweet. Stella blew on it before trying a tentative sip.

'Lovely. I feel like it's very good for you.'

'It is. It builds up your immune system. It will stop you getting sick.'

Once she'd had a few sips of her own tea, Katerina ate her pastry quickly before settling back contentedly in her chair.

'Now I feel human again,' she said with a sigh. 'I won't need to shop again for several days.'

Stella felt herself relaxing, too. In her own surroundings, Katerina seemed less intimidating somehow and perhaps more open to questions.

'Did you and your husband live here, before he passed away?' Stella continued, pushing back her own chair and resting a foot on the opposite knee.

'We did. We moved here when we married. I'd lived with my family in town up to that point. It was wonderful to have our own place.'

'And do you spend much time at Villa Ariadne when it's unoccupied? Or maybe it's always full? It's so beautiful, I wouldn't be surprised.'

Katerina raised her eyebrows, which, still dark, contrasted sharply with her grey-white hair.

'Oh! It's often empty,' she replied, as if the answer were obvious. 'Not because people don't want to come. We get many enquiries, but we only accept very special visitors.'

The 'we' dangled enticingly in the air between them, but Stella's fingers had been burned when she'd asked about the owners earlier and she decided not pick up on it.

In any case, she was just as intrigued by the rest of the old woman's statement.

'What do you mean by "special"?' she asked. 'How do you know?'

Katerina took another sip of tea, her black eyes sparkling mischievously.

'Let's just say, it's an intuitive thing. We can always tell from our visitors' correspondence who will fit right in and gain the most from coming here.'

'Have you ever made a mistake?'

The housekeeper thought about this for a moment before shaking her head.

'Not really, no. Perhaps one or two didn't get as much out of their stay as I'd hoped. But mostly they leave in a better place than when they arrive.'

She was sounding peculiarly prophetic, like Marina, which prompted Stella to enquire now about the artist.

'She means no harm,' Katerina insisted when she heard about Marina's alarming warning. 'You shouldn't take offence.'

If she were surprised by what had passed between the two women, though, she didn't show it, which made Stella wonder if she'd heard already.

'How well do you know Marina?' She deliberately didn't disclose what April had told her of their relationship. 'Is she a friend of yours?'

Katerina breathed in and out deeply. 'In a manner of speaking, yes. I've known her all her life, since before she was born, in fact. I was friends with her mother, Cora.'

'And was Marina always, um, a bit different?'

This was met with a nod. 'She was nothing like Cora. She took after...'

Her voice trailed off and Stella desperately wanted to hear the rest.

'Took after who?' she said eagerly.

Katerina reached into her pocket and pulled out a grey woollen pouch, which she rolled between her fingers. It seemed to contain several small items and Stella wondered what they were.

'You said you saw the paintings of my lady in the villa?' the housekeeper commented.

'Yes.'

'Well, take a good look at them when you go back and see if they remind you of anyone. The nose, the eyes, the lips. I think you know what I'm driving at?'

Stella's eyes widened in astonishment. 'Marina's the daughter of your former employer?'

A slight incline of the housekeeper's head confirmed the truth.

'Are others in the village aware of this? Does Marina even know?'

'Marina, yes. Everyone else, no.'

'But why? Why was she given to Cora and her husband? What was the reason?'

She almost added, *And why are you telling* me, *a virtual stranger?* but stopped herself. She felt privileged to be party to the information, for whatever reason, and didn't want to break the spell.

'Ah, well that was because my lady wasn't supposed to be able to have children. She and her husband were childless. When he found out, he agreed to keep it quiet on the one condition – that his wife give up the baby and have no contact with her whatsoever. I was entrusted with the job of arranging where to place her. Mr Makris and his wife were the obvious choice, as they were childless themselves, and I knew Cora would be a wonderful mother.'

'Is Mr Makris Marina's father?'

Katerina frowned again and opened the woollen pouch, taking out a silver pendant, which she ran through her fingers like a rosary.

'He is, though he doesn't deserve to be. It's a mystery to me how anyone so beautiful and talented could come from someone like him.'

Stella's mind was buzzing. She had a million more questions, but Katerina was beginning to tire.

'I think that's enough,' Katerina said, finishing her tea and replacing the cup on the table. She gave a weary little smile. 'Don't you?'

'Just one more thing,' Stella gently pleaded. 'Did your lady, as you call her, think she had special powers as well?'

'Certainly,' the old woman replied decisively. 'She could see things before they even happened. She saw my husband's death at sea, but unfortunately, I didn't take heed. At that time, I thought she was, what do you call it? Fey. I think that's the word. Now, I know better, of course.

'I don't have her gift; very few do. But I used to know when she'd had a vision. Her eyes would glaze over and she'd whisper things to herself. Sometimes, she'd become upset and I'd have to comfort her. I was the only one who could. She always wanted me by her side in those moments.'

Stella was silent for a few minutes while the information sank in, then her stomach clenched and she stared at the housekeeper in sudden panic.

'If she foresaw your husband's death, maybe Marina's right to warn *me*? Do I need to take her seriously? I've never really believed in things like that before, but should I be cautious this time? Should I get everybody home?'

Katerina took another deep breath before shrugging her thin shoulders and raising her hands, palms out.

'I'm sorry, I can't answer that. It's for you to decide. You must make up your mind and do what you think is right.'

Stella felt dizzy and her leg started bouncing up and down involuntarily, making the table shake.

'Can't you give me some guidance? I don't want to ruin the kids' holiday unless I have to.'

'Listen to your own intuition. Trust your gut.'

Katerina fixed Stella with an enigmatic gaze, which made her fists clench. She tapped her fingers on her thigh repeatedly.

'You know what to do. You just have to figure it out,' the old woman added.

12

Stella's mind was in turmoil as she left the cottage and started to make her way back down the mountain. Just when she thought she'd conquered her fear of Marina and her creepy predictions, here was fresh information and cause for worry.

She trusted Katerina far more than the artist, whom she'd only met briefly a couple of times, but should she really pay any heed to the old woman's psychic nonsense?

It was most likely pure coincidence that Katerina's husband had drowned soon after the lady of the house's prophecy. In fact, Stella was surprised a woman of Katerina's evident intelligence set any store at all by someone's supposed ability to see into the future.

But then again, was it worth the risk to dismiss it all as rubbish and ignore Marina's warning? If something terrible did happen, Stella would blame herself forever.

She was busy pondering all this when she walked through the gates of the villa to see Lily hurrying towards her, brandishing a mobile.

'I saw you through the window,' she said, thrusting the phone in Stella's hand. 'It's Dad. He wants to speak to you.'

The blood drained from Stella's face and she started to shake, remembering the husband and wife rule she and Al had put in place: *No contact unless it's an emergency.*

'What's happened?' she asked, staring at her daughter, icy with fear.

Lily's eyebrows shot up.

'Mu-um! Calm down! He just wants a word about Hector.'

Relief washed over Stella and she exhaled loudly before glancing at her daughter, who gave a small, exasperated smile before turning tail.

Stella finally put the phone to her ear, feeling little bubbles of hope start to fizz in her stomach. Now the panic was over, it occurred to her that Al was the only person in the world who'd truly understand her dilemma and tell her what to do.

'Hello!' she said eagerly. 'How are you?'

Walking swiftly over to a patch of grass in the shade under an olive tree, she sat down, with her things on the ground beside her, so she could fully focus on the conversation.

'Sorry, I didn't mean to give you a fright—' he began.

'Oh! No problem at all,' she interrupted, unable to disguise the keenness in her voice.

'I'm okay,' he went on. 'You?'

He sounded a bit stilted, but that was understandable, given the circumstances. Stella hesitated, wondering where to begin, and before she could reply, he jumped back in.

'As Lily said, I wanted a quick word about Hector. She mentioned he wandered off somewhere yesterday and you had to look for him. Is he all right?'

'He's absolutely fine.' Stella was anxious to get this over with as quickly as possible, so she could tell Al what was really troubling her. 'He was on the beach. We had a good, helpful chat, actually. Listen, I've got something—'

They were disturbed by a woman's voice in the background.

'No thanks,' she heard Al reply crisply. 'I'll be with you in a sec.'

Stella's pulse quickened and anxiety nibbled at her insides.

'Where are you?' The question escaped from her lips before she could catch it.

'Still in Cornwall. Like I said, the signal's terrible here so if I suddenly—'

'Who with?' She wanted to sound nonchalant, but the crackle in her voice gave her away.

Al cleared his throat. 'With, um, my neighbour. Sasha. She lives in the flat above mine. We've become quite good friends. She needed a break, too...'

'How nice!' A feeling of dread descended on Stella and she could hardly breathe. But she was determined to seem in control and forced herself to sit up straight, jutting her chin. 'I hope the weather's being kind to you?'

It took a great deal of effort to free the words.

'Very. It's quite mild. A bit cloudy but it hasn't rained.'

'That's lucky.'

'Look,' he went on, seriously, 'I didn't want to disturb your holiday. But when Lily said—'

'You were worried, I understand.' She sounded staccato and faltering; she barely recognised herself. 'He's been moody and difficult since we got here, but I think I've got to the bottom of it.'

'Really? Go on.'

'I-I can't talk about it now,' she stammered. Sasha. The name was whirling round her head, which had started to spin, and she feared she couldn't hold it together much longer. 'It's not the right time.'

'Why?' There was a pause, then, 'Stella, are you all right?'

A thick mist seemed to creep over her eyes, disfiguring her vision.

'I-I need to see the others. I've been out all day. Thanks for phoning. I hope you enjoy the rest of your holiday.'

With that, she just managed to make out the off sign on her phone and press it, before flinging the mobile, face down, on the grass.

Her heart was thudding and her chest was so tight, it was as if she'd run a marathon. Clenching her fists, she dug her nails into the palms of her hands to stop them shaking, and gasped for breath.

The blood was pounding so loudly in her ears, she couldn't think, couldn't even cry. Something was crushing her ribs and she feared her heart was about to burst open.

Through the fog, she heard her own faint voice telling her to breathe slowly, in and out, in and out. She started counting backwards – one hundred, ninety-nine, ninety-eight, ninety-seven, ninety-six, ninety-five – and gradually, her pulse began to slow.

Of course she'd suspected Al was seeing someone, but she had secretly been hoping she was wrong. The truth hurt like hell.

How foolish she'd been to imagine there could ever be a reconciliation! After some of the unkind things she'd said to him, it was a miracle he was even talking to her.

The saying – *you don't know what you've got till it's gone* – never rang more true. He'd always had her back and she'd trusted him completely.

He'd been a great husband and dad and he'd tried so hard to be there for her when Harriet died, but she'd scorned his love and driven him away. She didn't deserve him.

Cupping her forehead with her palms, she stared at the ground. All the light seemed to have gone, leaving her with nothing but her own black thoughts.

Another nasty saying came to mind – *you've made your bed, now lie in it.*

Letting out a groan, she rose clumsily and picked up her things. Everything felt heavy and seemed to hurt: her head, back, shoulders and knees – and most of all, her heart.

Whatever happened, though, she couldn't show Lily and Hector she was sad. She needed to disguise her suffering and be strong for them.

As she made her way slowly towards the villa, she made a conscious effort to smile and walk tall. No one would see her despair or guess what had caused it. She was going to have to put on the performance of her life.

* * *

A loud splash followed by a burst of girlish laughter told her at least one of the children had jumped in the pool.

Instead of going into the house, she ventured straight to the back garden, where she found Hector, Will and Amelia watching Lily attempting a handstand in the water.

Her legs waved wildly and before long, she toppled over.

'That was rubbish!' Will shouted gleefully when she came up for air. 'Ten seconds. A five-year-old could stay up longer than that!'

Lily stuck out her tongue.

'Come on, Hector!' she said. 'It's your turn.'

It was only then Stella noticed her son was in his bright-blue swimming trunks for the first time since they'd arrived in Crete.

Even more surprising, at Lily's command, he leaped into the pool, spraying water everywhere. Then he bobbed down, headfirst, and raised his legs and feet skywards.

He was even worse than his sister, flapping his skinny, white, hairy limbs wildly and lurching clumsily to one side before keeling over.

The other three shrieked with laughter.

'Five seconds!' Will roared delightedly. 'Team Johnston's a complete flop. Amelia, show them how it's done!'

Stella laughed, too, despite herself, when Amelia jump bombed into the pool and started a water fight with Hector and Lily. They were like little kids.

'Hi, Mum!' Hector said when he noticed Stella at last. He moved away from the girls and came to the edge of the pool, resting his elbows on the side. 'I didn't realise you were back.'

'I haven't been for long.'

'Good walk?' He looked and sounded so normal, he was like a different person. For a few delicious seconds, Stella completely forgot her misery as warmth spread through her body and her eyes lit up.

'Yes thanks. I bumped into Katerina and went back to her house for a cup of tea.'

'Nice.' Hector looked doubtful. 'I think?'

Stella nodded. 'It was, actually. She's got this funny old place in the middle of nowhere.'

All of a sudden, a vision of Al with Sasha in a remote part of Cornwall popped into her head, and blackness descended again.

'I'm just going to get some water,' she said quickly, her bottom lip trembling. 'I'm really thirsty.'

She could feel her face crumpling as she left the garden. It would have been a big relief to let the tears flow uncontrollably, but as she approached the kitchen door, she spotted Jon, reaching for something in the fridge.

Her stomach churned and she was about to dart to the left, out of sight, but he must have heard her because he turned his head.

On seeing her, his face brightened then almost immediately fell again when he clocked her expression.

'Hi,' he said flatly, his body tense and rigid. 'Where have you been? I haven't seen you for ages.'

'I went for a walk.'

He moved aside while she fetched a glass from one of the cupboards and poured herself some water from a bottle on the worktop. She wasn't going to tell him about Katerina or try to make small talk. She just wanted to get away.

The safest place would have been her bedroom, but she didn't fancy being alone with her thoughts. Better to re-join the children and try to blend into the background.

The heavy silence that followed when she picked up her glass and walked back to the door made her feel panicky and claustrophobic.

'I'm sorry I've upset you so much,' he said suddenly, forcing her to pause. 'I know I shouldn't have spoken to you about my feelings. I regret it now.'

At that moment, she hated him with a passion, not for what he'd said but because he'd picked the worst time for another weighty conversation. She didn't want to hear his apology, welcome as it was. She could barely hold herself together.

'Thanks,' she managed to reply numbly. 'Can we talk about this another time?'

The crack in her voice had returned and it was lucky she had her back to him, so he couldn't see her eyes brimming over.

'Of course.' He inhaled sharply. 'I-I think it would be better if I left, don't you?'

Her skin prickled and her palms felt sweaty. If she turned to face him, he'd see her tears and then she'd have to explain.

'Yes... Maybe. I don't know.'

It wasn't the response he wished for and he made a deep-throated groan, which made her insides curdle. She felt cruel, but didn't have the strength to offer words of comfort; she needed comforting herself.

Still clutching her glass of water, she left the room without speaking, sensing him staring after her, shrouded in a cold mist of abandoned hope.

* * *

That night, at supper, Louise announced she intended to take her children on a hike the next day to a different gorge. She made it clear this was a family only excursion and Amelia and Will had obviously been primed, because neither demurred.

Lily, sensing something was up, made no move to muscle in on the trip or try to dissuade her friend from going.

Instead, she looked wide-eyed and a bit puzzled.

'What shall we do, Mum?' she asked, childlike.

'I don't know. What do you fancy?' Stella replied, not looking up from her plate. 'We could go back to Sweetwater Beach if you like and do some more snorkelling?'

Hector, displaying a new-found geniality, actually supported the idea, and Stella suggested picking up some things for a picnic on their way to the taxi boat.

As there was no longer any pretence, in private at least, that she and Louise were on the same wavelength, she realised they'd probably spend the rest of the holiday going their separate ways as often as possible.

Perhaps the atmosphere would improve when and if Jon went home. But Stella was now so devastated about Al, she didn't know if she had the energy to try to patch things up with Louise, or even cared enough.

Jon hardly spoke a word. He hardly ate, either, but sat swigging red wine until his lips stained violet and his teeth turned black.

He made no mention of any plans to fly home, but when he went upstairs to bed, Stella spotted him clumsily picking up the towel and yellow swimming trunks he usually left outside to dry.

It made her wonder if he'd booked a ticket for tomorrow, but she couldn't face asking.

She was exhausted when she finally got to bed, but tossed and turned all night and barely slept. She still wasn't sure whether to finish the holiday or go home early, but the news about Al and Sasha had rather taken over and she decided to delay the decision for now.

Listening to podcasts provided some distraction from the washing machine in her head, but all too soon, her husband's handsome, gentle face would reappear, and she felt as if her heart would crack into a thousand little pieces.

It was a relief when light finally started to filter into the room and she rose and opened the shutters. Watching the sun rise, spreading its golden glow across the mountain and olive groves, helped to lift her spirits a little.

She showered in cool water, washed her hair and put on a clean pair of denim shorts and a pale-pink shirt, rolled up at the sleeves.

No matter how desperate she felt inside, she was determined today would be a happy one for her beloved children. The show would go on.

* * *

Louise, Will and Amelia left at around 7 a.m. Stella heard their feet scrunching on the gravel drive and saw them set off in walking boots and sunhats, carrying their backpacks.

There was no sound coming from Jon's room when she tiptoed downstairs and made herself coffee, which she took into the garden.

About an hour later, she went to wake Hector and Lily, as agreed. Hector's room smelled of cigarettes and stale sweat, but she held her tongue and was relieved when he rose without complaint and pulled on his crumpled clothes, lying on the floor beside the bed.

Lily was grumpy and monosyllabic until she'd had a glass of orange juice and a couple of pieces of toast and honey. Then the three headed out in the cool morning air. No one asked if Jon were coming or even mentioned him.

There was a commotion outside the mini-market in Porto Liakáda, with April talking in a loud, agitated voice to a group of tourists holding maps and water bottles.

They were shaking their heads, and as Stella came closer, she heard them say in American accents they hadn't seen anyone, while April kept repeating, 'He can't have vanished into thin air!'

When Stella approached to enquire what had happened, April threw up her arms in despair.

'It's Meaty! He's gone again. He must have sneaked out of the house when I was changing the baby's nappy. He didn't want to go to school, the little bugger. He's for it now!'

'Oh dear!' Stella glanced round rather half-heartedly because she doubted he'd be anywhere nearby. He was probably up the mountain now and wouldn't venture down till school was over.

'We'll look out for him when we go to get the boat,' she promised, before stepping into the shop, followed by Hector and Lily.

They bought fresh bread, local cheeses, ripe red tomatoes, olives, crisps and grapes, along with plenty of cold drinks.

April's husband, Georgios, served them, but he didn't seem particularly worried about his son.

'Ah, he'll turn up; he always does,' he said in broken English, shrugging his shoulders. 'Kids! What can you do?'

As they strolled towards the quay, carrying their supplies, Lily gave a shout.

'Look! He's there!'

To Stella's surprise, Meaty was sitting on a low wall, his legs dangling over the side and his bare feet almost touching the water.

When Stella told him his mother was looking for him and he'd better get home sharpish, he scowled and stuck out his bottom lip.

'I'm not going to school. I *hate* school!'

'But you have to; every child does,' Stella said gently. 'It's the law.'

'Can't he come with us today? He'd love it at the beach. He's probably too late for school now anyway.'

Lily's question came out of the blue and Stella hesitated, frowning.

'I don't think—'

'Plee-ase!' Meaty begged, fixing on her with his big, round, melting brown eyes.

Stella was powerless to say no.

'Run and ask your mother. It's up to her. Lily, you go with him. Be quick!'

It wasn't long before the pair reappeared, with Meaty carrying a small rucksack and beaming from ear to ear.

'She said I can come if I promise to go to school tomorrow.'

'And will you keep your promise?' Stella asked, giving him her best stern and masterful expression.

'Yes,' he replied solemnly, lowering his long, black lashes.

Having him with them turned out to be a good thing. He made everyone laugh and keeping an eye on him stopped Stella from dwelling too much on her troubles.

Hector seemed to enjoy having a small boy to tease and play silly games with, and it gave Lily and Stella some time to talk on their own.

'What's the matter with Louise?' Lily asked, lying face down on her towel, tanning her back. 'She's gone all weird and cold. She won't look you in the eye. It's obvious she's fuming about something.'

Stella decided there was no point hiding the truth now it seemed Jon would be leaving. She explained Louise had wanted her to tell him to go sooner, but she'd refused and they'd rowed about it.

'I'm not surprised she has such a problem with him,' Lily retorted. 'Everyone does.'

Stella sighed. 'I just feel so bad him being here has caused so much nastiness. I wanted to help him, for Harriet's sake more than anything.'

'It's not your fault, Mum,' Lily said kindly. 'You didn't know this was going to happen. He must've gone a bit mad.'

'I fear you're right.' Stella scratched an old mosquito bite on her thigh, which had started to itch again. It stopped irritating, but the scab came off and a thin trail of blood dribbled down her leg. Annoyed with herself, she licked her finger and tried to wipe away the evidence.

Her legs were a mess, covered in scrapes and bruises. Al would have told her off.

Him again. She swallowed down the painful lump, which had wedged itself in her throat, like a hard, tight plug, and focused on the turquoise sea.

Will and Meaty were a little way out but still in their depth. They weren't moving but appeared to be chatting. She smiled, wondering what about.

Thank God she'd found Hector on the beach and had the conversation with him, she thought. She was truly grateful for that.

The four of them ate their picnic, swam together and separately and snoozed in the sun. By about 3.30 p.m., Stella's skin was beginning to feel hot and tight, despite having slathered on high-factor sun cream and covered up for a while in her cotton shirt.

'We should probably go,' she told Hector, who was beside her now, while Lily was near the water, covering Meaty in sand.

'It's been a great day, Mum,' Hector said warmly. Stella reached out, put her hand on his, and squeezed.

By the time they'd packed up, waited for the taxi boat and got back to Porto Liakáda, the heat of the day was over and the sun was beginning to cast longish shadows.

'I'll drop Meaty off and pick up a few things for supper,' Stella told Hector and Lily. 'You head back now. I know you're tired.'

'Are you sure? We can help with the shopping?' Lily offered, but Stella shook her head.

'It's fine. I can manage. We don't need much.'

April had the baby on her boob and was serving a male customer at the same time when Stella and Meaty entered the mini-market.

Meaty immediately started telling his mum all about his day in short, animated sentences, which were quite hard to follow as he spoke so fast.

It seemed April had already forgotten about his naughty disappearance and as soon as the customer left with his purchases, she turned to Stella with a big grin.

'Thanks, love,' she said, unlatching the baby and deftly plugging him onto the other boob. 'He's obviously had the best time ever.'

They talked for a little while and April insisted on fetching a Coke
from one of the giant coolers and presenting it to Stella as a thank you.

'You can have a beer or a little bottle of wine instead, if you prefer?'
she offered, but Stella shook her head, pulling back the tab on the can,
which made a pop, and taking a grateful swig.

She didn't realise how long they'd been talking until her phone rang.
It was Hector, and he and Lily were already back at the villa.

'The front door was unlocked,' Hector said uncertainly. 'We thought
Jon was in, but Lily went past his room and the door was open and it was
a real mess in there. He'd thrown a load of clothes and stuff on his bed.
There's an envelope addressed to you on the side table. It's sealed. Do you
want me to open it?'

Stella's legs felt wobbly and her mouth went dry.

'No, don't do that,' she said quickly, anxious to protect her son from
anything unpleasant that Jon might have written. 'I'm still in Porto
Liakáda. I'll come back now. Have you checked everywhere – the garden,
the pool?'

'Yeah. He's definitely not here unless he's hiding up a tree or
something.'

'Okay, I won't be long,' Stella added shakily.

After saying goodbye to April, she hurried towards the steps, almost
knocking over an elderly gentleman with a stick, which he waved crossly
at her.

'I'm sorry,' she cried, pausing only to check he was all right before
rushing on.

To her dismay, she noticed Marina on the quayside, in the spot where
they'd first met. It would be hard to miss her in her bright-orange dress
and jangly silver bracelets, her long, dark hair blowing gently in the
breeze.

Luckily, she was sitting at her easel facing the water, but before Stella
could dash up the steps out of sight, Marina swung round, as if she'd
been startled by something.

Though the two women were some distance from each other, their
eyes met. Stella felt her gaze locking and found she couldn't look away.

She walked slowly, almost robotically, towards the artist, sensing herself being dragged, as if by a magnetic force.

When she was standing in front of Marina, she realised the artist had a peculiar glazed look, as if she were focused on something far away.

'What is it?' Stella asked fearfully.

'Stay close to the sea tonight,' Marina replied darkly, still staring into space. 'I see danger. Don't leave the water's edge.'

For a moment, Stella couldn't speak. Shock had destroyed her vocal cords.

'What do you mean?' she asked at last in a shrill voice. 'Which sea? This sea? What danger?'

In an instant, Marina's glazed look vanished, as if a switch had been flicked, and she concentrated fully on Stella.

'I'm sorry, I can't tell you that,' she said softly. 'I wish I knew. All I can say is, you must not go back up the mountain now.'

All of a sudden, Stella saw the ridiculousness of it all and gave a cynical laugh. 'Your advice changes all the time. Can't you see how you contradict yourself? Only a few days ago, you were warning me to be wary of the water; now you're telling me to not leave the waterside. Why should I listen to you at all?'

Marina shrugged, which only maddened and confused Stella all the more.

'You don't have to listen. You can walk away right now and return to the villa without ever looking back. The choice is yours.'

13

For a while, Stella paced noisily up and down the quayside. She was hoping Marina would take pity on her and reveal any other scraps of information or insights she might have forgotten to pass on. Either that or admit it was all a joke in very bad taste and apologise for causing such distress.

But the artist, seemingly oblivious to Stella's presence, merely turned round and resumed painting. If Stella hadn't been in such turmoil, she'd have laughed out loud. How could anyone behave normally after trying to frighten someone out of their wits? You'd think Marina would at least have the decency to offer Stella a seat for a moment and make sure she was all right.

Conscious of the unopened letter from Jon waiting for her at the villa, she was faced with an impossible choice: whether to rush home to see what it said and check he was okay, or heed Marina's silly warning and remain by the sea.

She called Hector again to find out if Jon had returned, but the answer was no.

'I need to stay by the sea for a while,' she said, almost without thinking.

'Why?'

'I've had some news. It's fine, I'm sure it's nothing. I'll explain when I get back. Go ahead and eat with Lily if you're hungry. I'll keep you posted.'

With her stomach in knots and her brain racing, Stella decided to sit in a café for a while to try to calm down and clear her head.

She ordered a cup of soothing mountain tea and sipped it as the sun went down, painting the sky tangerine orange, crimson red and finally, velvety raven black.

Paralysed with indecision, she felt the best course of action was to do nothing for now, but pay attention to Katerina's words and wait in hope for the way to become clear.

The irony of the situation wasn't lost on her. After all, it was only two days ago she'd flown down the mountain to search for Hector. On finding him safe and well, she'd resolved to see sense and forget all Marina's stupid comments about the sea.

Yet now, here she was again, panicking about the artist's words, allowing them to mess with her mind even as she told herself they meant nothing.

What had got into her? She must have gone soft. But having heard what had happened to Katerina's husband, Stella felt unable to walk away from here. It was as if she were being held back by invisible hands.

She was beginning to feel chilly and once she'd paid up, she decided to stroll the length of the high street, keeping a close eye on the sea at all times.

The light coming from cafés, shops and restaurants was enough to illuminate the water, which shimmered beneath the stars and spread out, as far as the eye could see, like a giant sequinned shawl.

Mr Makris was standing at the entrance of his shoe shop, surveying the passing crowd. He looked very tall and distinguished in a mushroom-coloured knitted waistcoat, with a jaunty yellow cravat round his neck.

The old devil, Stella thought, remembering his illicit romance with Katerina's boss.

She smiled and nodded an acknowledgment and he waved back, which was a mistake, as he'd been propping himself up against the door-frame and almost lost his balance.

Fortunately, he just managed to grab hold of the frame again and right himself in the nick of time before there was a nasty accident. Relieved, Stella strolled on.

The crowds had thinned by the time she got to the start of the public beach and she stopped, wondering whether to continue.

With nobody else there, the place looked lonely, cold and dark. Even so, she removed her sandals and padded in bare feet across the shingle, until the sharp stones hurt too much and she put on her shoes again.

The crescent moon shone brightly, so she could at least see where she was going. All the parasols were down, secured in the middle by strong rope, and the white plastic sun loungers had been lined up in a row, some way back from the swell.

Walking past, she hugged her arms round her to try to keep warm. There was quite a strong wind here, away from the main buildings, which was making her shiver. Some of the waves rose surprisingly high before curling over and crashing towards the shore.

When she reached the place where she'd found Hector, she thought about turning back. She was quite far from the town now and didn't want to lose sight of the restaurants and people completely.

However, something made her decide to press on to the dark-grey, rocky point, which jutted some way out, almost into the sea, turning the beach into a cove and providing a natural boundary.

Instead of skirting round the headland and risk getting wet, she clambered over, curious to discover what lay beyond.

Something sharp scraped her knee and she yelped, quickly climbing higher until she was almost at the top.

It seemed like an age since she was on Sweetwater Beach with the children, and all she'd eaten since lunchtime was bread and cheese. Her stomach was empty and her skin prickled from the sun and salty sea, but she seemed to be flooded with adrenaline and had a surge of new-found energy.

Soon, she was high enough to peer over the edge of the promontory. At first, all she could see was another, much smaller, enclosed cove, where the waves reached further up the sand, almost smashing into the craggy cliff behind.

On closer inspection, however, she thought she saw something move at the foot of the cliff: a small, white figure.

It was a man, who appeared to be walking, naked, out to sea. Was he really going for a swim at this time of night on his own? The water would be so cold now, and who knew what currents swirled beneath the surface? And there was no one else around to help if he got into trouble.

Stella's heart started thumping and a gasp rose to her throat where it remained, trapped, for several seconds before she exhaled.

For a while, she couldn't move, but stayed rooted to the spot, gaping. The man didn't stop, or seem to react at all to the icy water, but continued walking slowly and purposefully into the waves. It was as if he'd been pre-programmed, like a robot, and nothing would swerve him from his mission.

In an instant, her brain switched gear and she knew without a doubt what she must do. After shinning over the top of the rocks, she scrambled down the other side and ran as fast as she could across the shingle towards the man.

'Stop!' she cried, but the wind carried her voice away and he didn't hear.

By now, he was up to his shoulders, bent over slightly and pushing hard against the powerful waves, intent on beating the tide at its own game.

Although Stella couldn't make out the man's features, the closer she got the more convinced she became that her initial suspicions were correct: it was Jon.

Fear curled its freezing fingers round her insides and her breathing accelerated. She felt as if she were suffocating, yet her muscles had never worked harder or more effectively. She was flying across the beach as if she'd been supercharged, her only goal to reach Jon before it was too late.

On arriving at the water's edge, without thinking, she stripped off her shoes, shorts and top and flung them, along with her backpack, onto the ground.

Then she waded into the sea, barely even noticing the cold, though it made her gasp involuntarily.

'Jon! Wait!' she screamed again and again, until her throat was raw, but he seemed to have blocked ears and didn't turn.

All that was visible of him now was his head, and still he kept on walking at the same relentless pace. Any moment, he'd dip below the surface and she wouldn't be able to find him.

It had taken her only about five minutes to scramble down the headland and reach the sea, but it seemed much longer. When she was in deep enough, she plunged headfirst into the swell and swam frantically towards Jon, kicking her legs as hard as she could and extending and pulling furiously with her arms.

He was fully submerged now, save for the crown of his head. To her horror, he ceased moving at this point and she realised he wasn't even trying to stay afloat; he'd surrendered himself to the waves.

She could hear herself crying, making great big sobbing sounds, but no one was listening and it was no use.

All of a sudden, her outstretched hands touched soft, yielding flesh. She grasped blindly before grabbing, wrapping both arms tightly round his chest, her fingers intertwined. Then she used all her strength to tip him on his back, raising his chin with one hand so his nose and mouth were out of the water.

He inhaled sharply before coughing and spluttering, spewing out salty brine. Relief spread through her and she had a few moments of sweet clarity, when she was able to recall a long-ago lifesaving lesson at school: *keep holding on to the chin, not the throat; use sidestroke or backstroke to tow the casualty.*

Briefly, the method seemed to work, then without warning, Jon made an eerie, high-pitched, wailing sound and started to struggle, his body twisting, his arms and legs flailing.

In panic, feeling her grip loosen, Stella let go of his chin, seized him round the waist with both arms and held on for dear life.

She could just about touch the bottom, but he was rearing up and down, like a bucking horse, writhing and trying to shake her off. She kept going under, swallowing gulps of water, and her lungs started to burn like hot lava, but still, she wouldn't let go.

Even in this state of terror, she was repeating the same words in her head, like a mantra – *I'm not going to let you die... You're not going to die like this... I promised Harriet.*

But she was getting weaker, she could tell. Her body was starting to give up on her. Then, perhaps, they'd both sink down, down, together.

In her exhaustion, she began to think this might be a relief. She could leave all her troubles behind: Al, Hector, Louise. She could forget them all and just slide gently, her pulse starting to slow, her airways closing, her mind going blank until at last... oblivion.

A nasty thought crept its way into her consciousness: Marina had won. That weird, frightening woman must have told her to stay by the sea so she'd drown.

Out of nowhere, a manic laugh bubbled and burst in Stella's throat, then she began to cry once more, her tears mixing with the salt water before being washed away.

She'd been duped, and she didn't even believe in psychics. The whole world had turned upside down and she was doomed to leave, without ever having the chance to set it right again...

Her body felt so heavy and her muscles useless. Her arms and legs went floppy, like a rag doll. She felt herself begin to drift away from Jon as the tide took control, pushing and pulling her at will. Not long now, she thought, in a kind of dream. Soon she'd fall into a timeless sleep...

Something yanked at her flesh and began dragging her backwards, brutally hauling her from her peaceful slumber. She wriggled weakly and tried in vain to push the thing off, all the while thinking – *leave me be. I just want to rest.*

There was a shout: 'Stella!'

She was choking, drawing in great gulps of breath. She could feel herself being scraped over sand and pebbles, tiny stones digging into her back, buttocks and thighs. Someone forcing her to sit up, wrapping her in fabric, wiping away her salty vomit.

Dazed, she watched Hector struggling to pull Jon up the beach towards her. She was puzzled. Why was Hector here? She didn't think he'd been with her before. And if he was saving Jon, someone else must have rescued her. But who?

The person with her was now prising her arms into a T-shirt and fleecy sweatshirt, stretching them down over her head. She was shivering so much, she could hear her teeth clattering together.

'Here, let's get these on.'

It was a male voice. Familiar. Comforting. He'd walked round to her other side and was crouching by her feet, pushing them clumsily through the legs of some jeans that weren't her own.

She blinked a few times, thinking it was Al, her husband, but it couldn't be. He was in Cornwall. With Sasha. She must be hallucinating. Perhaps that happened when you almost drowned.

'Can you stand up?'

She tried but was too weak, and she let him lift her off the ground like a child, hooking her arms round his neck while he wrestled her into the trousers.

They were much too big, so he set her down again gently before tightening them round the waist with the belt and putting her in socks, too.

The whole exercise must have been quite an effort with her so feeble and useless, but he didn't complain.

'Al, is it you?' she heard herself ask, bewildered. She was still shivering, but a little less so, and her breathing was becoming easier. 'What are you doing here?'

He didn't answer but told her to wait, before hurrying over in just his boxers to help Hector get Jon into some clothes, too.

Jon was making odd moaning noises and she heard him repeat 'I'm sorry' over and over. He was alive, thank God. She must have done something right. But she still didn't understand about Al. Perhaps it was all a dream. Maybe she was dead.

There was a lot of shouting and strange voices. A group of men was running towards them, carrying things – blankets and stretchers. She felt herself being lifted onto a soft bed and wrapped tight in crinkly foil, so she could hardly move. Soon, the men were jogging back the other way with her, taking care not to bump her around too much.

'Al?' she whispered piteously, frightened she'd imagined him.

'I'm right here, Star,' he replied, coming alongside.

A warm, fuzzy feeling enveloped her, and her skin tingled. Star was his nickname for her. She hadn't heard it in such a long while.

'I'm so sorry,' she said, fighting back the tears pricking in the corners of her eyes. 'For everything.'

He touched her cheek, one of the few bits of her that was still exposed.

'Shh. Don't talk now. We'll speak properly later.'

* * *

The rest of the night passed in a bit of a blur. They were airlifted by helicopter to the nearest hospital, where they underwent medical tests. After around eight hours of observation, they were declared fit to go home.

Medics advised getting checked over by a local doctor in two to three days, unless the condition of either of them deteriorated, in which case they should return to the emergency department without delay.

Stella was exhausted but slept fitfully, jerked awake by her own screams. The events of the evening kept replaying in her mind, bringing back hideous memories of her time in the black water, fighting to keep Jon alive, gasping for air.

She was aware of Al's comforting presence beside her, but didn't try to have a meaningful conversation. She did ask why he'd come to Crete, though, and how he'd managed to find them.

'You sounded weird on the phone when we spoke yesterday,' he explained. 'I was worried, so I rang Hector. When he told me what was going on with Jon, I decided to catch the next available flight.

'Neither of you were at the villa when I arrived and Hector said you'd told him you wanted to stay close to the sea for some reason. It sounded odd. Then I read Jon's letter and heard about the artist's warning. Basically, Hector and I put two and two together and ran here as fast as we could.'

Stella's eyes widened and she tried to sit up. 'You read Jon's letter? What did it say?'

Al shook his head.

'Lie down. You need to rest. Jon's fine. You did an incredibly brave thing. Try to sleep. We'll discuss this another time.'

Too weary to object, she did as she was told and started to drift off. But her eyelids soon sprang open again.

'What about Sasha? Where is she?'

She glanced nervously round the white hospital room, half expecting to see the other woman walk through the door.

Al frowned. 'She's in London. She went back when I left.'

Stella nodded dumbly.

'So is she—?'

The words had hardly left her lips before her husband interrupted.

'Hush. Don't think about that now.'

He put a finger gently on her mouth to close it and before long, darkness descended and she was whisked away by sleep.

* * *

Returning to Villa Ariadne felt, to Stella, like coming home. She'd been gone less than twenty-four hours, yet the place felt quite different with Al there and both her children fussing round.

She and Jon went to their rooms, where the others brought them fresh vegetable soup, cooked by Louise, and delicious soft bread.

Lily sat on the end of the bed and wanted to hear every last detail of what had happened.

'You could've died,' she said with tears in her eyes. 'I couldn't bear it if you'd gone. I'd want to die, too.'

'Don't be silly,' Stella replied gently, reaching out to hold her daughter's hand. 'You're strong. You'd be okay. Luckily, I'm still very much here, though.'

Later, Louise came to collect the tray and empty dishes. Stella noticed she'd removed all her gold earrings. Perhaps she felt they weren't appropriate after the events of yesterday. She seemed humbler somehow, lowering her eyes when she spoke to Stella.

'I'm sorry I was such a cow,' she said, fiddling with the frayed edge of her denim shorts. 'I know you were really worried about Jon; that's why you invited him. I should've been supportive. Instead, I made things much more difficult for you.

'I, I guess I always was a bit jealous of Harriet, as you said in the garden that night. I'm not proud to admit it, but it's true. You two were so close. I never had someone like that in my life, not even you. I wanted to be your best friend in the world, but I knew with Harriet around, I couldn't be.

'Then, when she died, I suppose deep down I thought I stood a chance. But you talked about her all the time and you were so bereft, it was obvious no one would ever take her place. I tried to accept it, but I felt resentful and a bit left out, like I could never live up to her standards. I know that sounds incredibly childish.'

She spoke from the heart and was so humble and remorseful, Stella couldn't help but accept her apology.

'Thanks for being so honest,' she said with a smile. 'It can't have been easy. I'm grateful.

'I need to apologise too,' she went on with a sigh. 'I know I've behaved really badly over the past eighteen months. I've felt sorry for myself and I pushed Al away when he was only trying to support me. I also demanded far too much of you and others, expecting you to be there for me all the time when you had your own stuff going on. I'm sorry I said those dreadful things about Josh, too. I wanted to hurt you and it was spiteful and mean. You're also right about Hector and Lily. I have neglected them, and I'm sure that contributed to Hector's meltdown. I'm going to do my best to put that right from now on.'

Louise nodded. 'That's great to hear. They'll really appreciate it and I know everything will be all right with Hector. The other thing is, I didn't understand Jon was in quite such a bad state.' She shuddered. 'I didn't think he was going to do something like that.'

'No one did,' replied Stella. 'Well, only Marina, maybe.'

Louise's eyebrows shot up. 'Her?'

'Yes. I mean, she was right about telling me to stay near the sea, wasn't she? Otherwise, Jon mightn't be with us any more.'

Louise frowned. 'I suppose so. I'm still inclined to think it's just coincidence she saw danger in the water, then he tried to drown himself, but we'll never know. I guess there are some things in life you can't explain. The main thing is, thank God you're alive to tell the tale.'

Stella smiled again, before knitting her brows. 'How is he?'

'Okay. Very apologetic. We're taking it in turns to sit with him. Don't worry, we won't leave him alone for a minute. I don't think he's going to do anything silly again, though. He said it was a moment of madness and he seems really regretful, especially about putting you in such danger. He says he just wants to get home and sort himself out.'

'He needs to see someone – an expert. I'll make some enquiries when I'm feeling better.'

'We're already on it,' Louise replied. 'Al and I. And Jon's agreed to it, too. We're going to try to make an appointment for him as soon as he's back in London. We're trying to persuade him to change his flight and travel home with us.'

Relief washed through Stella, who took a deep breath. Jon was no longer solely her problem; she had help now. And she and Louise were going to work through their issues and be okay. Her body seemed to grow lighter; she hadn't realised quite what a burden she'd been carrying. She felt as if this was the first time in months she could properly relax and let go.

News of the rescue had travelled fast round the village and Katerina arrived with a big bunch of flowers she'd picked from the mountainside.

Later, April turned up with all four children in tow and a cake from her shop, which the older kids devoured in front of Stella, scattering crumbs everywhere.

Baby Nikos sat on Stella's lap, playing with her necklace, and Meaty was fascinated by Al.

'He's *your* husband?' he asked Stella in a puzzled voice. 'So how come he wasn't here and he is now? It's a good job he came at just the right time, isn't it? If he'd come tomorrow, he'd have been, what do you call it? A widow?'

'A widower, yes,' Stella said with a laugh, glancing at Al, who smiled, revealing the gap in his front teeth. She'd forgotten how much she liked that gap. It made him look cute.

'Quiet!' April said crossly to her son. 'Stella doesn't want to think about being dead.'

'I don't mind,' Stella replied truthfully. 'He's saying it like it is. I admire his directness.'

The final visitor was none other than Marina. Louise hurried upstairs to ask Stella if she wanted to see her, and Stella said she did.

Al insisted on being there, partly because he was intrigued to meet the artist, but he also wanted to be sure she didn't say anything to upset his wife.

'You've had quite enough shocks since you arrived.'

His eyes widened when Marina entered the room, wearing one of her trademark, multi-coloured tie dye dresses.

She looked very beautiful and delicate, like an exotic bird, with her slim, tanned limbs, silver jewellery, long, straight nose, big black eyes and her shock of wavy hair reaching almost to her waist.

She'd walked all the way from the village carrying one of her large paintings, which she propped up against the wall where Stella could see it.

'It's for you,' she said with a smile, before settling on one of the chairs nearby. Al was beside Stella on the bed. 'I hope it will remind you of Porto Liakáda – in a good way.'

Stella stared at the abstract canvas in a simple, white wooden frame. It was the one she'd seen Marina working on by the quayside, a joyful splash of bright, swirling colours: yellow, orange, red, violet, silver, turquoise and deep blue.

'It's the sea here, isn't it?' she said, losing herself in the picture. 'It's just how I saw it when I first arrived. It's beautiful, but I can't possibly take it from you.'

'Tsk.' Marina shook her head. 'It's a gift. Accept it.' She gave Stella a meaningful look. 'I want you to remember our sea as a happy place.'

'Thank you.' Stella was still gazing at the iridescent colours. 'I'll treasure it always.'

Marina had been focusing on Stella the entire time, but now glanced round the room, taking everything in.

'Katerina has a good eye,' she commented appreciatively. 'I love everything she's done with the house.'

Stella raised her eyebrows. 'Oh! So she's responsible for the interior design? Not the owner?'

Marina seemed surprised. 'Katerina *is* the owner. I'm sorry, I assumed you knew by now. Her employer left the house to her in her will, along with a large sum of money. She trusted Katerina completely to do something good with the villa, knowing she'd have no use of the place herself.

'Katerina doesn't like grandness, you see; she prefers the simple life. She doesn't tell many people that Villa Ariadne is hers. In fact, the villagers have no idea, though a few might suspect it. One day, it will come to me, and I'll try to do the same as her and rent it out to the right people, those who really need it.'

'How does she choose the people who need it?' Al, who'd been quiet up to now, was leaning forwards, elbows on knees, head cocked inquisitively.

'Oh, Katerina doesn't choose,' Marina replied enigmatically. 'The villa decides.'

With that, she rose swiftly, kissed Stella lightly on the cheek and shook Al's hand, affording them no time to ask further questions.

'I'll leave you to rest,' she said, straightening her dress and walking towards the door. 'I'm glad you're recovering so well.'

It wasn't until she'd gone that Stella and Al were finally alone to talk.

'How peculiar!' Al said, scratching his head. 'I don't know what to make of her. What does she mean – the villa decides? It sounds like absolute rubbish, yet she seems so intelligent and plausible.'

'I agree,' Stella replied. 'That's why I did what I did and looked for Jon. I wanted to believe she was a total fraud, but something in me kept saying maybe she wasn't, maybe I should listen.'

Al frowned. 'Still, I can't swallow the stuff about the villa having some weird power of its own. It's just a house, for God's sake. Bricks and mortar – or whatever it's made of. It didn't choose for you to come here. You looked online and bingo! You found it. It was the right price, available and it suited your needs; that's all there is to it.'

Stella went silent for a moment, lost in thought. She was remembering Katerina's words when they first arrived.

I think you'll like it here, all of you. Villa Ariadne is a very special place. It's like nowhere you've ever been before.

This trip had certainly been like no other holiday she'd ever had, and it wasn't over yet.

A cloud seemed to appear from nowhere, casting shadows round the room. She looked at Al's handsome, gentle face and wanted to cry.

'There's something I have to ask you,' she said, swallowing. Her heart started to go bumpity-bump. 'I don't want to, but I need to know the truth.'

14

Al's mouth twisted anxiously and his eyes darkened. He was still beside Stella on the bed, but he backed away a little, as if to protect himself.

'What?' he asked, fixing on her features, searching for clues. 'What do you need to ask me?'

She clenched her fists and stared hard at her lap; she couldn't watch him while he gave her the news she so feared.

'Are you seeing someone?' she said quietly. Her mouth had gone dry. 'Is Sasha your girlfriend?'

There was a sharp intake of breath, then he made a noise, like a small cry.

'What? Oh I see!'

Stella glanced up; she couldn't stop herself. He was staring at her steadily, determined to catch her gaze.

'No,' he said firmly. 'Absolutely not. We're just friends. She's been a good mate to me these past few months. She invited me for coffee the day I moved in. She sat and listened to me blubbing about you for ages. It must have been really boring, but she was very patient. Since then, we've been out a few times for walks and to the cinema, that sort of thing. She says I need distracting.'

Stella nodded uncertainly. She'd never known him lie and desperately wanted to believe him, but couldn't.

'But you went on holiday together,' she pointed out, swallowing. 'She must be keen on you. You must like her, too, even if nothing's happened yet...' Her voice trailed away, leaving a question mark hanging in the air.

'Nothing has happened, I assure you. I mentioned you were going on holiday with the kids and I was thinking of hiking in Cornwall to cheer myself up. She loves walking, too, and asked if she could come along, so I said yes. Simple as that.'

'Do you want something to happen?' Stella persisted. It was her turn to stare at him, now. She looked deep into his eyes and he didn't flinch.

'I only want *you*, Stella,' he said in a low voice. 'Besides, Sasha's gay. She split up with her long-term girlfriend about a year ago. She was really cut up about it. She's been licking her wounds ever since.'

Stella was so surprised, she was temporarily lost for words.

'But I thought... Lily said...' she eventually managed to splutter.

'What did Lily say?'

She couldn't help noticing the corners of Al's eyes starting to crinkle. Was he finding her amusing? The cheek of it! And to make matters worse, she could feel herself blushing.

Straightening up, with her chin raised, she tried to summon as much dignity as she could.

'She said Sasha offered to give her a makeup lesson.'

This sounded naïve and a bit foolish, even to her, and her blush deepened.

'Yes, but that doesn't mean we're going out.' He gave a teasing smile. 'You silly goose.'

She wanted to be annoyed with him, but the funny insult made her face light up and a laugh exploded in her throat, which she choked on halfway through. As it happened, the honking noise that came out sounded remarkably like a goose. This was getting worse.

'I, I just assumed,' she stuttered, desperately trying to compose herself. 'I mean, I was sure you'd find someone else really quickly because you're such—'

'An irresistible hunk?' This time, he laughed out loud. 'I've had women propositioning me left, right and centre. They've been climbing over each other to get to me. The Swedish nymphos are the worst.'

The image of hordes of amorous women fighting over him made her giggle, but then his expression changed and he became deadly serious.

'Honestly, Star, there's no one but you. There never has been, not since we met. You're the one who went off me, remember? It's you who wanted us to split.'

At this, tears pooled in Stella's eyes and trickled down her cheeks. In a flash, all merriment had vanished. Her emotions were in uproar, see-sawing wildly, and she felt stupid and cursed herself for causing so much pain.

'I know it's all my fault,' she said miserably. Her nose was dribbling, too. She was an utter mess. 'I was horrible to you. I'm not surprised you couldn't take any more. I regret it so much.'

'Do you?' He shuffled closer before reaching out and using his thumbs to gently wipe away her tears.

'Yes,' she replied hotly. Her throat burned and she realised she was shaking, despite the warm weather.

'Stella?' His gaze was fierce and penetrating, but she didn't shrink from it. Her heart was battered and bruised and she knew he was the only one who could heal it.

For some moments, her eyes remained locked on his, willing him to trust she was telling the truth.

He must have been convinced at last because without another word, he leaned forwards, cupped her face in his hands and kissed her, ever so tenderly, on the mouth.

'I love you,' he said softly. 'I thought I'd lost you.'

Stella's cheeks flushed and her body felt as light as candyfloss, while her insides seemed to dance an Eightsome Reel.

'I love you too,' she replied, scarcely able to breathe.

She couldn't hold back any longer and flung herself into his arms, holding him tight with her cheek against his chest, inhaling his familiar, clean, earthy scent. She could hear the strong, steady beat of his heart and wished she could stay here forever and never move again.

For a few, ecstatic minutes, it was as if their souls combined, like copper and zinc. No longer two separate beings, they were one and the same, melded by a type of alchemy to form something shiny, strong and new.

'Will you come home?' she asked in a small voice, still pressed against his chest, which was slightly damp from her tears.

He kissed the top of her head again and again with fervent kisses.

'I thought you'd never ask.'

* * *

Al had already offered to stay with Hector that night so they could chat, which meant he and Stella couldn't be together. In any case, it would have been difficult to hide what was going on between them from the others, and they weren't quite ready to make their reunion public.

Parting company at bedtime felt like agony to Stella, but she was still tired from her ordeal and soon fell into a deep, dreamless sleep.

The following morning, she woke in high spirits and hurried downstairs to sit by the pool under a parasol.

Her heart was so full, she was sure she must look different and everyone would notice.

She still hadn't seen Jon since the accident, however, and knew she must rein in her happiness for his sake. Only now did she feel strong enough to read his letter, which Al went inside and fetched for her.

It was, as she'd suspected, a suicide note addressed to her. Her hands trembled as she scanned the words, written in Jon's small, neat script.

I've come to accept that you don't and never will love me... The prospect of our being together one day was the only thing that made my life worth living... I can't go on... You mustn't blame yourself... This is my decision and mine alone... Please tell Jemima I love her and look after her for me. I know you will...

'It's so sad,' Stella said with a shudder, folding up the letter and handing it back to Al. 'He must've gone out of his mind, or he wouldn't have dreamed of doing such a terrible thing to Jemima.'

'I think this has given him a massive shock,' Al replied, replacing the letter in its envelope and tucking it safely in the back pocket of his shorts. 'He knows he needs help. He realises he came very close to drowning and nearly killed you, too. I don't think he'll try anything like that again.'

'Bloody hell, I hope not. Thank God you're here. Did you tell him about us?'

Al shook his head. 'We should speak to the children before anyone else. Let's do it when they come for breakfast.'

Lily and Amelia ventured down first, followed by Will. It was after 11 a.m. by the time Hector appeared and he was taken aback when Al asked him and his sister to join their mother by the pool.

'Why?' he asked suspiciously.

Al couldn't help grinning. 'We've got something to tell you.'

Both children stood at the end of Stella's sunbed, fidgeting nervously. They tried to act cool when they heard Al was moving back home, but the glint in Hector's eyes gave him away.

'So are you and Mum...?' he started to say, wanting to be sure he hadn't misheard.

Al, who was perched on the end of Stella's lounger, glanced at her with a smile and they nodded in unison.

'But I thought...' Hector's voice trailed off. He still had doubts in his mind.

Stella did her best to reassure him.

'Everything was so difficult after Harriet died,' she explained, looking from Lily to Hector and back again. 'Grief does strange things to people and I was in a very bad space. I'm sorry I put you all through that. I'd like to think we can turn over a new leaf.'

Al beckoned to the children and Lily swiftly joined him on the end of the lounger. He put an arm round her shoulders before patting the other side of the seat.

'C'mon, Hector. There's room for three. You can just about squeeze in.'

It was a tight fit and the lounger threatened to tip up, but nobody cared. Hector looked sheepish when Al hugged him, but didn't protest.

Meanwhile, Stella watched on, smiling, scarcely able to believe this was happening.

After lunch, she plucked up the courage to go and see Jon. Louise had been sitting with him, but she rose when Stella entered.

'I'll leave you to it,' she said, giving Stella a look that meant *good luck*. Stella smiled bravely back.

Jon was sitting up in bed, with an open book on his lap. He appeared pale and tired, Stella thought, but otherwise reasonably okay. He'd clearly washed and put on a clean white T-shirt, which she reckoned was a good sign.

'How are you feeling?' she asked, settling on the chair Louise had just vacated.

'Not too bad thanks. You?'

'Pretty well actually. Almost myself again.'

'Good.' A look of pain crossed his features. 'Words can't express how sorry I am,' he said quietly, allowing his head to drop. 'You nearly drowned because of me. What I did was selfish and unforgiveable.'

He drew in his legs and curled up in a ball, his forehead resting on his knees.

'Please don't blame yourself.' Stella reached out to touch his arm. 'You're not well. You haven't been for some time. But with the right help, you're going to get better. We all want to see you happy again.'

At this, he made a choking sound and tears started to slip down his face. Stella inhaled sharply. She'd rarely seen a man cry. Her body stiffened and she clasped her throat involuntarily.

'I've been such a fool.' Jon glanced up, red-eyed, and tears splattered down the front of his T-shirt, leaving dark spots.

She desperately wanted to comfort him, but feared choosing the wrong words. She thought rapidly before speaking.

'Jon,' she said at last, in a firm tone that forced him to stop crying and focus on her. 'Look, I've made mistakes too. Lots of them. Since Harriet died, I think we've both been a bit mad and done stupid things. But at least we can acknowledge it and everything's in the open now. It's time to pull ourselves together and sort ourselves out, don't you think?'

He'd clearly heard but his eyes were downcast and he didn't reply. Stella hesitated before pressing on.

'There's something else you need to know. Al's moving back home. We should never have got separated. I wasn't myself. It was a mistake.'

Jon remained silent and stared at her through puffy, bloodshot eyes. It was impossible to tell what he was thinking. Stella felt herself shrink, afraid of what was to come. She glanced nervously at the closed door, wondering if he might flip again and she'd need to call for help.

Finally, after what seemed like an age, he wiped his nose with the back of a hand and gave a long, haunting sigh that twisted her heart, as if it had been gripped by a fist.

'I'm glad for you,' he said dully. 'If it's the right thing for you, it's great news. Thanks for letting me know. I promise I won't ever mention my feelings for you again.'

Stella exhaled deeply. She hadn't realised she'd been holding her breath.

'You'll meet someone else,' she went on cautiously, feeling as if she were tiptoeing over loose stones, waiting to trip. She was watching his face all the time, looking for clues, but he didn't move or even blink.

'There'll be someone out there for you, I know it. In time, you'll forget about me. You'll look back on this holiday like a weird dream.'

To her great relief, he didn't try to argue with her, but shook his head slowly several times. Her pulse, which had been sprinting, started to slow a little. At least he knew about her and Al now, she thought. She'd made her point and Jon had taken it better than she'd expected. This was surely some progress.

A tap on the door made them both look up, and Louise entered.

'Can I get you anything?'

She'd come to check on them. Stella smiled gratefully.

'No thanks. I think I'll head back downstairs. Al said he'd come and chat with Jon when I've finished.'

'I'll be fine on my own,' Jon mumbled. Snot dribbled from his nose, leaving a slimy trail. Stella had to look away. 'I'm not going to do anything stupid.'

'We know.' Louise looked doubtful. 'But we'd rather keep an eye on you for now.'

Stella started walking towards the door but Jon called out, so she stopped and turned.

'Thank you,' he said with a crackle in his voice. His face was red and blotchy.

She was surprised. 'What for?'

'For saving my life. I was being selfish; I wasn't thinking about Jemima. I will now. And another thing – I-I didn't really want to die.'

He managed a small, brave smile, which made Stella's own eyes well up.

'Good.' She sniffed hard, to hold back the tears, and gave him the biggest, brightest smile she could muster in return. 'You've no idea how happy that makes me feel.'

* * *

When the temperature started to drop in the late afternoon, she and Al decided to go for a stroll. She wanted him to experience the sights and smells of this little corner of beautiful Crete and watch the sun set over the mountain.

They took a rug, a bottle of white wine from the fridge and two glasses, which Al carried in a basket over his shoulder.

'That's Eleni Manousaki's house,' Stella said as they approached the tumbledown stone cottage. 'She's ancient and lives all alone. I don't know how she manages.'

The windows were open and the brown shutters folded back, so the elderly woman must have been around. Sure enough, they spotted her soon after at the side of the house, dressed all in black and bent almost double, scattering corn for the chickens.

A goat, with a bell round its neck, was tethered to a wooden post nearby and signalled their arrival with noisy, insistent bleating. Stella waved when the old woman looked up and she nodded and grinned in return, flashing her rotten teeth.

'Jesus!' Al said when they were out of hearing. 'She doesn't go in for dentists, does she?'

Stella laughed. 'No, but she looks after her goat and chickens and never asks anyone for anything. I think she's amazing. I won't have a word said against her.'

Before long, they left behind the centuries-old footpath that led to the village and headed right, into a clearing carpeted with yellow flowers.

In the distance, the mountain peaks were still covered in snow, and the limestone rocks seemed to change from blue-ish black to light grey.

The view was quite breathtaking and Al suggested they stop right there to enjoy it. He spread out the green fleecy rug in the shade of a lone olive tree and they settled down side by side. There wasn't a soul in sight, their only company a herd of goats some way off, breaking the silence with their jingling bells and intermittent baa-ing.

'Wine, madam?' Al said, producing the chilled bottle from his basket with a flourish and pouring her a glass.

It seemed to her to be more delicious than any wine she'd ever tasted, but this was probably because of the perfect setting – and the fact her husband was close by.

She was wearing a cream T-shirt and her loose linen khaki shorts. When she straightened out her legs, which had picked up quite a tan, Al stared at them and tut-tutted.

'You've really been in the wars.'

He was referring to the array of unsightly cuts, mosquito bites and bruises that began at her ankles and ran at regular intervals all the way up.

'I did that on the very first day, walking up a big flight of steps with our bags,' Stella said ruefully, following his gaze, which had fallen on the large bruise on her right knee, now faded to a purple-ish grey.

'And what about this?' he went on disapprovingly, pointing to a long, ugly scab on her other knee.

'I caught the toe of my boot on a tree root. It really hurt.'

'Oh dear. You look like you've been in a fight.'

'It was much worse when I first did it. There was blood everywhere.'

'Clumsy girl.'

She noticed that twitch in the corners of his mouth, and wondered.

'Okay, now tell me about *that* monstrosity.'

This time, he put a finger on her thigh, where a large, red mosquito bite seemed to glare at them angrily.

'You've been scratching it, haven't you?' He was frowning, pretending to be annoyed, but his mouth twitched again. 'You've made a right mess. I've told you before to leave your bites alone, otherwise I'll have to put you in mittens.'

She almost laughed but decided to play innocent instead, pulling a sulky face.

'I can't help itching,' she whined. 'Mosquitoes seem to love me. I think I must be allergic because the bites literally drive me mad. I have to hack at them. I don't even know I'm doing it. I probably do it in my sleep. At least the itching stops when they bleed, otherwise I'd go crazy.'

'Haven't you heard of anti-itch cream?'

'Yes, but I can never find it when I need it.'

'Hm.' He glanced at her reproachfully. 'I bet I'll find another dreadful wound up here.'

This time, he lifted the hem of her shorts, leaned over and peered inside, at the same time sliding his hand up her inner thigh, right to the top.

A giggle bubbled in her throat. 'Oh!' she cried, acting shocked, but she didn't try to make him stop.

Before long, his inquisitive fingers started to explore inside her knickers, making her wriggle with desire. Then he moved even closer, leaning forwards and pressing his mouth hard on hers, his tongue searching out her own.

His breath smelled sweet and nutty and he tasted slightly of salt. In and out went his tongue, giving teasing little flicks with the very tip that made her giddy.

The tingle between her legs turned to a burning throb that almost hurt, it was so powerful. She opened her legs wider, instinctively pushing up with her hips and squirming with pleasure.

She was imagining his hard, swollen penis and full balls, vulnerable and firm at the same time, his surprisingly silky pubic hair, which was either brown or rust coloured, she could never decide.

Her eyes were closed and she was totally in the moment, held captive by her longing. The world around her went blank and it was as if nothing existed but the two of them and their fierce, fiery lust.

All of a sudden, she became aware again of the faint jingling of bells in the distance and a thought popped into her head: there might be a farmer nearby, or Eleni could have followed them.

'Wait!' she said, pushing Al off and glancing nervously left and right. 'We can't do it here. Someone might see us!'

'Only a bunch of old goats,' he replied, with a wicked grin. 'I don't think we need to worry about them.'

She was about to protest further when he gave her a playful shove, making her roll onto her back. Catching her head before it touched the ground, he made his palm into a pillow, while the other hand wandered up her T-shirt and into her bra, then down again, into her white lace knickers.

He was like a starving man, greedy for every last inch of her. She could hear his breathing becoming faster and more urgent, and her own pulse was rushing, too.

Soon, he was pulling down her shorts and slipping off her knickers. He didn't have a problem; they seemed to slide off as if by themselves.

She heard him undo his flies and pull himself out with a grunt, then he was on top, supporting his weight on one elbow. His pelvis and lower body were pressing down on her, his hard penis pushing into the flesh of her thighs and pubis.

He entered with a mighty thrust which made her gasp and she called out in surprise. Tears pricked her eyes, but they were tears of joy, not sorrow. She'd forgotten how good he felt and realised how much she'd missed him.

He came quickly, in just a few, fevered moments, but she didn't mind. They'd have time enough for slow, leisurely lovemaking later, or tomorrow.

'Mmm! That was delicious,' Stella said with a sigh, feeling warmth spread through her body, like melting chocolate.

Grinning with satisfaction, he kissed her on the forehead before rolling onto his back, spent.

Stella crept into his arms and he held her without moving, while his body cooled and his breathing return to normal.

She would have liked to stay there for hours, maybe even wait till he'd recovered and was ready to do it all over again. But she was anxious about being disturbed and forced herself to sit up and dress.

'You were *very* naughty,' she said, straightening her waistband, smoothing down her hair and coming over all prim.

The sun was much lower now, and the sky was awash with bold splashes of fuchsia pink, tangerine orange and ruby red.

His eyes glittered and a mischievous smile lit up his features.

'Excuse me, I think *someone else* was totally up for it, too. Horny as hell! I certainly didn't hear any complaints.'

15

The second week of the holiday could hardly have been more different from the first. The two families spent long, lazy days by the pool or ventured into Porto Liakáda to go to the beach or buy food.

Jon had agreed to catch the same flight back as the others. He was subdued and didn't join in the games or conversations, but he did do his fair share of meal preparation and clearing up.

Al and Stella were like newlyweds, constantly touching each other and sharing jokes. One afternoon, they lay side by side on the same sun lounger while Al played with Stella's hair, running it through his fingers.

Hector was sitting nearby, looking at his phone. He'd been finding his parents' PDAs hard to cope with, and he finally snapped.

'For fuck's sake,' he said, sticking a finger down his throat and pretending to throw up. 'Will you two just stop it? It's disgusting!'

Al laughed but Stella jumped up and scurried to another seat.

'Sorry,' she said, fiddling with the strap of her swimsuit, feeling her cheeks heat up. 'Um, anyone fancy a cold drink?'

A couple of days before they were due to go home, she suggested making a dinner reservation for their last night in one of Porto Liakáda's best restaurants.

There was a full moon, and they were all together round the garden table, having just finished eating.

'I'd like to invite some other people if that's okay?' Stella said. 'April and family, Katerina, of course, Marina...' She glanced at Louise, who nodded almost imperceptibly. 'Maybe the shoe shop man, and the local men who came to help us on the beach. I want to say thank you to them.'

Lily made a face, wrinkling her sunburned nose. 'Can't it just be us?'

'I think it's a great idea,' Al countered, breaking off a corner of the bread he'd left and popping it in his mouth. 'We should show our appreciation. We'll pay.' He looked at Louise, who raised her eyebrows in protest. 'Of course it's on us.'

Being sensitive to Jon's feelings, he didn't add, *After all, you weren't the one who caused all the trouble*, but everyone knew what he meant.

April gave Stella contact numbers for the five men who'd rushed to the rescue when they saw Al and Hector hurtling to the beach, and realised someone was in trouble.

On leaving the store with the information scribbled on a piece of paper, Stella bumped into Marina, who gladly accepted her invitation and offered to tell Katerina about it, too.

The only person who couldn't make the dinner was Mr Makris, from the shoe shop. Stella suspected Katerina might have had a word with him, perhaps via his daughter. The old woman wasn't exactly his greatest fan.

In the event, there were twenty-six acceptances, including April's four children, who couldn't be left out, plus five local men and their four wives.

Stella asked for three large tables to be put together on the veranda, overlooking the water, and the chef agreed to provide a range of sharing dishes and plenty of Cretan wine.

When the time came, Stella was looking forward to the evening's celebration, having spent the afternoon packing and tidying up. She hummed to herself while she was getting ready, and carefully applied some creamy brown eye shadow, mascara and blusher, which she hadn't worn all holiday.

Seeing herself in the mirror, she couldn't help noticing her eyes had a new-found sparkle and her skin glowed. Even her hair, which had been flat and bodiless, seemed to have sprung back to life and turned thick and glossy. It was amazing what love could do to you.

Al came out of the shower with a turquoise towel round his waist just as she was putting on her favourite jumpsuit, pale pink and strappy.

He was tall and broad-shouldered and his fairish skin had turned light golden brown. His stomach wasn't quite as flat as it had once been, nor his chest quite as firm, but he was her man and he was gorgeous. He made her burn with lust.

'Settle down, I know what you're thinking,' he said, clocking her expression and grinning. 'But we haven't got time.'

'Aww.' Stella stuck out her bottom lip. 'Just a quick one?'

She tried to grab his towel, but he hung on tight and wrestled her off.

'Don't! We're in a rush! Later,' he promised.

They sauntered down the well-worn path to Porto Liakáda with Lily and Hector. Louise, her children and Jon followed behind.

The air felt warm and delicious on Stella's skin and the wildflowers appeared brighter and more dazzling than ever before. She seemed to bounce along, her feet hardly touching the ground, as if she'd swallowed a giant dose of endorphins, or been pumped full of magic gas which made her float.

Right now, she thought, life was just perfect, as if happiness had spread itself, like Joseph's technicolour dream coat, over everything.

Of course joy was fleeting, the same as any other emotion, but she decided she'd suffer a thousand setbacks just to hold on to this glorious feeling for as long as possible.

They were a little late to arrive at the restaurant and some of their guests were already seated under a cheerful blue and white striped canopy, overlooking the sea.

Waiters had put together several large tables, as Stella had requested, covered in white linen cloths adorned with jars of fresh wildflowers and flickering candles, as it was already quite dark.

April, her husband and children were occupying one end of the table, close to Marina and Katerina. Baby Nikos had been provided with a highchair and looked very pleased with himself, clutching a big a set of keys which his parents must have given him.

He kept dropping them, then one of his siblings would have to bend down and pick them up. He was clapping and laughing, finding it all highly entertaining, his brother and sisters rather less so.

April had clearly gone to some trouble with her appearance and was wearing a revealing strapless black top showing lots of cleavage, and heaps of makeup. She'd also washed and blow-dried her blonde hair. It was the first time Stella had seen it down, and it made her look younger and prettier.

Her husband, in a jacket and open-necked shirt beside her, appeared proud and proprietorial, with an arm round his wife's voluptuous, bare brown shoulders.

Meanwhile, Marina was in a silky, voluminous, bright-pink and orange shirt, with several buttons undone at the neck and rolled up at the sleeves.

Katerina had opted for a neat, cream, short-sleeved blouse. It wasn't particularly dressy, but she'd picked some rather beautiful, eye-catching gold and amber earrings, with a matching necklace, and looked smiley and relaxed.

Stella hadn't quite finished saying hello to the group when the five rescuers and four wives arrived together.

Black haired, deeply tanned and sporting bushy beards and moustaches, the men made quite an entrance, talking and laughing in loud voices and slapping the waiters on the back.

Judging by their exuberance, Stella guessed they'd been on a pre-lash, probably without their less boisterous wives, who were following behind.

She soon gathered that none of them spoke much English, so it was going to be difficult to communicate. Hopefully, some of the bilingual guests would help translate.

In any case, she thought, the occasion was more about raising a glass and buying the men a slap-up meal to say thank you, rather than attempting to have deep, meaningful conversations.

She also wanted to thank the kind villagers who'd expressed concern for her and Jon, and she'd even brought them little gifts.

One of the waiters arrived with carafes of local red wine, white wine in ice buckets and jugs of water, while another fetched baskets of fresh crusty bread and jars of local extra virgin olive oil for dipping. Stella and Louise suggested their families fan out and find places to sit, where possible, amongst the locals. Once everyone was settled and drinks had been poured, the volume started to rise. There were quite a few other diners, but luckily they were making plenty of noise, too, and Stella reckoned it was unlikely her party would annoy anyone.

She'd already agreed with Jon and Al that she'd make the speech. Jon didn't want to say anything, and Al felt it would be more appropriate coming from his wife.

To psych herself up, Stella reminded herself this wasn't about her; she was here to show heartfelt gratitude.

Without the help of the local men, it would have taken far longer to get her and Jon back to the village and airlifted to hospital. They might have died of hypothermia. And the villagers in general had shown great kindness and hospitality.

Before the food arrived, Al gave Stella a nudge and she rose to her feet, feeling self-conscious. Hector, across from her, pinged his glass with a spoon and the guests fell silent.

'We're leaving tomorrow,' Stella began, feeling herself turn pink. 'Unfortunately, I've fallen in love with Porto Liakáda and I don't want to leave.'

She paused, noticing Katerina whispering in the ear of her next-door neighbour, one of the rescuers, who nodded, before passing the message along. Soon, the whole table erupted into laughter and cheering, and several people slapped their knees or banged their knives and forks. Even the waiters, in white shirts and black trousers, grinned and clapped.

When the cacophony died down, Stella cleared her throat and smiled.

'I wanted to take this opportunity to say a massive thank you to you all for helping to rescue me and my friend Jon, here.'

She gestured to him and he put his hands together, as if in prayer, and bowed his head.

'Thank you also for being so welcoming when we arrived. Thanks for your beautiful scenery and fabulous food, and heartfelt thanks to all you lovely people. We'll be back!'

With that, she raised her glass and said, 'To you all!'

This didn't take long to interpret and after just a few moments, everyone raised their glasses and cried, '*Yamas!*' and, 'Cheers!'

The food began arriving as soon as she sat down, and it was a proper feast. They started with a selection of Cretan meze: *Dolmades*, delicate little parcels made of courgette flowers and stuffed with rice and herbs, which melted in the mouth; *Dakos*, a hard barley rusk topped with the sweetest-tasting chopped tomatoes and tangy, crumbled, Cretan *mizithra* cheese, plus olives, capers and rich, golden, extra virgin olive oil; Tzatziki, made with thick Greek yoghurt, garlic, cucumber and more olive oil; a salad of smoked aubergine, nutty-tasting tahini, chives and parsley; fried aubergine with dry *mizithra* cheese and the lightest, crispiest fried calamari.

The wine flowed and when Stella's faltering attempt to communicate with one of the rescuer's wives came to an end, she sat for a few moments in silence, gazing round her at the animated faces and soaking up the warm atmosphere.

Jon was engaged in what looked like a lively chat with Meaty, April's son. The boy was waving his arms round and at one point, Jon threw back his head and laughed.

Stella's insides glowed like sunshine and she whispered silently to Harriet: 'I wish you were here, Harry, but look! He's going to be all right; we all are. Sometimes, miracles do happen.'

Later, they ate light, sweet-tasting grilled octopus with olive oil and lemon juice, *Souvlaki*, or skewers of barbecued pork and chicken, sea bream baked in the oven with onions, garlic, red wine, honey, paprika, cinnamon, oregano and basil, and *Kleftiko*, a rich, flavoursome, slow-cooked lamb in tomato sauce, served in a clay pot. The meat was so tender, it fell apart on the fork.

By the time dessert came, some of the diners had no room left. However, the hardiest ones nibbled on *Sfakian* pie, filled with local cheese and topped with honey, or sweet *Kalitsounia* pastries, washed down with *raki*, the local fiery brandy flavoured with aniseed.

By now, eyes were bright and faces flushed. Nikos, the baby, had fallen asleep on April's chest, while the next child up, a little girl, was nodding on her dad's lap.

They must have been exhausted, because they didn't even wake when a troupe of black-clad Cretan musicians turned up with a *laouto*, or Cretan lute, a lyra, or type of violin, and a long-necked tamboura. They set up in a corner of the restaurant and started playing a range of wild folk songs, led by a male vocalist with long black hair and a deep, sonorous voice.

People clapped along and laughed at the funny lyrics. Some even rose from their chairs, joined hands in a circle and began to perform a rhythmical dance. This started slow, but speeded up as the tempo increased and one of the men stepped into the centre of the ring and started twirling wildly in the air.

When he'd finished, the whole restaurant erupted in cheers, which made the baby wake and scream. Unable to console him, April signalled to her husband and the other children, who rose reluctantly and made their way towards Stella.

'Thank you,' April said with a big smile, before kissing Stella on the cheek. 'We've had a smashing time. See you again next year, eh?'

'I hope so,' Stella replied, smiling back.

The family's departure seemed to act like a cue for the others, who began to gather their things together and get up. Stella and Al stood at the end of the table to say goodbye, shaking hands and embracing everyone warmly.

Katerina and Marina were the last to leave, and Stella thanked Katerina for giving the two families and Jon the opportunity to enjoy beautiful Villa Ariadne.

'Ah, you must thank her, not me,' Katerina said, smiling mysteriously. 'She knew you needed a helping hand.'

Stella glanced at Al, who looked slightly bemused, then at Marina, who linked arms with the housekeeper, drawing her close.

'I will,' Stella said, holding Katerina's gaze. 'I promise.'

* * *

They had a very early start the next morning. Hector was the last one down and Stella stood shivering on the gravel drive with the others while they waited for him.

Katerina had asked Stella to leave the keys in the special lock box at the side of the house. She said she'd be down later to clean the place and change the bedding, ready for the next visitors.

Once they were all assembled with their bags, Stella decided to do one last sweep of the house, to make sure they hadn't left anything behind.

As she strolled round the bedrooms, checking the electrical sockets for forgotten phone chargers and under the beds for stray items of clothing, she found herself reflecting on who the villa's next guest or guests might be.

Would they have got themselves into a terrible muddle, like the one she'd been in when she arrived? And would Villa Ariadne sort them out?

Downstairs, she took a last look at the paintings of Katerina's employer, then at the one of Katerina herself, in her youth, looking young and beautiful.

She thought of the child, Marina, born in shame to the lady of the house, and given away. Katerina had always watched over Marina and her fragile birth mother. She'd given her life to this villa and faithfully kept its secrets.

Could a building have feelings and powers? If so, this one was full of compassion and healing. In her heart, Stella knew she might revisit Porto Liakáda, but she'd never stay here again; Villa Ariadne had worked its magic on her and her family. Someone else needed it now.

Outside in the cold air again, she closed the door for the last time and turned the heavy key in its lock.

'Goodbye, Villa Ariadne,' she whispered to herself, popping the key in its lock box and waiting for the click before twisting the combination digits.

A slight breeze rustled the leaves of the surrounding trees, sounding like a gentle sigh, which resonated throughout her body. She closed her eyes and melted into its tender embrace.

Little by little, the sigh morphed into a soft, sleepy song, like a lullaby, swirling in the air all round her. She pricked her ears, listening carefully to the whispered lyrics, trying to make sense of them.

Just then, a loud voice pulled her from her reverie and made her start.

'Hurry up!' Al called. 'Or we'll miss the ferry.'

'Coming!' Stella replied.

As they set off down the path towards Porto Liakáda to catch the ferry back to Hora Sfakion, she turned to take one more look at the place where they'd spent the past two weeks. So much had happened, it seemed they'd been there for an age, and she felt like a different woman.

'Thank you for everything,' she murmured. She could swear the villa, with its grand, welcoming windows and wide, tree-lined drive, smiled back.

'Sorry?' Al, at her side, turned to look at her.

'Oh! Nothing.'

Smiling to herself, she picked up her wheelie bag again with one hand and took her husband's hand in the other. It felt warm and safe.

'Let's go home,' she said.

ACKNOWLEDGEMENTS

With grateful thanks to Mike, my mum, my beloved family and my dear friends for their support and encouragement, for making me laugh and buoying me up when I need it. Thanks, also, to my fabulous former agent, Heather Holden-Brown, and her friend and successor, Elly James.

Heather was the first person to believe in my writing and has been with me from the dawn of my novelist's career. I was lucky to have her and am equally fortunate to have been taken on by the indomitable and super-talented Elly.

Finally I'd like to thank Amanda Ridout, Rachel Faulkner-Willcocks and all the team at Boldwood Books for welcoming me into their fold and working so hard to shape, refine and market my novel. They've brought it, kicking and screaming, into the big wide world and now it's up to you, dear reader, to help it grow! I'm lucky to have you, too.

ABOUT THE AUTHOR

Emma Burstall is the bestselling author of women's fiction, including the Tremarnock series. Emma studied English at Cambridge University before becoming a journalist for local and national newspapers and women's magazines. She lives in London and has three children.

Sign up to Emma Burstall's mailing list here for news, competitions and updates on future books.

Visit Emma's website: www.emmaburstall.com

Follow Emma on social media:

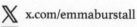 x.com/emmaburstall
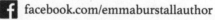 facebook.com/emmaburstallauthor
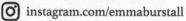 instagram.com/emmaburstall

LOVE NOTES

LOVE IN EVERY CHAPTER

WHERE ALL YOUR ROMANCE
DREAMS COME TRUE!

THE HOME OF BESTSELLING
ROMANCE AND WOMEN'S
FICTION

 WARNING:
MAY CONTAIN SPICE

SIGN UP TO OUR
NEWSLETTER

https://bit.ly/Lovenotesnews

Boldwood